THE SCIENTIST, THE PSYCHIC, AND THE NUT

a novel

Charlene Bell Dietz

QUILL MARK PRESS · ALBUQUERQUE

LIBRARY OF CONGRESS CONTROL NUMBER: 2019938974

Dietz, Charlene Bell
The scientist, the psychic, and the nut: An Inkydance book-club mystery\
Charlene Bell Dietz.—First Edition
ISBN 978-1-9452-1255-0 (hardcover)
ISBN 978-1-9452-1256-7 (softcover)
ISBN 978-1-9452-1257-4 (electronic)

1. Multigenerational—Fiction 2. Caribbean Islands—Fiction 3.Murder—Fiction
4. Mystery—Fiction 5. Science Caribbean Flora and Fauna 6. Hotel 1829—Fiction
7. The Baths, Virgin Gorda 5. Mad Dog—Fiction 8.Guavaberry Spring Bay, Virgin Gorda

Quill Mark Press
933 San Mateo NE, Suite 500-159
Albuquerque, NM 87108

AUTHOR'S NOTE: The characters in this book live only in my imagination. Many of the locations and places are factual, but used fictitiously. Unfortunately, a few years ago category five hurricanes two weeks apart, Irma and Maria, devastated these islands along with several of the buildings mentioned in this book. Hotel 1829 on St. Thomas, once full of charm, no longer welcomes overnight guests but has become a museum and storage facility. These hurricanes totally wiped out the Mad Dog Restaurant at the top of The Baths on Virgin Gorda. I'm delighted to learn it has been rebuilt and recently reopened for business under new management. The first time I visited Mad Dog the gentleman who owned it gave me a hibiscus blossom for my hair. His name wasn't Mad Dog, but I honored him by giving one of my fictitious characters this name. The open-air market in Charlotte Amalie used to be made of wooden stands with awnings. Now it's a permanent structure selling fruits and vegetables. As far as I know, Guavaberry Spring Bay on Virgin Gorda remains as I knew it. May my story treat you to an island vacation or at least bring back memories if you walked some of these streets and beaches and swam in these bays.

BOOK DESIGN Lila Romero
BOOK COVER PHOTOGRAPHY Pixabay: Free-Photos and Sarah Larkin

The Scientist, the Psychic, and the Nut

DEDICATION

As one we snorkeled, swam, and laughed into the night,
making every moment a Double Feature.
David and Susan Hettema
Charlie (we miss you, guy) and Mary Ann Domina

ACKNOWLEDGEMENTS

Thank you to my writers' support group: Patrica Wood, Margaret Tessler, Dianne Flaherty, Linda Triegel, Rita Herther, and Babs Langner.

My Beta Readers:
Mary Ann Domina
Marlene Kurban
Dianne Flaherty
JoAnne Bell
Nancy Lockridge
Ann Zeigler

To fear love is to fear life, and those who fear life are already three parts dead.

—BERTRAND RUSSELL

1   Denver, 1996

Beth shoved in front of Harold. "What a bunch of bull. The last thing anyone would accuse me of being is paranoid. It doesn't mean someone's not stalking me."

Her husband, Harold, muffled a chuckle, pulled her aside, and opened the door. He strode out into the normal world of sunshine, looked around, and motioned her to follow.

She trailed out behind him through the funeral home's double doors. Only sedans and stately spruce trees lined the street, as she would expect.

No one would bother to stalk me—unless, of course, it's someone deranged.

"Where's your proof, dear?" Harold pulled out his car keys. "Don't scientists insist on evidence?"

His timing of this particular conversation rattled her. His insensitivity to her grief shouldn't require Beth to defend her professional conduct.

She craved solitude . . . some alone time to sort out this new circus raging in her mind. In the last twenty-four hours, much of what she knew about her life had been destroyed.

If I'm the daughter of this redoubtable woman, then who in the world is my father?

"Proof or not," she said, "with all that's going on, I don't need some crazy guy following me."

Harold took her elbow to guide her down the steps. "Yesterday I read an article about how mourners fear the fragility of their own lives. They see the world as dangerous. Guess your suspicions these last few days are natural—I can understand your being hyper alert."

She pulled back. "Not just the last few days, Harold, but for weeks now—more like months." Her urge to throw something intensified.

Anger—one of the first stages of grief.

An ache started in her throat. She swallowed hard against its constriction.

"Hey," he faced her and whispered, "I'm your partner, remember? We're together in this."

"It's hard," she began, squeezing her eyes shut, "finding out my aunt is actually my mother just in time to bury her."

The ache spread up to the bridge of her nose, causing her eyes to water.

He wrapped his arm around her, and she rested her head on his broad shoulders. He patted her back. "Mary will always be your mom. Moms are there for the twenty-four-hour work—the dirty little jobs along with the joyful celebrations. Give her that."

"My aunt's my mom and my mom's my aunt and they're both dead." Beth gave a tiny *pffft*. "Is there something constructive I'm supposed to say about this?"

She straightened. Being tall, she could look at him eye to eye.

What had happened the night before made no difference to the robin chirping high up in the spruce, or to the traffic making its way through Denver. Even with the sun doing its best today, the mile-high Colorado air wrapped a chill around her. She nestled back into Harold's strength.

He drew her face up and winked at her. "M'lady, as your fair knight, I suspect the stress of these last few days has colored how each of us views our realm."

She managed a conciliatory smile but found no humor in their longstanding jests. Again, his timing. He needed to work on it—but then he had to hurt as much as she did.

Beth buttoned her jacket and puzzled at the incomprehensible. Everything around her, except for Harold, escaped her awful sadness.

He waited.

She linked her arm with his and inhaled the cool, high-altitude air, relieved to be away from the perfume of fresh-cut roses displayed with white lilies. Fragrances of love transformed into reminders of loss.

This is how it is when your mother dies.

He escorted her to the car. "I do understand. You're grieving, and now you're disheartened because you're afraid you'll find it impossible to learn anything about your biological father."

"And you continue to underestimate me, kind sir."

"Jeez. This tendency of yours . . . it's become a habit."

"A habit? I haven't a clue . . . What are you talking about?"

He glanced down. "Forget it. Let's talk later."

She huffed and squeezed his arm. "You might as well be telling me, 'I'm not hungry for your cheese soufflé, dear. Let it cook in the oven until tomorrow.'"

He opened the car door for her. She cupped her hand over his.

"Do you think I can actually forget there's something you won't talk about now?" She didn't move. "Tell me about this tendency of mine."

He looked away, down the street, then back at her. "Never valuing what you have—you know how you obsess on things."

Beth studied her husband, then she climbed into the car.

"Maybe just this once," he leaned in and said, "you could pretend there's no biological father."

She knew he was watching her.

He touched her cheek with the back of his hand. "This time, can't you let *us* be enough?" He closed her door.

She shut her eyes and leaned her head against the cool glass of the window.

Why can't I have both?

"Now you're not speaking to me." He slid behind the steering wheel.

"We're hurting." She straightened. "We're saying things we wouldn't normally."

"But I'm right. If she were here, Kathleen would agree."

"She's gone, Harold. She has no say in anything anymore. You're through using her to champion your causes."

"You're saying we should ignore what she—" He cleared his throat and started the car. "Kathleen understood how out of balance your priorities are. You purposely placed yourself in danger and then expected me to understand. Who else would put their life in jeopardy to save some science institute?"

"It's not some science institute. It's my home away from home. Kathleen knew how much my research meant to me. She cheered me on. She didn't care about the theft of proprietary information or, more simply, economic espionage, but she knew the importance of not ignoring evil." Beth sighed, then said, "And I loved her even before I found out she was my biological mother . . . Let's drop this."

"Yet you won't." The finality of his words flooded her with heat.

"Depends on what you expect me to ignore."

"Your father's identity. With all the men in Kathleen's life, maybe she didn't even know."

What the—? Her cheeks burned. "You know as well as I do how principled she was."

"Beth, you're naïve. Kathleen—a 1920s flapper. Anything could have happened back then—and it probably did."

"We all do stupid things when we're teenagers. Besides, she was much older when I was born." Beth needed to soften this conversation.

Harold remained silent while he maneuvered through congested traffic.

"For a most noble knight," she said, "you're being rather disloyal, talking about your best drinking buddy this way."

A few minutes later he turned onto Colorado Boulevard. This afternoon his usual energetic, outdoorsy face appeared defeated. Until now she hadn't noticed the deep wrinkles around his eyes. He had a few more on his forehead, almost hidden by his unruly, black salt-and-pepper-streaked hair. Still, his easy-to-look-at strong features would carry him well into his old age.

They would both miss Kathleen's nightly stories over cocktails. She knew this without a doubt. He had loved not only Kathleen's company, but he had loved her counsel too. Actually, he had simply loved *her*.

Beth touched his hand. "I'm giving you a heads-up here. Kathleen has a trunk in her apartment, and there's more on the way. She's bound to have letters or something."

"Please don't go all obsessive."

"I do have a right to know. And don't give me crap about my real father being the one who raised me. That's not the issue. I'm owed this truth. My parents and Kathleen deprived me of a huge part of my life. You can't do the same."

"Dammit, didn't you learn anything from her?"

Beth needed to change the tone of this conversation.

"Easy there, my love." She folded her hands and looked away. "You're edging on harshness. You know Kathleen's always in my head. My mom—Mary—was formal and practical. But Kathleen, she always challenged me—and I've never known anyone as unflappable. How could two sisters be so different? No wonder I felt out of sync with what Mary expected of me. She groomed me to live within mannerly boundaries, but my inherited genetics scoffed at society's norms. No wonder I'm always conflicted. When Kathleen first slammed into our lives, and after I got to know her—"

"Which took you way too long. She knew you didn't want to be responsible for the *old aunt*."

"I apologized for that—you don't need to remind me."

Harold chewed at his lip.

She hated snipping. Grieving hurt enough. She didn't need to add to their pain.

He glanced at her, then said, "We do have other things to talk about."

Like Kathleen's funeral tomorrow. Then what?

The hollowness within her didn't compare to the emptiness she found all around. Last year, when her mother died and Kathleen showed up as her estranged aunt, it had all taken a huge toll on Beth's marriage, on her work, on her emotions.

Beth wanted some thinking time. The thought of concentrating on some complicated biomedical research weighed her down. She blinked at that thought. She had to wonder for a moment at this change in her attitude. Maybe she needed a break from the science institute. She could retire, but this thought quickly passed.

Beth couldn't imagine sitting at home all day with nothing to do, and she dreaded the evenings ahead—she and Harold consoling each other in their grief.

For months Kathleen's outrageous tales had entertained them at the end of their workday. Beth thought of it as Kathleen's cocktail hour. Her aunt would sit in the wingback chair smoking Pall Malls, turning the air blue. Harold would pour Coke and rum over ice in tumblers and add slices of lime. And then Kathleen would tell her flapper stories. Their sides would hurt from laughing. Yet some of her escapades kept them on the edge of their chairs with fear, like the time Kathleen had saved her best friend Sophie from the mob. She had hustled Sophie off to hide out in the Caribbean and recuperate with a dashing, rich man. And Kathleen's mink coat had somehow ended up in Lake Michigan. Beth pulled her bottom lip in, realizing those devil-may-care girls could have been murdered.

How brave of Kathleen to live her dreams, regardless of the dangerous Roaring Twenties.

Beth would miss Kathleen scolding and nudging—her subtle directing of Harold and her along the pathways of their lives.

A flash of green in her side mirror caught her attention. Beth's heart thumped. She scrunched down for a clearer view.

"Harold, quick. Make a right at the next corner."

"What? Why?"

"Do it. It's imperative. Please."

Imagination?

He stopped for the red light, then he turned onto Hampden Avenue. She studied each vehicle when it came around the corner behind them.

Paranoia?

"I have your evidence." She was becoming jittery. "See the grass-green pickup behind that Subaru?"

"You're being stalked by someone in a beat-up old truck?"

"I've seen it before, several times this last month."

"Who's driving it?"

"I wish I knew. I can't even imagine."

Death is more universal than life;
everyone dies, but not everyone lives.

—A. SACHS

2

Smells of peat moss and fresh-turned earth seeped from the mound hidden under the carpet of artificial grass. Beth elected to ignore the odor. Her gaze slid from the casket and fell on the limp, lavender tulips in her arms, and then it went back to the casket. Kathleen deserved different flowers, something more flamboyant, more reflective of the woman's spirit.

She slumped against Harold, stoic in his grief, and wished the afternoon would be over.

I will lift up mine eyes unto the hills. From whence cometh my help . . .

Beth sorted through the minister's words and stared out over Denver. She let her mind wander over the front range of the Rocky Mountains west of the city. The peaks held traces of snow. No comfort came today from anywhere, including *the hills*. These mountains wouldn't bring back the wisdom, the stories, the guilt, the frustrations, and all the love being buried today.

A flash of anger surged through Beth. She wouldn't have known about her adoption if she hadn't been a snoopy little girl. When she was a nine-year-old, she had found part of a torn note from Kathleen to her mother. Both her mother and, later, Kathleen had refused to talk about it. They had also ignored her questions about the strange inscription on Beth's mother's watch. Beth glanced down at it, now on her own wrist. Words on the back of this watch read, *For where thou art is the world itself.*

Where did this watch come from, and who put those words on it?

Until a few days ago, none of this had meant anything. Kathleen's cocktail-fueled conversations had helped Beth put together the piece of the aunt-mother puzzle.

My help cometh from the LORD, which made heaven and earth.

The minister's words didn't comfort Beth. She created celestial tones from Mozart's "Requiem" in her mind and stared at a couple gathered around a nearby tombstone. A flash of putrid green moved along the road behind some trees beyond the couple. The pickup disappeared down the hill.

A chill went through Beth. Then she relaxed. Not even a certified loony would follow her to a funeral.

She turned her attention back to the service. Beth wanted more time to know Kathleen as her biological mother, not as her outlandish aunt who once stole a gangster's limo.

The bridge of her nose prickled. She could hear Kathleen's delighted voice telling stories. She could hear Kathleen's reprimands followed by her consolations. She could hear the music in her mind as breezes danced through the spruces.

Behold, he that keepeth Israel shall neither slumber nor sleep.

With time, would Kathleen have told her she was Beth's mother? Would Kathleen have told her the identity of her lover, Beth's father?

Now the name of her father could be buried today too—forever.

Her suit collar irritated her neck. The chill of the wind didn't cool the embers of frustration deep inside. She wiped at her cheek with the back of her hand.

She heard music. *Not Mozart.*

This music didn't come from her mind—not harpsicords, flutes, or violins. Beth glanced around but couldn't see the source. Confused, she fixed her eyes on the minister.

The minister's words mingled with soft, breathy, melodic notes. They hadn't authorized music for this private graveside service. Only her best friends and a few coworkers attended.

Mournfully drawn-out tones of an alto saxophone slid into Kathleen's ceremony.

He will not suffer thy foot to be moved: he that keepeth thee will not slumber.

Then full-bodied notes gained in volume and complexity. They competed with the minister's words. He stopped, glanced around, then raised his voice. The saxophone melody escalated and transformed into fast-paced jazz. She recognized it now: "When the Saints Go Marching In."

The minister's face was flushed with splotches of red. He raised his voice louder and kept his head lowered as if not to lose his place.

The LORD is thy keeper: the LORD is thy shade upon thy right hand.

How rude, she thought. Beth glanced up at Harold, then back to the minister. *Why would anyone be so disrespectful?*

She set her jaw and stared at the minister's bible.

The sun shall not smite thee by day, nor the moon by night.

Harold touched Beth's arm, and she looked up at him again. He nodded, directing her to look to the right and a little behind.

There—a heavyset, blonde woman dressed head to toe in black stood yards away on a small, grassy rise surrounded by towering blue spruces. Music poured from her vintage, silver saxophone.

The LORD shall preserve thee from all evil: he shall preserve thy soul.

Beth felt her mouth open in disbelief. The late afternoon sun caught the bell of the saxophone. She shut her eyes against the blinding glint. She swallowed hard and forced her attention back to the minister.

The LORD shall preserve thy going out and thy coming in from this time forth, and even for evermore.

Everything went silent. She looked again. The woman, her saxophone, and the jazz music had vanished.

The leaves of memory seem to make a mournful rustling in the dark.

—HENRY WADSWORTH LONGFELLOW

3

Harold followed Beth along the speckled navy-blue and tan carpeted hallway to Kathleen's apartment. Beth turned the key in the lock.

"You didn't need to come with me." She opened the door.

"The first time back here since the funeral has to be tough. Thought some emotional support might help." He held the door for her and stifled a cough.

She waved the air with her hand. "I'd prefer support from an oxygen mask. Good grief. Her cigarette smoke closed up in here makes this room toxic." Beth pulled open the draperies, allowing golden light to flood the cloudy living room. She unlocked the glass patio doors and slid one aside.

"Damn. Weeks later and the air's still blue." Harold knelt down next to the trunk in the middle of the living room.

Beth joined him. "I think you came with me because you're as curious as I am."

He shrugged and fiddled with the latch.

She said, "Kathleen enjoyed her independence here in this apartment. I thought she finally seemed happy."

"Trunk's locked. Do you have the key?"

"I'll have to find it. There's probably three of them." Beth headed to the one-butt kitchen and began pulling drawers open. "We'll keep it quick. I need a sense of what we'll be dealing with when the other two trunks arrive."

"What's in this?" Harold pointed to a ceramic box sitting on the lamp table. Beth shrugged. He raised the lid and dangled three brass keys from his fingers. She caught her breath and grinned. He handed them to her.

Beth wrapped her hand around them, feeling their tiny but solid weight in her palm. She knelt beside him and inserted them, one by one, in the lock of the trunk until she found the one that fit.

Beth lifted the lid, and heaviness flooded over her. She needed Kathleen in her favorite chair by the glass doors, chain-smoking and dishing out scandalous tales of her youth. The two of them were supposed to unpack her trunks together.

Harold patted Beth's shoulder, stood, and sat in his favorite wing-back chair.

How many hours had he sat there, drinking rum and Cokes with Kathleen, listening to her stories?

Beth forced herself back to the business of the opened trunk and peered inside. Feeling like an intruder, she lifted out tissue paper and removed a red velvet cape. She draped it over the arm of the chair. Something inside her shifted. Beth continued to poke into and through Kathleen's things. How would she dispose of these personal belongings?

Harold examined the cape. "Was this a theater costume?"

"Probably not. Bet it's something she wore to the opera."

A few months ago, when Kathleen had fussed about the trunks being stored in Chicago, Harold had arranged to have them shipped to Denver. Every item Beth removed from the trunk pained her—they each held a special story about this teenage runaway, this flapper. She wanted more fascinating tales about the mob, the speakeasies, and Kathleen's escapades.

The lump in Beth's throat kept her quiet.

She lifted out a long, satin wraparound dress, emerald colored and with a plunging neckline. "Good God, what do I do with this?"

"Just your style."

Beth's pulse quickened as she silently fingered through layers of linens, furs, and more stylish dresses. She couldn't imagine her life filled with such elegance.

"Seriously, you'd look glamorous in it. But where would you wear it?"

She sat back on her heels, and a tiny huff of laughter slipped out. "It's the right color for a Christmas party."

"You do remind me of her in many ways."

Beth cocked her head.

"Your long legs, your hand gestures, and she said her hair was the same rich chocolate as yours used to be before you started coloring the gray."

He dodged Beth's playful swat.

Harold continued, "Kathleen plunged in and righted all wrongs, no matter how dangerous. Think of how you—"

"Harold, stop."

"Like her story about hiding in the supply closet to put on a maid's uniform in some Chicago hotel so she could rescue her friend from the mob—that crinkled my skin because I could see you doing something screwy like that. And then you did. Wonder how much of her stories were true."

"My research had been sabotaged and proprietary information was stolen. What else would you have me do?"

"Tell your boss, call the cops, don't get locked in a dog kennel . . . at least let me know what you're planning."

Beth shook her head and groped down toward the bottom of the trunk, below the clothes. She touched something firm. A book. She nudged the clothes aside.

"Here's something." She lifted out a photograph album. Scalloped, white-edged black-and-white photos, held down with tiny black corner holders, covered the soft-dark pages. She reminded herself to breathe.

The first page showed a photo of a young child all bundled up in a snowsuit with two cocker spaniels on each side.

"This one's of Kathleen as a toddler. She told me her parents had two cockers."

"She's a snuggle bunny. Pretty cute."

"Harold . . . I'm sorry I never took you seriously about wanting children. You would have made a great dad."

"Our life is good. I'm okay with it."

She stared at him. What else could he say about her not having children? She glanced down at the album and turned the next few pages.

"I know what you're thinking." Harold sat next to Beth on the floor.

"Three guesses, and I bet you'll be wrong."

Beth turned more pages. She didn't feel like talking.

"One of these men might be your father."

"If you were in a tank with sharks, you'd have just been eaten." Beth kept turning the pages.

"Funny. Look, this one's pretty dapper. Why not him?"

"This time your parachute didn't open. Besides, he's way too short and old." She slowly turned another page and studied each photo.

"But all these guys, aren't you thinking anyone of them could be—" He pointed out a photo of two guys standing next to a car and another one of some man. The mysterious-looking man, his features obscured by darkness because of sunlight coming from behind, stood on a veranda overlooking the ocean.

"That's three. You're losing because you're stuck on the wrong question. Not smart."

She felt him shift away. She set the book on her knees and faced him.

"Our game-show questions don't help grieving." She stood and stretched. "I'm looking for the saxophone lady. I suspect she showed up at the cemetery because of Kathleen. What's the connection?" Beth swallowed, blinked, and said, "Who the hell is she?"

"Could she be the one in the green truck following you?"

"Geez, why would she?" Beth knelt back on the floor, tapped her finger on a photo, and said, "I believe this is the wrong time frame. How old would you guess the lady in black with the saxophone is?"

"A little older than us, maybe in her mid-sixties. What happened to those photos?" Harold pointed to a couple that had the faces cut away. "Why are their faces missing—who cut up them up?"

"Those are the holey people." Beth smirked. "Kathleen told me rather than throw a perfectly good photo away because she didn't like someone, or how someone looked, she would take her fingernail scissors and cut away—eradicate them. Look at the wide lapels and short ties. These women are wearing hats and gloves. Not our generation."

"Can you remember when you first saw the truck?"

"Like you remember the first time you saw a big-horned sheep. I didn't think much about it until months later because it was so out of place at the time. Kathleen had come to Denver to live with us, and I was overloaded with all the problems at the science institute. It was the night you and Kathleen got into that horrid argument, and she stormed out of the house. She had called a cab and disappeared. I went to look for her and found her at the Brown Palace Hotel."

"I hated that night. You didn't come home until early the next morning—drunk."

"First time ever and worthy of forgiveness." She slipped him a smile. "Kathleen and I had much to learn and discuss."

"Did the truck follow you to the hotel?"

"When I neared the Brown Palace, this beat-up green truck pulled in behind me, then it chugged around and rumbled down the street. All the other vehicles were sedans, SUVs, and limousines. It fit in like a turtle at a high-school prom."

"Yet, it's a busy place down there. Lots of traffic. Could be a wrong-turn coincidence."

"Nice try, Harold. When I took Kathleen to the emergency room weeks later, I went out to move my car from the emergency drop-off to a better parking place, and a green pickup pulled out and left the lot in a cloud of exhaust."

Harold remained silent.

"Okay, it's all speculation, but I swear I saw the same truck again the last time I went to the hospital to see Kathleen, and again just before her fiasco with the assisted-living home."

He rested his elbows on his knees. "I have to say, the color is not only unique but nauseating. If you think you've seen it before, you probably have."

"That cemetery needs better security."

Beth closed the album, looked at her watch, then felt around further down in the trunk. This whole business exhausted her emotionally. She could return and do this tomorrow.

Her fingers touched something hard, not an album. She pulled it out from under all the clothes—a photo in an ornate frame of a lovely, round-faced blonde in a black, sequined dress.

"Look." Beth handed it to Harold. "She seems so young."

"Sophie—a professional photograph." He turned it over, checked the back, then studied the face again. "Kathleen mentioned Sophie's beauty."

"She's written something on it. I can only make out her signature." Beth took the picture from Harold and held it up to the light.

Kath, thanks for being there. Love, Sophie.

Beth reverently placed the photo up on the table next to Kathleen's favorite wingback chair.

"Kathleen's stories about rescuing Sophie had to be true." She flipped through a handful of loose photos. A snapshot of a lovely, three-storied home surrounded with palm trees caught Beth's attention. A young smiling woman wearing a dark skirt and a white blouse held up a tray of cookies—a maid. The next photo was of a younger Kathleen. She reclined in a one-piece bathing suit near a swimming pool with a book and a cigarette. A palm tree shaded her.

"Bet she's on St. Thomas." Beth thumbed through more pictures of white beaches, calm bays, tall palms, and fluffy clouds.

Harold now sat next to her, studying each photo after she finished.

"Here's a photo for you." She handed Harold a photo of a boat, maybe for fishing, with billowing sails. A strange name, *Dusky* something, had been painted on its side. He had always wanted to go deep-sea fishing.

Harold pointed to one. "See this."

"More boats at a dock."

"Look closer. Read the sign."

"Red Hook. Kathleen's favorite place—she told us several times to take the ferry from Red Hook to St. John."

Harold sorted back through and found snapshots of beaches and bays. "I bet one of these is where she and her lover drank cuba libres and danced in the sand at midnight."

Beth's heart quickened. She led a mundane life compared to Kathleen's. Beth gave a little smirk, wishing she had inherited some of her mother's insouciance. She picked up the album again and turned its pages.

Where are all the photos of Kathleen's handsome young men?

Dost thou love life? Then do not squander time,
for that is the stuff life is made of.

—BENJAMIN FRANKLIN

4

"When will you close out the apartment?" Harold held Beth's purse while she locked Kathleen's door.

"I called the manager and asked if we could keep it for the rest of the month. I'll need time to sort through and figure out what to do with her things. Besides, I don't know when her other two trunks will be arriving."

They walked in silence to the car.

He started it and backed out of the parking space. "Do we need anything from the grocery store?"

"Let's just go home. I've had all I can take today." She leaned forward and studied what she could see in her side mirror.

"I've already checked. No green pickup." He patted her knee.

"After the science institute problem, your believing me means more than you can imagine." For a long time, only Kathleen had believed her about someone sabotaging the research.

Kathleen . . . all her precious treasures in those trunks.

Beth wished she had taken the photographs to study later. The photos of those places brought Kathleen back—close—keeping her a part of their lives. How Kathleen had loved the ocean and beaches.

She touched Harold's arm and pointed. "Pull in that strip mall over there, please."

"Shopping?"

"We're both miserable. It's time for us to do something different."

"Isn't your timing off?" Harold turned into the parking lot and parked in an empty space. "We're not exactly frolicking in congenial moods here."

"Humor me." She leapt out and leaned into the car, staring at him. He unbuckled and climbed out.

She guided him down the walk to the third unit from the end.

"A travel agency?"

"You're your own boss—give yourself a week off." She squeezed his arm.

"Beth, what's this about?"

She suppressed a tiny grin. "We're long overdue for a vacation."

Kathleen had chided her to stop ignoring their marriage.

Harold stopped, planting his feet squarely on the sidewalk. "Where would we go? Don't we need to research or at least discuss this? Besides, there's Kathleen's dog. Saucy needs someone to care for her. Did you even think about her? And you talk about my timing . . . bad idea, Beth."

"Laura will take care of Saucy for us." Laura lived across the street and was Beth's best friend. "Nothing else to think about. It's time you and I stopped worrying and started living."

"But we should plan and—"

"Nope."

"I hate it when you give me a one-word answer," he said.

"For years you've been hounding me about wanting to travel. Even Kathleen chastised me about not making time for you." She stood aside for him to open the door. "She told us exactly where we should go. Certainly you remember."

"Nope," he mocked her as she entered the office.

"Then think of this as my surprise date for you." She led him over to a desk covered with brochures. The travel agent wore dark-rimmed designer glasses, and stood up and extended her hand. Beth didn't catch her name, but she shook her hand anyway.

"Where do you want to go, sir?" Travel-Agent-Woman said after she waved them into chairs.

Harold looked at Beth and then at the travel agent.

"I read that men never want to go on cruises," he said. "It's always their wives or girlfriends who get the idea."

He glanced over at Beth and said, "After the first cruise, it's the men who want to go on another. I suspect it's the all-you-can-eat atmosphere that entices them." He looked at Beth again and shrugged. "I don't know where we're going, honestly. I'm with her—she's in charge."

Travel-Agent-Woman shifted her gaze to Beth. Harold took one of Beth's hands. He held it firmly and grinned one of those sly ones that were so hard to conceal.

"We need to go to Red Hook." Beth winked at him, then she turned to Travel-Agent-Woman. "It's on St. Thomas, where we can take the ferry to St. John—we've been told there's this lovely little bay with turquoise water—I'm sure you know the one. That's where we're going. I want to be drinking cuba libres and dancing on white sandy beaches at midnight with *him*."

I do desire we may be better strangers.

—WILLIAM SHAKESPEARE

5

Beth slept most of the way on their flight from Denver to San Juan, Puerto Rico. When they arrived, she and Harold hustled along the tiled floor to the far end of the terminal.

"Beth, if you insist on carrying your purse over your shoulder then please keep it in front of you."

She pulled her purse around, clasping her hand over the top. This trip came with her own personal, exceptionally cautious bodyguard. Harold kept telling her stories about the prevalence of illegal drugs and thuggery in the Caribbean Islands.

He studies everything way too much.

A flight of steps led them down to the airline counter where they were sent out the door onto the tarmac.

"Feels like someone turned on the furnace," Harold said.

She dabbed at the perspiration collecting on her neck. Salt air mixed with the pungent fumes of fuel spills on the asphalt made breathing unpleasant. She took shallow breaths.

They strode toward the small aircraft waiting to take them to St. Thomas. Her shoes made a tapping sound as she hurried up the airplane's aluminum steps. Beth squeezed down the narrow aisle until she found their assigned seats. Harold accepted the window seat. Settled, they fastened their seat belts. Others jostled briefcases and purses as they leaned down and squinted at row numbers.

"This one seems to be mine." A trim woman in a white suit with a coral blouse that enhanced the glow of her mocha-colored skin lowered herself into the seat across the aisle from Beth.

"And you could not have found a better one." Beth felt her mood shift—a slight change, more tranquil. Deep inside tiny shreds of sadness trailed off behind her. Bits of her demanding professional world disappeared. She couldn't and wouldn't even want to explain it.

"Is this your first time to St. Thomas?" The woman asked as she pushed a coral and turquois purse under the seat in front of her then buckled her seat belt. Passengers moved between them down the aisle, preventing Beth from answering.

Most of Beth's grief hovered somewhere back in Colorado. She held her breath and listened. Saxophone jazz, not her usual symphonic music, played in her head. The aisle cleared for a moment. Beth leaned toward the woman.

"My husband and I haven't had time for vacations. This will be our most excellent adventure to date."

"You picked a magical place, even with the tourists." The woman's eyes widened. "Sorry, I meant—" More passengers moved past.

Beth enjoyed this small connection with her unknown neighbor. Their great island adventure had sprung off to a happy start. It was her turn to ask a question.

"Do you go to St. Thomas often?" She wished the plane would start so they'd turn on the air conditioner.

"I live there. I've just spent the week with my first grandchild. I bet I become this airline's most frequent flyer to Puerto Rico. You're from the states?"

She broke off the conversation because other passengers were still coming down the aisle. A thin, dark woman in a red-flowered dress stopped before the new grandmother.

"Shalee—why you not talk to me in the terminal? I know you seen me, girl." She leaned closed to Shalee's face, her black eyes flashing.

The grandmother pulled a magazine from the seat pocket, held it between them, and thumbed through it.

"Shalee, it's me, Malaka." Malaka pushed the magazine down and moved her face close in. "When we little and fought, we still spoke. Why you be mad?"

"Ma'am," the flight attendant said as she touched the standing woman, "you must move on."

"Shalee, you hurt my feelings. Why?"

"Excuse me, ma'am." The flight attendant put her hand on the woman's back. "You're blocking the aisle."

"We've nothing to say, Malaka—machetes in church, and that lovely woman disappearing." Shalee went back to her magazine.

"That wasn't me! Wasn't anyone I hang with. Don't you blame me."

"You must find your seat." The flight attendant's voice was now searching for control.

"Those boys," Malaka said. "They are not my boys. Just because Enrico run off with his no-good pa, don't make Joman bad too."

"Get on, Malaka," Shalee said. "You're holding up the passengers."

Malaka straightened, glared at the flight attendant, scoffed at everyone, then started down the aisle.

"You," she said over her shoulder to her former friend, "you wave one of Missus Abu's stupid chickens over it, girl, then you get on!"

Shalee burrowed her gaze deep into the magazine, ignoring Beth and the rest of the plane's passengers.

"Beth, look at this." Harold pointed to something out the window, but he whispered in her ear. "Told you St. Thomas could be dangerous."

"Right, Harold. That's why so many tourists spend big dollars there."

"Machetes? In church?" His voice turned to a soft mumble.

She shook her head, closed her eyes, and waited for the plane to take off.

The flight attendant started his safety spiel.

When he finished, Harold asked, "So what did you find?"

"Excuse me?" She hated this questioning, but she had promised herself not to be snippy. She owed him. He had been way beyond understanding when her job kept piling on worry after worry. He and Kathleen . . . because of Beth's busy schedule, he not only became Kathleen's best drinking buddy but eventually her caregiver.

"The cemetery," he said. "I know you stormed over there to find out about the woman with the saxophone."

"The keeper didn't know what I was talking about. How could he not know who was on the premises? Isn't that part of his job?"

"Did you go through those other two trunks yesterday?"

"I couldn't make myself. I . . ." The sadness came back.

He patted her knee and waited for her to continue.

"I didn't even open the third trunk." Talking and breathing drained her energy.

This feeling must come from sorrow, or maybe anger.

Resentment wouldn't alter the deep love she felt for her adoptive parents, but she feared her current mood might destroy this vacation.

Beth forced herself to continue. "There's so much, and considering all I didn't know about Kathleen being my biological mother and not my aunt—until a few days ago—"

This awful emptiness, would it always haunt her?

"It's tough."

She nodded.

He slid his arm around hers and clasped her fingers. She nestled into his comfort as the plane rolled down the runway, lifted into the air, and banked over the ocean. They were now headed toward the islands that Kathleen loved. These islands where Kathleen had told them she had lived with her one true love.

These islands had stored secrets for fifty-some years about her real mother. Her biological father must have played here on the beaches with Kathleen—or possibly he even still lived here.

"Harold, why would Kathleen keep my adoption a secret after my mother's funeral—I guess I should say after her sister's funeral?"

"Mary *was* your mother. She raised you. Back in the forties and fifties parents didn't tell their children they were adopted. When I was a second grader, one of my friends found out he was adopted. His parents said they didn't want to tell him because he'd be preoccupied about who he really was and wouldn't do well in school. Naturally, all the rest of us second graders figured we were adopted too. Second grade was a horrible year for all of us. It's not like today."

"Except what was there to lose after my mother died? She could have told me then that she was my biological mother. Why did she let me go on believing she was my aunt?"

"Do you think your cranky attitude at being *stuck* with her might have had something to do with it?" he said. "She probably didn't want to play the guilt card."

"I'm feeling cheated out of a relationship." She glanced over at the woman reading across the aisle. "Guess I swindled myself."

"Back to my original question, what did you find?"

"I found more photograph albums and more photos with the faces cut out." The humor of this erased Beth's annoyance in answering Harold's questions.

"Hot damn, the woman took after her parents." He grinned.

"My grandparents didn't cut up photos they didn't like. They burned them. Kathleen kept the good ones of herself."

"And you learned what?"

"Here's something." She dug in her purse. His questions were starting to overwhelm her. She handed him what she found.

"A matchbook cover—Hotel 1829?"

"In St. Thomas. I've booked us a room there for a few nights."

"Thought we were headed to Kathleen's beach on St. John," he said, "before we go play over in Virgin Gorda."

"You said you've always wanted to go deep-sea fishing, guy. I've booked you a day trip out of St. Thomas."

"Seriously?" He grinned, looked out the window, then turned back and studied her.

She cocked her head.

"Are you going fishing too?"

"Thought it would be fun to poke around St. Thomas before we go to the other islands."

He smiled, sat back, and watched the ocean below.

"Besides—"

He turned to look at her.

"I want to check out a few things—historically. St. Thomas must have changed since Kathleen lived there. We're talking fifty years ago. Think how much Denver's changed in that time."

"I see." He turned away.

She waited. He remained silent.

"What's wrong?" She wouldn't let herself feel guilty about this.

"Our situation has reverted back to normal."

"What's wrong with our *normal* situation?" She touched his arm.

He stared out the little window.

Damn his stubborn streak.

"You're upset. I haven't a clue why. Don't be unfair."

"Because you—" He sighed. "Our vacation seems to have changed from a holiday into a quest to find your biological father."

"Not at your expense. You'll be fishing, while I spend a few hours in the library. Kathleen said she lived with Martin on St. Thomas. You can't expect me to let that go."

"And do you know for sure Martin was your father?"

"Well, no—I'm assuming. Maybe. If Martin wasn't my father, it could have been Ed. He was the newspaper guy in Chicago that loved her."

"Remind me, why we are flying all the way to the Caribbean?" he pulled out a magazine from the seat pocket and thumbed through it. "Sounds like we could just have our rest and recuperation in Gallup."

"What are you talking about?" *Gallup?*

"I thought we were off to recapture the romance in our marriage," he said, "to run barefoot on some white sandy beach, make slow passionate love behind a coconut tree. Instead we're off on a mystery hunt for some guy who's probably long dead. You haven't any idea who he is or what he did. You don't know if he even cared."

"My biological father, Harold. You make this sound cold and calculating."

"I don't want your hopes ruined." He returned the magazine and shut his eyes.

Why was he making this so complicated?

She sighed. This last year had pretty much left their marriage in shambles. She watched him. He seemed to be sleeping.

How could Kathleen wind her way so tightly into Beth's heart and also become Harold's best friend? Without her here, the world wasn't large enough to hold this emptiness, and not knowing anything about her real father added to it.

Every time she glanced over at Harold, his eyes remained closed.

Beth's stomach clenched. For her to have any kind of comfort, she must first know something about her biological father.

She felt Harold shift positions. He now watched tiny ships in the rippled water far below.

Beth leaned over, took her purse out from under the seat, and pulled out a brochure. She squeezed his arm. He turned and stared at her, and she handed him the trifold information.

Her heart glowed with love for him, and she knew he loved her.

He grinned and settled back to study information about deep-sea fishing. She put her head on his shoulder, breathing in his familiar smell, and waited until he put the brochure in his shirt pocket.

She sat up straighter and said, "You've missed our camping trips and trout fishing, haven't you?"

He nodded and looked back out the window.

"Harold, those things you listed, you know, behind the coconut tree and the mystery hunt . . . I don't see why—can't we do it all?"

The world is a book, and those who do not travel, read only a page.

—ST. AUGUSTINE

6

Beth and Harold's taxi navigated the streets of Charlotte Amalie, St. Thomas. After a short ride, they parked in front of an intimidating set of steep, red-brick steps. Judging from the abundance of gray cement and the different hues of red brick, these steps had undergone numerous repairs. They led to wrought iron grillwork that encased an open-air veranda.

"Interesting, Beth," Harold said. "The matchbook cover didn't say anything about hauling our luggage up these steps."

"Yet still, doesn't it take your breath away?"

"These steps will."

"Don't worry, mister." The cab driver opened his door. "I've got it."

Beth stepped out into the heat of the afternoon, and they climbed the stairs.

"This grillwork, Harold, it's lovely." She opened the gate to the veranda.

"It'd be more attractive if it weren't to keep corrupt people out," he said.

She smirked, then went inside.

Heavily varnished tables and chairs, hanging Tiffany lamps, painted pots filled with greenery, and deep-set, dark-shuttered windows welcomed guests onto the veranda and to this old hotel.

The three crossed the veranda and stepped into the hotel's dark interior. The cab driver set their luggage on the stone floor in front of the reception desk, which also served as the bar.

Harold peeled off some bills and handed them to him.

"It's enchanting." Beth glanced around.

The driver thanked Harold and left.

"We're checking in," Beth said to the desk clerk. "Mr. and Mrs. Armstrong from Denver, Colorado."

The man started their registration process.

"Didn't you notice?" Harold said. "Many of the businesses have heavy grillwork, too."

"Caribbean style, guy." She winked at him.

"Is Caribbean style also no air conditioning?"

"You're being grumpy. Don't be anxious—we'll be fine."

"How many nights?" The clerk looked up with pen poised.

"Three," she said. "The reservations are under Armstrong. We'll be back here again next week to spend Saturday night. Our flight leaves early Sunday morning."

"Someone will take your bags up for you. Your room's up this stairway two flights to the right." He handed Harold an old iron skeleton key.

"This really brings us back into something out of the past." She started up the stairs. "All the stonework, the steps, the colors—I love it."

The deep-pink stairway adorned with plants, tile, and pottery was a focal point from the lobby. After less than a handful of steps, it branched to the right and the left. They took the steps to the right.

"I hope they don't call this a luxury hotel." Harold turned the key in the keyhole. "We do have an in-room bathroom, right?"

"The brochure said you'd find a beautifully appointed and quite large communal bathroom seven flights up on the top floor."

"This hotel doesn't have seven floors." He opened the door, and she brushed past him, crossed the large darkened room, and opened the shutters.

Harold peeled more bills off and tipped the man for their luggage. Then he plopped on the bed and gave her a lecherous grin.

Finally, this guy might relax and actually enjoy this trip.

Beth sprinted over, taking his face in her hands. "When we get back, if Orin says the board won't promote me to that administrative position, I'm going to look for another job."

Harold's mouth opened; no words came out.

With a flip of her hand, she said, "Don't look so shocked. Maybe it is time for a change. Bet other research institutes would beg to have me."

"You've worked there since you graduated from the university. It's been your life."

"And like my home away from home." Beth swallowed hard. Something unsettling churned inside. She didn't know if it came from the events surrounding the funeral or from her knowledge that the blasted good-old-boy system would never let her be promoted.

"I can't believe you'd risk giving it all up."

"So, tomorrow you go deep-sea fishing." She started unbuttoning her dress. "Then the next day I've booked a cab to take us to Red Hook, and there—"

"We catch a ferry to this lovely little bay—ah, to hear Kathleen tell that one more time." He rose to help finish the unbuttoning, stopping just long enough to kiss her shoulder.

She let the dress slide to the floor. "Bet she took a rum bottle rather than snorkeling gear."

He watched her, then said, "Like she would party all night on that beach without her rum?" He removed his shoes and stretched out on the bed. "Bed's comfortable."

"We both miss her." The lump in her throat came back. She needed it to go away.

"Kathleen lived in a different world," he said. "Chicago, Detroit, life in the fast lane, especially for a seventeen-year-old. How old was she when she came to these islands?"

"Probably in her late twenties, early thirties—not sure." Beth fluffed up the unused pillow. His deep-set eyes sparkled. Even after long hours of travel, he seemed full of curiosity and vigor. His classic features told of too many hours spent outdoors fishing, mountain climbing, and camping.

He needs to use sunscreen.

"Look at us." Harold laughed and said, "Coming to the Caribbean in our mid-fifties. This is about as geographically exciting as it gets for us."

"Maybe." She fastened her eyes on his. "However Harold, I guarantee, there's more fun ahead."

His silence seemed filled with expectations.

She glided the back of her hand over his cheek and whispered close to his ear, "I thought I'd take a shower in a little while, then change into something cooler. What's your plan?"

It is human nature to think wisely and act foolishly.

—ANATOLE FRANCE

7

Later, when the hot afternoon sun poured into their room, Beth locked the shutters and turned on the lights. She finished drying her hair and dressed while Harold showered. Then they headed down to the bar in the lobby.

Beth sipped her cold drink and studied framed photos on the wall at the end of the dimly lit hotel bar.

"Harold, look at this."

"A musician."

"A woman saxophone player." She moved closer to the photo.

"You're grasping. There must be thousands of women saxophonists."

"Look at the background."

"People drinking at a bar—oh, it's this bar." He glanced around.

"It's her, Harold."

"Too much of a coincidence." He went back to squeezing the lime in his rum and Coke.

She jammed her finger on the photo and stiffened her back.

He shook his head.

"I know it's her, and there's a connection between this musician and Kathleen. I feel it in my bones."

He screwed up his face. "A scientist who believes in mystical vibes?"

She had to laugh at that.

"Here's to our most excellent Caribbean adventure." She clinked his glass.

They sipped. His eyes twinkled.

"But, my love, it isn't her," he said.

"Watch this," she whispered in his ear, "Mr. All-Knowing."

Beth strolled down to the far end of the short bar and signaled for the bartender's attention.

"Sir?" She pointed toward the saxophone photo. "When was that photo taken?"

"Probably—maybe three years ago?"

"Dang, I just can't remember her name. Who is she?"

"That's Sylvia, do you know her?" He sliced more limes as he talked.

"Only heard her play for a few minutes. She's talented." Beth winked back at Harold.

"She's free entertainment when she's on the island. And she's good."

"And these are good cuba libres. What's her last name?"

"Don't know."

"I'd like to talk with her. Do you know where I could find her?"

"Nope."

"I think she's a good friend of my aunt—and my mother." *Damn it.* "Anyway, both have died, and I think she would like to know that."

"Sorry."

Did he mean sorry for the deaths or sorry because he refuses to tell me?

"Harold, how long ago was it when we last saw Sylvia?" *And please, dear God, don't say at my mother's funeral.*

"About two weeks ago. It was—"

"That's it—thank you, Harold. Two weeks ago this last Tuesday, in Denver."

The bartender finished putting the lime slices in a container, sealed it, then wiped up the juice.

"Guess she travels a lot. How often does she come to St. Thomas?"

"Don't know."

"Then could you answer this? When was the last time she was in here?"

Silence.

"Surely you can tell me something about her."

Harold's ice clinking in the bottom of his empty glass was the only sound.

"I want to tell her about my mother and my aunt. I think they really must have liked her. Okay?"

"Missus, I can't help you."

Beth glanced at Harold. He didn't look up. She turned back to the bartender.

"When I said they were dead, I hope you don't think I was implying she had anything to do—"

"Didn't give it a thought." He took his towel and wiped up the condensation her glass had left on the bar. Then he nodded to Harold, the nonverbal way to ask if he wanted another drink.

Harold shook his head and shrugged his shoulders in sympathy for all of Beth's questions.

"Dammit, Harold. I'm not prying. I'm just interested, okay?"

"Okay," the bartender said, "but no."

If I gave him a tip he'd know something. Beth downed the last of her drink and put it on the bar where he'd just wiped. She grabbed it up again, quickly rubbed off the spot with a cocktail napkin, and handed him her glass.

He folded his towel, gently placed it next to the cutting board, and raised his gaze to her eyes. He was more than a bartender who wouldn't share his answers. He seemed competent, wise, and rather kindly. She felt a twinge of guilt and wished she hadn't tried to manipulate him.

"I'm being ugly—I'm sorry." She glanced away. "My mother died. I'm—I'm distraught, and I have too many questions."

"Lots of tourists come in here," he said, "and ask all sorts of things. I'm happy to answer them if they're general in nature. But Sylvia's a respected person here. You can't buy her privacy from me."

Beth pulled her lips in and nodded.

"Let's go eat." Harold walked over to Beth and nudged her. "Is there a restaurant on site?"

"You'll find restaurants a few blocks down the hill and over that way."

Harold glanced at the shuttered windows. "It'll be dark when we return. I've heard some things . . ."

"No worries," the bartender said. "St. Thomas, like all these islands, has some problems with drug dealers and theft, but the tourist trade is important. You'll be safe, especially if you stay in the main downtown area and regular tourist places."

Beth continued to sit and gazed all around. Being in this bar, this hotel—Kathleen probably sat and drank her cuba libres right here. Beth tingled with expectations. She felt so close to learning what she didn't know. She sighed. Harold might get mad, but she couldn't keep quiet.

"Would it be prying if I asked about the history of this island? For instance, does the hotel have old photos of people who stayed here, maybe even forty or fifty years ago?" Beth glanced sideways at Harold. "Could there be some photos in boxes in the basement—"

The bartender laughed.

Beth looked at Harold and shrugged. "Never mind."

"You need to check," the man said, "with locals who are working on preserving the history of the island. Here's a number to call." He penned a phone number on a cocktail napkin.

Beth nodded a thanks and shoved it in her pocket.

This time Harold nodded at the bartender, then held out his hand for Beth. Still grinning, she stood.

"How will we get back in?" Harold said. "Looks like this place is locked tight."

"Just ring the bell."

Once I've made up my mind, I'm full of indecisions.

—OSCAR LEVANT

8

Harold paid their bar tab along with a healthy tip, waved to the bartender, and he and Beth went out onto the veranda and opened the gate. The heat from the afternoon sun hit them like a stoked-up furnace.

"Whew, we're not in Denver anymore," she said. Then she figured it out. Islanders shut the sun out during the day. Clever. The prevailing sea breezes at night lowered the island's temperature and humidity.

"Give up about the saxophone kook, okay? You're making people nervous."

"I sure didn't win him over. By the way, the hotel does have air conditioning."

"You're joking."

"It's called shutters."

When they reached the bottom of the steps, Harold put his arm around her, and they strolled across the park to the main street. He used to do this many years ago when they walked across their college campus. Beth couldn't remember his doing it since then. The weight and warmth of him calmed her.

Beth leaned in close. "The cemetery groundskeeper had never heard of anyone showing up unannounced and playing a musical instrument," she said. "This is why I know the saxophone lady must be connected to Kathleen."

He squeezed her shoulder. "I'd have to agree."

"Sylvia's blonde, overweight, plays a sax, and spends time where Kathleen used to live. I bet Sylvia knows a lot about Kathleen and my father."

"What does her being blonde and overweight have to do with anything?"

"Didn't you notice? The woman at the cemetery was blonde and overweight."

Harold slipped his arm down and took her hand when they stepped off the curb. They headed toward the main street along the waterfront. His silence bothered her.

He's worried I'll ruin our vacation looking for Sylvia.

"This *is* our time, Harold. It's *our* vacation, okay?"

He nodded and continued walking. She needed him to understand.

"I do owe Kathleen a little of our time here, don't you think? Even if I don't find Sylvia, I shouldn't pass up this opportunity. Look at everything Kathleen gave us—you'd have to agree she did save our marriage."

He nodded again.

"If I could find out a little more about Sylvia, then maybe I'd know more about the man Kathleen loved enough to make a baby with—"

He stopped walking, faced her, and shook his head.

She glanced away, out to sea. *Why can't I make him understand?* She wasn't being obsessive. She was on to something.

Three boats floated in the harbor. Red and gold faded lettering caught her attention.

"Look—there—" She grabbed his arm. "Over there. After fifty years—" She struggled not to squeal.

"At what?"

"Silly. The name on that boat, *Dusky Angler.*" She started down toward the waterfront.

He caught her, spun her around facing him, and said, "I'll not be silly if you'll be rational."

"The old boat over there, it's in one of Kathleen's photos—I remember the name *Dusky.*" She headed toward the seawall.

He pointed left to a larger harbor. "But look at all of those great yachts over there."

[35]

She ignored him. "This must be where the local boaters make quick downtown stops to pick up supplies."

She charged forward, snapping photos of the *Dusky Angler* while it rocked gently in the bay.

When he caught up, she asked, "What do you know about boats, and ships, and sailing things?"

He pointed to some newly painted trim. "Look. Someone's fixing it up. I'm surprised this old tub even floats."

"This isn't a tub." She enjoyed the tinge of excitement in his voice. "It's quaint."

"This used to be an old fishing boat." He shielded his eyes and squinted. "Do you have the photo with you?"

"I wish. Geesh, why didn't I think to bring some of them?" She had put all of them back in Kathleen's trunk. Maybe he'd be a sport about this after all.

He touched her arm. "The owner may not like us poking around."

"We're not hurting anything." She moved closer to the gangplank.

"Boat etiquette requires you never board without the captain's permission." He craned his neck to see if anyone was on deck.

"Do you think this old thing even has a captain?" She stopped and snapped a couple more photos.

"Whoever owns it *is* the captain. Man, I'd like to go on board too, but you can't without permission."

"Maybe I could—if I wanted." She tilted her chin up and snapped a photo of him.

Harold scowled. She grinned, looking out over the sea.

"Fine. I won't. I'm not rude." She gave him her over-the-shoulder smile, along with a sassy wiggle of her hips. "I'm not boarding—I'm photographing."

"And," he pointed across the main street to an upstairs seafront restaurant, "I'm not photographing. I'm hungry."

～

They checked out the menu at the bottom of the stairway and then went up and pushed through the door. A waiter escorted them to a table with a window view where they could look out over the ocean. The *Dusky Angler* bobbed next to a small, dingy-like floating vessel— not much more than scrap wood with an outboard motor.

Beth sipped her merlot and watched Harold stir his cuba libre. She liked this restaurant with its linen tablecloths, candles, napkins, and the table settings that sparkled.

"Maybe someone who works here knows about that boat," she said.

"When does this vacation actually start?" His words felt curt.

"Excuse me, sir." She looked wide-eyed at him over her wine glass. "I thought it started when we checked into our room, and we closed the door."

"Well, there's that." He nodded, keeping a tight rein on his grin. "I do stand corrected."

The waiter appeared with their dinners, filled their glasses, and disappeared.

"You'll meet the deep-sea fishing group tomorrow morning at nine thirty. They'll feed you lunch, and you'll be back around sundown. I tried to book you on the early-morning one—better fishing then. They were sold out."

He sipped, put his glass down, and reached for her hand. He held it, then turned it over and traced the lines in her palm. The muscles in his face contracted.

"My prince seems troubled. Sir, is there a dragon somewhere in your midst?"

He looked up, let loose her hand, and picked up his fork.

"Harold, what?" She knew his contrary expression.

"I'm not so sure I should go fishing."

"But—you've said you wanted to do this. Many times. Now that it's arranged you don't think you want to—"

"I want to—it's just—"

What was it he wasn't saying? She took a bite and stared at him.

"This is not like a decision to give up bowling at the last minute."

He shook out his napkin and replaced it back in his lap.

"How long are you going to make me wait?" she said.

He shrugged.

"Are you afraid you'll be seasick?" She leaned in and said, "There's medications, like meclizine, for that."

"Don't be angry, but I need to be here."

"You're not making any sense." She touched his hand. Her words were soft. "What's wrong?"

"It's you. I can't leave you for a whole day in this place. And now you'll be furious because you say I'm overprotective."

She leaned back and studied the ceiling—she watched the fan below the lights slice through the air and fling tiny reflections over walls and tables. She drew in a breath and forced herself to think— *think sweet thoughts of him.*

"Beth—I didn't want us to be this way—not on this trip. But if I'm gone for nine or ten hours, then—"

"Do you think I'll sit in a park all day and wait for your return?" She shook her head. "There are gadzoodles of activities I could choose. I've planned a whole day for myself."

He leaned back and studied her before saying, "Asking everyone you see annoying questions?"

She buried the murderous urge he evoked. Tomorrow was her only day of freedom during this whole trip. She itched to snoop in the island's historical records. She took a deep breath and smiled sweetly.

He moved his plate closer and cut off a piece of tuna. She needed to give him something solid to think about.

"After we have breakfast, I'll see you off. Then I'm off too. I'll have a day of historical records and museum explorations, including a taxi ride to the aquarium. When I've exhausted all there is to see, I'll go for a swim—Magens Bay. It's one of the world's best beaches. When you return, I'll display a glorious swimsuit tan that will age my skin ten years and be a forerunner to melanoma. But hey, it'll be worth it to watch my Prince Charming check it out."

His face relaxed. "Helps me to know you've made plans."

She took a bite, swallowed, and said, "More plans."

"Lady, how long do you expect me to be gone?" He squinted—then she saw the twinkle.

"For the two of us—for the next day. We're to meet the snuba people at Red Hook, and they'll give us snuba instructions while on the boat ride to St. John." She grinned.

"Snuba?"

"You'll love it, Harold. It's a blend of snorkel and scuba." She read the expression on his face. "It's perfectly safe."

"Perfectly safe to you means I can plan on our lives being snuffed out by some bizarre activity."

The waiter had cleared their plates and now returned with the dessert menu.

"I have a question, but it's not about dessert," she said.

"Certainly, Miss."

"Do you know who owns that old fishing boat, the *Dusky Angler*?"

"Sorry, Miss."

"Then do you know someone who might?"

He shook his head and looked around the restaurant.

The headwaiter appeared.

"Is there a problem?"

"Not at all," she said. "I'm just curious."

"Is your dinner satisfactory?"

"Perfectly seared tuna," Harold said. "I'd recommend this restaurant to anyone."

"Is there a problem with the service?"

"Excellent service," Beth said, "but I need to know, does anyone know the owner of that fishing boat down there."

"There are several fishing boats docked. Are you interested in going deep-sea fishing? We can make arrangements for you. Tell me what hotel you're staying—"

"I'm only interested in who owns the one across from us at this end. That one—it's gone." She looked at Harold, then the waiters. "The *Dusky Angler*, do you know anything about it?"

"I couldn't really say."

"I took photos of it just before we came up here, and it was there a few minutes ago."

The two waiters exchanged looks, and one nodded.

"I'll bring both of you crème brûlée?" the second waiter said. "It's the specialty of the house."

When they left, Beth said, "Why is everyone so secretive?"

"Because, my love, these people don't know you. You make them nervous."

It's the good loser who finally loses out.

—KIN HUBBARD

9

Early the next morning Harold said he wanted the works for breakfast. They descended the brick stairway on their hunt for food. An image of greasy eggs made Beth's stomach churn, but she decided not to wave banners over their food preferences. Both remained silent while walking down one of the market alleyways.

"Stop a minute." Harold held her arm. "Take a whiff."

"Coffee?"

"Assorted choices." He pointed to a tiny cafe.

"Let's check the menu." She hurried ahead, surprised by his understanding of her needs.

"Bet this beats your usual blue-yogurt junk." He held the screen door for her. They moved up to the counter and waited to order.

Beth decided on fresh fruit with mango and coconut served in a small paper cup and a toasted English muffin. Harold did the loaded egg sandwich. They took their coffee and breakfast outside and settled on one of the park benches.

Beth cocked her head before taking a bite. "Listen to those birds. They sound different than the ones in Denver."

"Everything's different." He unwrapped his breakfast sandwich. "The humid air, the sights ... Imagine us in downtown Denver instead of here."

"I should get you out of our backyard more." She tousled his hair. Unlike Denver's brick-building obsession, these mint-green, bubble-gum-pink, and sunny-yellow paints on shutters and building facades added a sense of gaiety.

They finished eating and threw their containers and napkins in a trash can.

"We have time before I catch my cab," he said. "There's some sort of garrison over there. See? The brick building with the flags. Looks old. Let's check it out."

"Fort Christian," Beth said. "Read about it, and there's also a museum behind our hotel. We could take those same stairs up to Blackbeard's Castle over the top of that hill."

He looked across the park to where Beth pointed. Stone steps started at street level, took a steep climb, and disappeared behind their hotel.

"There must be over a thousand steps."

"Only ninety-nine, silly. Relax, we don't have time for them. We'll do the fort. Let me take your picture in front of it with the clock tower in the background." She waved him on. "Run over across the street."

Beth wanted it framed with trees on one side and the ocean on the other. He waited for the traffic to break, then found a spot and posed.

"Back up a little farther—to the right—there." She focused the camera.

"No photos!" Footsteps pounding hard sounded close.

She lowered her camera. The source of the tenor voice resonated from a dark, angry face surrounded by cast-iron dreadlocks. The man strode toward her. He exuded physical strength and mental authority. His bare, walnut torso glistened with oil above his tight, blue jeans. Heavy, gold jewelry hung from his muscular neck.

What's his problem?

"No pictures of I and I."

"I and I? Sir, I—I'm not—"

The Rastafarian lunged toward her.

She darted away, clutching her camera close. "It's the fort—"

"Hey—" Harold started to cross the street but had to stop for cars to pass.

Heat spread though Beth. She couldn't make sense of this encounter. When she glanced over, Harold was still waiting on the traffic. The man grabbed her arm, snatched her camera, slipped out the memory card, then flung her camera away.

She lurched for it—too late.

"What the—" Her new camera, now cracked and chipped, lay on the sidewalk.

The Rastafarian thug's face screwed up into a sneer, and he swaggered off.

"You—bastard!" Beth dashed after him. Harold yelled for her to stop, but she ignored him.

She grasped the man's sweaty bicep and dug her fingers in deep.

"What's wrong with you? You've ruined my camera. I didn't take any photos of you."

She heard Harold running up behind her.

The man stopped and listened, staring down at her face. He blinked, then in seconds he peeled her hand off, seized her wrist, twisted her watch loose, pocketed it, and heaved Beth away.

She stumbled to gain her footing but landed in the dirt. The thief shrugged, then sauntered across the park and up the street.

Harold had started after him, but he stopped and dashed back to Beth.

"Beth—oh God! Are you okay?" He knelt down. She held up her arm to check the damage while Harold brushed hair out of her eyes.

An ancient, heavyset woman in a calico dress appeared and bent over, studying Beth. Then she flicked leaves and dried grass off Beth's back. A young, waiflike girl wandered close. She peeked around from behind the woman.

"Missus, are you injured?" The woman asked.

"Nothing that won't heal." She burned inside. Harold held his hand out to help her up. "Just mad as hell." A lump grew in her throat.

The young girl spat in the direction of the Rastafarian. She squatted down in the dust, picked up a twig, and furiously scratched symbols in the dirt.

The thief, a block away, didn't look back. Beth sprung forward, yelling, "You coward! Give me my watch back."

Shaking his head, he flipped her words away with one hand.

"You're nothing but a dammed bully." Beth lurched in his direction, but Harold grabbed her. She struggled to pull his fingers off, but the Rastafarian had disappeared down a side street.

Her eyes begged Harold to let her go.

"Beth, forget it."

How could he say that?

The old woman stood close, clucking her tongue. The girl kept drawing crazy designs—crosses with curlicues.

Beth's ears were ringing. Nothing made sense.

People were staring at them from a distance. Beth wanted them all to go away.

Didn't Harold care about her watch?

"My watch, Harold—anything, but not my watch—" Her eyes filled. "I wanted pictures of this vacation—but you know how important my watch is."

"I'll buy you another one."

"Mother's watch—it can't be replaced." She wanted to throw something.

"There be a real shame in this." The old woman picked up her large cloth bag, shaking her head. "That good man not be himself no mo'."

"You know him?" Beth asked.

The child whispered, "He's bad. He's the one who made my mother disappear."

Beth stared at the girl. *What?*

"Hush. You don't know that for a fact, child." The stout woman fumbled in her cloth bag, pulled her hand out, and pressed something hard in Beth's palm. The woman mumbled something as she shuffled on toward the open market. The stands had opened even though the owners were still arranging their wares for the day.

Beth opened her fingers and saw the object the old woman had handed her. A brown nut lay in her hand, but her ring finger—

"Dammit, Harold. He took my rings too. How did he do that?" She pulled in her lips, looked back at the nut, then slung it toward her last view of the Rastafarian.

The child gasped, dropped her stick, and darted toward the street. She squatted and poked around, then grabbed it out of some weeds. Her lips pulled into a hard, tight line. Her dark eyes locked on Beth.

Beth shivered. Evidently she had trespassed somewhere on something she didn't understand.

The child looked at the nut before shoving it in her pocket. She was a creamier version of the dark nut. Her little pixie face put her age at about nine.

"Don't worry about your rings." Harold brushed dirt from her back, diverting her attention from the girl.

Beth looked back for her, but she had disappeared.

"There's a police station around here," Beth said. "I saw the sign. They'll do something about this if they value tourism."

~

A police officer handed Beth a sheet of paper and asked for a list of the photos on her memory card.

Beth ignored the stool at the counter and pulled the paper closer. She took a pen out of a holder—her mind filled with memories of last night, taking her camera with them to dinner.

"No—those photos were mostly of the boat, the *Dusky Angler*." Energy drained from her. Her watch, her rings, and the photos of Kathleen's past—gone.

Beth edged onto the stool and wrote with anger. The pen ran out of ink. She grabbed another and recorded what she could remember along with a detailed description of her watch and rings.

The officer filled out more forms and gave them to her. She read them and signed each one. He suggested she let her insurance company know.

That was it.

Harold and Beth walked out and down toward the waterfront, neither speaking.

"You don't want to be late." Her hand rested on his back.

"Whoa. I'm not going anywhere except where you go." He ducked away from her touch and faced her.

She figured he'd say that. She signaled a taxi. He pulled her arm down, but not before one rolled to a stop.

"Harold, you've always wanted to do this. It's your one chance. Go. I'm fine."

"After what just happened?" He clamped his lips tight.

The cabbie raised an eyebrow. Beth held her finger up to him. He nodded.

She hugged Harold. "And that's all that's going to happen. It was a fluke, wrong place, wrong time. You can let it ruin our vacation or not, right?"

Harold looked miserable.

"No choice, love. Off with thee. I want to enjoy this day full of our separate and most wonderful adventures."

"I am not leaving you. Too many unknowns here—this place—"
He held his arms out. "It's too dangerous."

"Then why are these islands so crowded with tourist? It's all good.
End of discussion. Now have fun." She pushed him aside and
opened the door.

"Remember that incident on the plane? Machetes? We're staying
together." He held her shoulders and stared into her eyes.

"I remember well, and Shalee seemed to be a very sweet woman—
just like the woman in the calico dress and the child. They came to
help us. Most of the people here are good people."

"Beth—I'm sorry. I just can't do this."

"Then it will be your fault for a most crappy vacation. You're too
afraid to have fun." She glared at him. "And this is only the first
day—we might as well go home."

He set his jaw and stared back.

"One rotten person—come on, Harold. See those tourists over
there, laughing, enjoying themselves."

The taxi driver squirmed and shot Beth a pleading look.

"Sir, just a moment longer. This guy is a big tipper." She tilted her
head toward Harold. The cabbie seemed satisfied and settled back to
wait.

"Harold, get real. Okay? Think of the times the institute sent
me out of the country to medical conferences. Who protected me
then?"

He remained silent.

"Remember the time I stayed in downtown Vancouver and a huge
riot broke out over the Stanley Cup? How about that conference on
telomeres in England? Just a few miles away the Manningham riots
started. You have to admit, this place is paradise in comparison."

He studied her face, then looked out at sea and shrugged. "Why
do you always get your way?"

"Here's your sunscreen." She pulled it from her beach purse. "Go.
I'm off to search for my father in historical records while you search
for fish. Please don't keep this nice cab driver waiting any longer."

Harold started to get in, then stopped. "You've got to curb your
inquisition. Stop making people nervous. Promise?"

"Funny man. I promise." Beth shoved him into the back seat and
leaned into the window of the cab. "He's catching the fishing boat
that goes out of Hull Bay in twenty minutes." And then to Harold,

"Use the damned sunscreen. And now, my handsome Prince, go catch us something worth frying."

One great use of words is to hide our thoughts.
—VOLTAIRE

10

Beth planned to go back to the hotel and call the number written on the napkin. Certainly they would have records about the island's residents in the late 1930s.

And, yes, Harold, I'll not be a pain.

Actually, the statistical chances of it all, discovering in one day who her real father might be, seemed impossible. She should have paid better attention to Kathleen and her crazy stories.

She remembered a few names—Martin, Ed, Max, Sully . . . maybe someone else. Her guess zeroed in on Martin because Kathleen talked about Martin as her own true love. And she did live with him here on St. Thomas. When? What year?

The excitement of unplanned possibilities in a foreign place made her giddy—a tribute to Kathleen's capricious life, so unlike her own. She drew in a deep breath. *This place even smells different . . . sea . . . flowers . . .* The open-air market begged her to come and take a look. She would spend a minute there before heading back to the hotel.

The stalls, draped with colored fabric, shaded the customers and workers. Vendors displayed island shirts, skirts, and locally made crafts, such as sturdy-looking brooms. The smells of fresh-cut wood, oiled leather, and dried, yellow grasses made into woven bowls caught her attention. Some of the grasses still showed tinges of green.

Beth found a sun hat, tried it on, took it off, placed it back on the hook, and fluffed her hair. She wandered over to a bin of tiny dolls labeled *Authentic Voodoo*.

The small, colorful cloth dolls were tagged for their specific uses. One label said it helped return lost objects. She picked it up, not to buy, but to examine it. She smirked.

Why would anyone think something like this could influence the location of solid matter? Maybe there's one for lost watches—or, better yet, fathers.

She felt a tug on her shirt hem. The waiflike girl looked up at her with those huge dark eyes. She shook her head, took the doll from Beth, and placed it back in the bin.

"Miss, that's tourist trash. I'll ask loa to help you." She scooted around another shopper.

Beth craned her neck to see, but there was no sight of her.

"Hello, again."

Beth glanced over her shoulder.

"You won't find her. She's quick." The smart-looking woman who had sat across the aisle from her on the plane held some multicolored woven goods over her arm.

"You're the new grandmother," Beth said.

"Loving it. Call me Shalee."

"I'm Beth. Do you know that child?"

"Her name is Natalie Baymon, but we all call her Gnat. She flits around unseen most of the time."

"What did she mean by saying she'd ask loa?"

"Gnat's an exceptional child who sometimes connects with Ayezan of the invisibles."

This stopped Beth. She didn't know how to frame questions about loa that wouldn't make her sound stupid or intrusive. Time to change the direction of this conversation.

"Gnat tagged along with an older woman earlier. Is that her grandmother?"

"Missus Abu? She more like Gnat's guardian angel. If anyone ever needed one, it would be Gnat."

"This morning Missus Abu appeared out of nowhere like *my* guardian angel." Beth held up her elbow.

"Ow," Shalee said. "Missus Abu's an enigma. Probably because she's lived here forever and knows everyone and everything—quite a good friend to have."

Friends. Shalee's conversation with Malaka on the plane.

"Each of us needs loyal friends—ones who won't betray our devotion to them."

Shalee tucked her lips in, glancing away.

Beth pointed to the cloths over her arm. "Those are beautiful. Did you weave them?"

"These table runners? Goodness no, I'm a bank teller with no creative talent. My neighbor makes these. She can't leave her home, so I bring them here for her. I'm taking them to that stall over there."

"Then I must buy one."

Beth folded her purchase and placed it in her shoulder bag. A small crowd gathered along the street near where the boats were docked the night before. A sound came from that direction, like a small animal or bird fluttering and squealing to be released.

Curious, Beth hurried closer and saw a small girl, pirouetting barefooted. *Natalie Baymon—Gnat.* She moved seamlessly into a flat-footed spin with some side steps. Gnat's eyes were shut, her head thrown back, and her shoulders and arms seemed to move on their own. A sonorous humming tone with clicks and squeaks came from her mouth. The little girl heard a rhythm all her own.

Beth stopped at the edge of the group of people and glanced at the viewers. Missus Abu was over on the far side of the crowd. She wasn't paying attention to Gnat. She was arguing with that Rastafarian thief.

Beth lurched, but she stopped when he yelled out, spun around, and strode off.

Missus Abu only shook her head, staring after him. Beth pulled her attention back to Gnat.

Beads of sweat collected on Gnat's pixie face. Dark strands of hair whipped and lashed with each jerk of her head. Someone started to beat on a drum, slowly working up to Gnat's frantic rhythm. A few others hummed or sang unrecognizable sounds that coordinated with the beat. Gnat danced faster. Why didn't someone stop her? She was bound to trip, or fall.

Beth studied the faces gathered around. She caught sight again of the calico dress. Missus Abu drifted away from the bystanders, moving in closer to the girl. Still she didn't touch or stop her.

The girl collapsed.

Beth couldn't see her now because of the crowd. She pressed through to the front.

A deeply wrinkled and tanned man, tall with thick silver-white hair, shoved up next to Missus Abu, who knelt next to the girl. He wore faded-blue cutoffs and a red, sleeveless T-shirt.

Missus Abu shaded Gnat from sun and onlookers. The two adults murmured to her for a minute. When the elderly man helped Gnat up, the crowd drifted away. The gentleman took Gnat by her hand and walked across the main street and down one of the side alleys. Missus Abu watched them leave. Beth noticed Missus Abu wasn't the only one watching.

Two shoeless and shirtless boys, a year or so older than Gnat, with white-toothed, winsome grins stood on the open stairwell of the restaurant across the street. Sunshine glistened off their cocoa bodies. The smaller one wore dreadlocks, but the darker, taller one sported black, sunlight-reflecting curls.

The adorableness of their dancing and gesturing disappeared when Beth understood the meaning of their antics. Their movements mocked and mimicked Gnat's.

After the gentleman and Gnat disappeared from view, the boys bent close to each other in an animated discussion.

Beth glanced at her wrist where her watch should have been. She ignored the flicker of anger. Stolen watch or not, she had spent enough time being a tourist. The calico dress caught her attention, as Missus Abu ambled up one of the narrow shopping alleys.

The two young boys climbed down from the stairway and followed her.

Puzzled, Beth tagged after them. When the old woman made a turn at the far end of the narrow cobbled street, the boys scooped up small stones and darted after her.

Beth sprinted up the alley, weaving past tourists. She turned the corner. Horrified, she found Missus Abu crumpled on the curb.

She heard the boys' laughter down the block. They pointed and danced like puppets on strings, then slipped out of sight behind a building.

"Missus Abu—"

Missus Abu held a blood-soaked cloth to her forehead.

Never tell the truth to people who are not worthy of it.

—MARK TWAIN

11

"Let me help." Beth took out her unopened water bottle and poured some on the cloth.

"I be fine. I now go home." Missus Abu held still while Beth cleaned around the wounds.

"You may need stitches. Is there a doctor nearby?"

"I take care of myself," she said. "I thank you for your help."

Missus Abu started to stand, then sat back down. She looked at her palms. They had specks of blood from the cement and gravel when she had caught her fall.

"Sit, wait a few minutes. Is there anyone I can get for you?"

"Help me up." Missus Abu picked tiny pieces of gravel out of her arm, then held it up to her.

"Where's home?"

"Down Wimmelskafts Gade a ways and beyond."

"You're not going on your own."

"Then you must tell me your name and who you be."

"I'm Beth Armstrong from the United States. I'm a research scientist here with my husband because we both needed a vacation. He's off fishing."

They shuffled together down the sidewalk in silence. After several blocks Beth spoke again.

"Do you know why those boys did this?" Beth looked around to be sure they weren't being followed.

"They imagine themselves be defenders."

"Defenders? Of what?"

"Of who they follow. Of the mighty one who creates their sorry lives."

"Are you talking spiritually, or about an actual person?" Beth glanced behind them again.

"It would be both."

"They're more cowards than anything, sneaking up behind you."

"They braver the more they grow."

"I'm beginning to share my husband's concerns about this island being dangerous."

"Not at all. Theirs be a simple way of life that's complicated to explain." Missus Abu nudged Beth to turn up another street, and they turned again. The street names changed before the streets ended, blending into each other.

Beth could see the main part of town below them. Missus Abu stopped, took out a key, and unlocked a small gate hidden behind gigantic emerald leaves. She pushed the leaves aside and beckoned Beth to enter.

Beth hesitated, then remembered Shalee's praise of Missus Abu. She followed the older woman into a miniature courtyard dappled with sun and shade. Half a dozen brown and red hens pecked about. The big daddy bird, bedecked with a huge scarlet wattle, stood on the back of a metal lawn chair. He eyed them with a proud cock of his head then crowed out to the world, announcing their arrival.

"I shall wash properly, then I shall fix us tea. You may come in or sit out here in the hounfour." She opened a screened door to a darkened house.

Hounfour? "I'll be fine out here. I love your chickens and plants." *I'll ask Missus Abu about Sylvia, and maybe she can tell me about St. Thomas in the 1940s.* Beth brushed some unidentified matter off one of the metal chair seats, tingling with expectations. *Maybe she even knew Martin.*

Before she sat she saw delicate white flowers of the dogbane family. Their rich, sweet fragrance caused her to inhale deeply. She should know their name. She wandered around, examining other plants, and then she sat, swatted at an occasional fly, and watched the hens cluck to each other.

Missus Abu reappeared with a teapot and two mugs. Beth was taken aback. She would never think to serve hot tea in eighty-plus degree weather.

Missus Abu, with a colorful bandana wrapped around her forehead in a turban, looked island fashionable. The small gash over her eyebrow, still swollen, had stopped bleeding.

"Do you want me to put a bandage or something on that for you? It looks so deep and painful." She would have a nasty bruise around her eye before morning.

"It be fine soon." She set the mugs down, changed the teapot to her other hand, and poured a military-green hot tea into each.

Beth inhaled the steam before she sipped. She thought the smell might hint at what she was about to drink. Its earthy bouquet left her with no clue.

"You not like most North American tourists."

"Why do you say that?" Beth sipped. *Wowee!* Every molecule in her body seemed to suck in and absorb something herbal. She wanted to laugh, but she forced herself to keep a neutral expression. This tea took her breath away. She instantly wanted more, and it didn't even taste good.

"You not like others. I watched you." Missus Abu picked up her mug. "You be interested in people. You ask questions, not talk only to other tourists."

Beth actually squirmed a bit in the metal chair. When did Missus Abu see her ask questions, and to whom? The desk clerk, the waiter—she had only asked questions of them and no one else. Missus Abu wasn't around then.

"My husband thinks I ask far too many questions. He's afraid I annoy people."

"If you have lots of questions in your head you need to let them out."

"Shalee. You saw me talking with Shalee." Beth smiled.

"You were interested in what she said, not what you could get for a cheap price. How you and Shalee be friends?"

Beth mentioned the conversation on the plane about Shalee being a new grandmother. Then she told Missus Abu what she heard about machetes in church. Was she betraying a confidence?

"I worry about that." Some of the white flower petals had fallen into Missus Abu's lap.

"Can you tell me?" Beth knew she shouldn't pry into island politics. Harold would have a cow right now. "I'm sorry, it's none of my business."

Missus Abu took a few of the fallen petals, sniffed them, and handed them to Beth for Beth to smell.

Creamy Gardena—no. Buttery fruit? Its specific odor escaped her.

"Those who believe they are one and also Jah do not agree to authority or organized religion."

"Jah?" Beth tilted her head. "Organized religion—isn't all religion organized?"

"When you hear someone refer to themselves as 'I and I,' they be one with God, or Jah. They disapprove of authority and structured religions. They see the Catholic Church the highest in structured religion and the pope the ultimate in authority."

"These men hack up people in church?" *This place wasn't safe. Harold was right.*

"Most Rastafarians love peace and don't want violence of any sort. Some boys strutted into the church the other Sunday and waved their machetes around. Then they left. There will come a time when very bad things happen somewhere on these islands."

"You're talking about the Rastafarian society, right? Shalee's friend, Malaka—is she a Rastafarian?"

"Shalee should not end her friendship with Malaka. Malaka be a good person. It's only a few that cause problems."

"Like those two boys."

Missus Abu shook her head. "Those boys live scared, so they listen to the wrong voices.

Beth didn't know how to respond. Instead, she said, "You're quite respected by Shalee. Thanks for being there when that jerk shoved me down." She immediately regretted calling the man a jerk. *Why not? That's what he was, wasn't he?*

"William be a good man, but he now leads a misguided life. Those boys follow him."

William? A guy like that has a sweet name like William?

"Those boys," Beth said, "aren't kids I'd want to invite over to play. Why'd they attack you?"

"Because I watch over Gnat. I don't stop her from her own way in this world." Missus Abu leaned back, savoring several sips of tea.

"Why do they care what that little girl does? I think they'd rather be swimming, playing basketball, or off shoplifting."

Missus Abu laughed at that. She poured them some more tea, set the pot down, then checked her palms. She held them up to show Beth. They looked normal.

"What did you put on them?" Beth studied the gash on Missus Abu's head. "Your cut looks much better too. Some of the swelling is down."

Missus Abu winked.

"Is it this tea?"

"Maybe a little, the tea, and some herbs my mother taught me to use, but mostly—" Missus Abu tapped her head.

"Your mind? Are you magical?" Beth couldn't believe she said that, let alone thought it.

"Some say so, but they be wrong. We not need magic or sorcery when we can be one with God."

"You mean like those boys, or William? Like that I and I thing you mentioned?"

"They think Jah is within them always. We know we each be connected to God through loa. Those boys dream to be like William, of his power and his way of life. They hang around him, do everything he does, but they be terrified of him when he be mad. When Gnat cut off her dreadlocks a year ago William be like he would kill everyone."

"Dreadlocks?" She had hundreds more questions now. "What's it to William how she wears her hair?"

"If you be a true Rastafarian, you have no rules to live by, but there are rules you obey regardless. You never put sharp objects near your head, no scissors or combs."

"Are you Rastafarian?"

"My way be much older," she said with a sigh. "My way be older than time itself. Rastafarians come to be less than fifty years ago."

"What about Gnat?"

"William be terrifying when angered, and Gnat knows exactly how to stir up William. He wants to blame me for what Gnat does." She picked up her cup and drained it, then clunked it down on the wooden table.

"He blames you because you don't restrain Gnat? Are you her guardian?"

"I keep her in my heart. Gnat knows those boys do anything to keep William from being mad, and that's how she tricks them."

Beth stared at Missus Abu. Then Beth reached over, picked up the pot, and poured more tea into their mugs.

"Missus Abu, why do you watch over Gnat? Where are her parents?"

The older woman sighed. "A big problem. I cannot watch with a mother's eye. Her mother disappeared, and this fey daughter of hers be insisting William be responsible." Missus Abu picked up a hen, put it in her lap, and stroked its feathers.

"Do you believe Gnat? Did William kill her or something?"

Beth didn't like the light feeling in her head. She held tight to her mug—blue ceramic, handmade, a tiny raised handprint placed where her thumb held the cup handle.

"William—he responsible if you look into the shadows that go back in time before the deed, but it be not William who wanted or did the bad thing. William hop and skip up and around about Gnat's finger pointing at him. Maybe she be the cause he smokes more and more ganja. She tells me her mother whispers to her from dark waters." Missus Abu shook her head. "Gnat's anger grows. William should fear her."

Seriously?

"You said Rastafarians strive for peace. Gnat, these boys, and William seem off track there."

Beth's head didn't weigh what it should. She must leave. She might float away any second now. Yet—the peacefulness in this walled garden anchored her down.

"Gnat chooses her own path."

"But those boys are violent." Who *was* the caretaker of that little girl?

Children need love and comfort and safety. Poor Gnat. Harold always wanted children. How would he feel about adoption?

"Except for a few, Rastafarians are at one with others. They like positive words and change down-feeling words to up-feeling ones. We say, 'Understand?' They say, 'Overstand?' None like rules, and they share whatever they have. If it be yours, then it be theirs."

"William's way of sharing felt pretty rough, not positive, and quite one-sided to me. I *overstand* a thug when I meet one." Beth watched a butterfly go to the delicate white flowers then fly away without so much as a sip.

She didn't want to leave. This garden gave her protection and peace.

The hen settled deeper into the folds of the calico dress and shut her eyes.

"Ganja not enlightening to William's mind anymore. He smokes more and more and becomes a different William. Gnat believes fire actions will change him back. You must watch. You would like to see her feet dance across burning cinders. She be doing this someday, and she be the destroyer of his ganja, too."

Friendship multiplies the good of life and divides the evil.
—BALTASAR GRACIAN

12

Sitting there in the hounfour, Beth's mind couldn't make sense of anything. She listened for her wooden-flute music. *Nothing, not even the saxophone sounds, only silence. Where had her music gone?*

She thought of something that might be pleasant and opened her eyes.

"Missus Abu, the silver-haired man down by the waterfront with Gnat, who is he?"

"Her grandfather. He takes her for ice cream. He talks with her for a time. She wore out from when she be loa for you."

"Loa? For me?"

"The intermediary for Bon Dieu." Missus Abu poured more tea into their empty mugs.

The images of Gnat dancing filled Beth's mind. Those strange movements must have been some sort of a ritual. Beth shuddered, realizing she didn't understand any of this. She needed to do something.

She sipped. Everything looked all right, but she imagined herself on an outer edge of something, standing there blurred, out of focus.

"Does she live with him—the grandfather?"

"She lives with many."

"Wait, who cares for her? Tucks her in at night? Sets boundaries for her? Who protects her?"

"Her grandfather talks with her, buys her sweets, and plays games. He knows she not be controlled."

"What kind of a guardian is that?"

"Hers one fine family, and I, the nanny for their daughter. She grew up, married a fine man, but it turned poorly, and now she disappeared last year. That's why Gnat be troubled. She be most angry with William. The grandfather and I be too old to be her guardian."

Beth didn't follow much of that, but now the adoption question hung even stronger in her mind. *Such an endearing child . . .*

She needed her flute music back. Beth wandered through what Missus Abu had said and kept coming back to her conversation with Shalee. Shalee had told Beth Missus Abu knew everyone. Beth's heart quickened. Here, in this garden with Missus Abu, Beth found her opportunity.

Opportunity for what? I've lost my question and my symphony. Wait. I had more than one question.

Missus Abu busied herself watching the bees.

"Shalee said you've lived here for a long time. She said you knew everyone." Beth took in a deep breath. She felt more grounded after getting those words out.

"Oh, that Shalee. I do not know everyone. The island has too many people here now."

Music, saxophone music from the funeral service—

"There's someone who comes to this island who interests me. I think she must have been a friend of my family's in some way. She's about my age, probably three or four years older. Unfortunately, I only know her first name, Sylvia. She's quite musically talented—the saxophone. Do you have any idea who I might be talking about?"

"I know her. She does not remember me. When she be a young girl, maybe Gnat's age, she played the piano. She sat at that big grand piano creating wonderful music, her feet swinging back and forth with her long curls bobbing up and down. She played the whole time her mother was in the study, talking with the mister."

"Her mother—?"

"The fuss, the horrible yelling, the little girl did not want to leave. 'I want to be in St. Thomas. I want to stay here.' She screamed all the way out the door. Her mother fought with her on down the steps to the big sedan. She hefted the child up and shoved her in the back seat. What a sight. The mother's hair fell down from that fancy do. She lost her bobby pins in that tussle. That little girl be loving her music and that big piano."

"You're sure the little girl is the same Sylvia?"

"She be the same. She comes here many times a year now she be an adult. She likes visits with Mister Davies. I listen to her, I see her, but I never talk with her. She doesn't know me because I be an invisible person."

Invisible?

"Do you know why her mother came here and how long ago that might have been?" Beth's heart raced—her questions brought answers.

"I should not talk why the mister sent for the woman." Missus Abu closed her eyes, then said, "She came in the spring when the new flowers bloomed. A few months later, in the summer, everyone be talking about the atomic bombs."

The time would have been the middle 1940s. "You say he sent for her?"

"These were sad years for him. He go to the states, come back, go back to the states—he a miserable man who didn't know what to do. After several years of his turmoil he sent for Missus Sylvia's mother. I believe he thought she could help him find someone that would make him happy."

"Do you know how he knew Sylvia's mother?"

"Long ago I used to be a cook for this fine family. This gentleman lived up high on the cliff. His home be very fine. Mister Davies thought the mother and Sylvia be staying for a while—enjoy the island. The maids prepared two guest rooms with windows to see out over the ocean. I made a beautiful dinner for all of them, but Sylvia's mother took the child by the hand and left before the cocktail hour. He went to his room. He did not come out for many days."

"Was he the grandfather? Who was Sylvia's mother?" Beth shook her head. Maybe if she stood and moved around . . .

Missus Abu stroked the golden-brown feathers on the back of the contented hen.

The shortness of shadows signaled it must be close to noon. The fragrance of the white flowers emitted their perfume of love.

The lover—

"Missus Abu, do you know a man who lived here long ago whose name was Martin?"

Missus Abu remained silent. She raised her gaze. Her black eyes stared deep into Beth's.

Beth flushed.

White noise filled her mind. White like those blossoms she couldn't identify. She prompted herself to remember where she was in space. She sat in a metal yard chair, in Missus Abu's garden, the hounfour, in St. Thomas, and the sun said noon.

A flash of something yellow over in the corner caught her attention. A baby chick peeked out from behind an overturned flowerpot.

How sweet.

That perfume, the smell, so sweet and strong. She turned and again took in the beauty of the flowers. Those white perfumed flowers were *frangipani.* The fragrance used to make French perfume, but it had no nectar for those butterflies. How could she have forgotten that?

So lovely—

"Missus Abu, thank you for the tea but I've stayed way too long. You've been kind to me—helped me understand." She set her mug down and stood. "I'm worried those delinquents might come back. What can we do?"

"They not brave enough to do more than sneak up and run." She placed the hen back on the flagstone.

Beth's mind focused on all that was around her. She felt sharp, energized, quite refreshed. Still something remained unresolved. She couldn't quite bring it forward . . .

The hen stretched one leg out behind, then the other. She straightened, fluffed her feathers, tilted her head, and pecked at something between the flagstones.

Missus Abu's ugly wound no longer looked swollen. It wasn't even red. She probably wouldn't have any bruising.

"I be safe. Gnat protects me."

"How does that sprig of a girl protect anyone?"

"No one wants William to be angry. When he be told about the rocks thrown by those boys, he be erupting worse than a volcano. There be only one person on earth who has no fear of William."

Missus Abu stood and moved past to unlock the gate.

"That be Gnat, the one person on this earth who be making William the angriest."

*The charm of fishing is that it is the pursuit of
what is elusive but attainable, a perpetual series of
occasions for hope.*

—JOHN BUCHAN

13

Beth strolled back down the hill, rounding the turns and passing commercial and resident buildings until she ended up on the sidewalk of the main street in front of the ocean. The *Dusky Angler* bobbed gently on the water, tied securely to a large cleat set in concrete. She strode toward it. It looked like no one was on board. She wished her camera hadn't been broken.

She moved in close and listened. No sounds. She looked all around her. No one seemed to pay any attention to her or the boat.

"Hello?" She needed to ask permission to board, according to Harold.

So why not get permission.

"Anyone onboard?"

She put her sandaled foot on the gangway and started up, knowing Harold would kill her for doing something like this. She only wanted to ask who the owner was back in the 1940s. What was the harm there? At the top of the gangway she called out once again.

"Hey, get off. You can't come aboard." The voice came from within. Dark dreadlocks framed a young boy's face, appearing through the cabin doorway. He moved out into the sunlight. This milk-chocolate child wore cutoff jeans and no shirt, and around his neck hung a white-braided string on which a cream-colored bone dangled. Beth recognized it as a Maori symbol of some kind.

Why would he wear a necklace from New Zealand?

"Are you alone?" she asked.

And why would someone leave a ten- or eleven-year-old alone on a boat?

"Lady, you've got to get off." He carried a paint brush dripping with varnish. He looked toward the street and then back at her. "Girls aren't allowed."

She stepped onto the deck, studying him.

He and another boy were the ones who threw stones at Missus Abu.

"You're bad luck. You can't come onboard." He waved his free hand at her as if he was shooing chickens out of the house. "Hurry, lady, you gotta go before they come back."

"Come on, I'm actually good luck." She smiled to reassure him. "Who owns this boat? May I talk with him?"

"I can't let them find you here." He chewed on a fingernail, looking up and down the waterfront. "You've gotta leave now. Go—"

His face screwed up.

Why, he's about to cry.

He backed into the doorway.

"Okay, okay." She threw her hands up. "I'm going. See?" He'd not be giving her any useful information. She trotted down the gangway and looked up in time to see a lanky teen and a heavyset kid on the other side of the street running through a crowd of tourists. They leaped off the curb and sprinted around traffic. One headed toward the seawall with something large and silver in his hand, while the heavier boy darted into a tourist-crowded store. When the tall, skinny kid with long dreadlocks neared the seawall he flung the object out into the ocean, barely breaking his stride.

This is becoming a most interesting day.

She continued her way down the sidewalk when two policemen popped out of an alley, stopped, and looked up and down the street. A few seconds later a priest came huffing out of the same alley. The policemen were busy questioning tourists, and the priest joined in with his high-pitched voice.

Evidently the tourists hadn't seen what Beth had seen. While the priest waved his arms, pointing in different directions, the heavyset teen ambled away from view among another family of tourists.

[63]

Beth glanced back and saw the mop-headed boy standing on the bow of the boat with the varnish brush still in his hand. He watched.

She had seen where the skinny thief went. She looked around for the policemen, but they had now disappeared too.

Beth should go to the station and tell them what she knew. But then, what would the police do? They would label her as a crackpot. She had already reported one assault and robbery today.

Nutty tourist woman convinced the island is thief infested.

Still, those two policemen had been chasing that thieving teen. She shuddered. Harold would say it was none of her business, and she had quite enough mysteries for one day.

She wanted lunch, and then she would go to the hotel, make the phone call to the Historical Society, and afterward she would browse around the library. Later she could take a taxi to the aquarium, but she had suspected from the start her beach plans wouldn't fit into the day.

If Harold enjoyed his deep-sea fishing experience as much as Beth thought he would, there'd be no guilt about how she spent her time.

Across the street, a fresh-fish vendor with his ice chest open sat on a stool next to his boat.

Gnat squatted, peering into his ice chest.

Perhaps not going to the beach or the aquarium might gain her something more important. She wandered over and stood at less than interactive distance. She fumbled in her bag while she watched Gnat point at the old man's catches and ask questions. The fisherman stood, stretched his back, and glanced around.

Beth feigned interest in a yacht sailing out in the harbor.

When she looked back at the two, he had squatted again. Gnat nodded, her head close to his. Then Gnat popped up, twirled around, and skipped toward the park.

Beth headed the same way.

"Gnat," she called. "May we talk?"

The girl froze, looked up, and saw Beth. She ambled over and studied Beth before she spoke.

"How are you this afternoon, Missus?"

"I'm fine, very fine, thank you." Beth didn't expect this type of mature greeting. "Is this day treating you well?"

"I've been working on that."

"Then let's pick a cafe somewhere nearby and have a sandwich or something." Beth said. "I'll pay."

The girl scrutinized Beth some more, then shook her head.

"Why not? Aren't you hungry?"

"You know my name, so you think we aren't strangers, but we are. Only loa knows you. I don't."

There was that loa thing again.

"If you had lunch with me then we wouldn't be strangers."

"If I don't know your name, even if we eat together, we'd still be strangers." Gnat stepped back and skipped a few more feet toward the park.

Just how old was this child?

Beth darted after her.

"Gnat, my name is Beth. You helped me in the market over there. Remember? You kept me from buying tourist trash this morning." Beth knelt to look the girl in the eyes. "Missus Shalee told me your name. I don't have any children. I don't know much about young girls, but I know I like you. I like how you say things and how you do things. Do you want to know something else—about me?"

Gnat tilted her head and waited.

"I hate eating alone, and I'm very hungry."

"Then we must eat." Gnat took her hand, and they walked together.

Inside a restaurant, which Gnat selected, they found a table and picked up the menus. Beth wondered if Gnat knew how to read. *Silly.* As smart as this girl was, she probably was born reading.

Gnat put her menu down and looked out at the people.

"Do you have a suggestion for me?" Beth asked.

"Chicken roti," Gnat said. "That's a Caribbean specialty."

Beth read the description.

"Missus Beth, please don't get it if you don't like curry. I detest it." Gnat positioned herself taller in her chair and craned her neck to see out the window at something farther down the sidewalk.

"I do like curry," she said. "What would you like to order?"

"Vanilla mango ice cream. A small one, please."

"Most certainly." The girl probably had her mind made up before they even sat. No reading required.

"If you'd like something more—maybe some—"

"I only like ice cream." She nodded toward the window. "Just look at those poopholes."

At first Beth though she had said "peoples," then "potholes," but when she saw two boys on the *Dusky Angler* it clicked.

[65]

"Why do you call them poopholes?" Beth experienced a tingling deep down. Gnat's personal opinion about those particular youth might clarify some of the matters Beth didn't understand.

"Because I shouldn't say the word that starts with an *a* until I'm older."

Beth chuckled.

Dead end.

They ordered and ate. Beth restrained from prying any more than she had. She even forced herself to keep her mouth shut about Missus Abu, the grandfather, and Gnat's dancing for loa—or was it more of a trance?

Instead they talked about the Grand Canyon, the Statue of Liberty, and Disneyland. Gnat wiggled around in her chair, licking drips of ice cream off her cone, begging Beth to tell her more.

Gnat grew quiet and stared out the window at the ocean, then said, "Someday I'll go to all those places."

"I hope you do. You could come stay with us, and I'd go with you."

The roti, spicy and tender, reminded Beth of Moroccan food. She hunted for other safe topics.

"Your turn to tell me something new. Tell me about the fish that fisherman caught this morning."

Gnat's gaze hooked onto Beth's. She tilted her head to the side a smidgen, then after what must have been some internal arguing with herself, she nodded. She swallowed her last bite of ice-cream cone, wiped her mouth, and folded her napkin.

"Sometimes they're sad because it's their friend, or maybe their mother."

"Who? The fish?"

"Sometimes that fisherman catches bad fish and that makes other fish happy."

"Like the big fish that eat smaller fish?" Beth remembered that old food-chain cartoon. It really was good to be the biggest fish in the pond.

"But, Missus Beth, when fish eat others in their reef they aren't really bad. Aren't they just hungry?"

"Seems that's a reasonable way to think. So what is a bad fish?"

"One who's a bully. I see lots of fish that are picked on by other fish."

"So fish have feelings?" Beth knew better. Fish, reptiles, and amphibians do their reproductive thing then continue their instinctive life with their ancient medulla oblongata brains.

Except—yes—except crocodiles, alligators, and some snakes. Yet, some frogs nurture their young, too—what else don't we know about these animals?

"These fish know things," Gnat said.

"Like what?"

Science postulated birds didn't think or have emotional feelings either. Anyone watching crows or ravens for any length of time knows differently.

Gnat leaned toward Beth and said, "Some know more than just the things they need to learn when they're born. Some fish hunt for beautiful things, and they even worry."

Gnat drank half her glass of water. She set the glass down, looked out the window then around the room, and leaned even closer to Beth.

She whispered, "Some are really smart."

Beth looked around like Gnat had.

Geesh. This child is contagious.

Beth whispered back, "Can you tell me more?"

"I sometimes swim to the water rocks, climb up and over, and squeeze way down to get out of the bright glow of day. I squat and hold very still. After a while I see things. Sometimes I have to wait a long time."

"Most grown-ups aren't that patient, are they?" Beth offered her one of the remaining potato chips.

The girl shook her head.

"Grown-ups see big things. They see the flounder buried in the sand. They see it on its side, peeking out with both eyes."

"Now there's a strange fish," Beth said. "Do you know that one eye of the flounder actually migrates to the other side of its head by the time it's fully grown?"

"I know a stranger one. If you taste it, even touch it, you could almost—maybe even die." Gnat's eyes appeared huge on her little angular face, and her voice rasped out the scary words. "They're puffers."

Beth folded her napkin and waited for this conversation to be taken where she knew it was bound to go, to some sort of mystical level.

"One fish, this one that I know, one of those puffers—she loves music," Gnat whispered. Then she sat back, jutted her chin up, and grinned.

This stray little elfin girl completely charmed Beth yet unnerved her at the same time.

Beth leaned forward and pulled in her eyebrows.

"She listens to me." Gnat looked around. "She does. Honest. My voice sounds different way back in those water rocks."

Gnat slipped off her chair and almost climbed into Beth's lap. She was so close to Beth's face with her whispering Beth could smell her sweet ice-cream breath.

"Missus Beth, this one fish always swims up close when I sing."

"And you're sure it's the same fish?" Beth hated to even ask, because Gnat exuded such honesty and sincerity.

"She has this little scar on her tail fin." She pinched her finger and thumb almost closed to show. "I'm always afraid she won't be there. A mean fish picks on her, and I worry it might eat her. It would die if it did, but still I don't want her hurt. I sing and sing, and after a few minutes, she'll be there under the water. She's so close I can see that piece missing out of her tail fin, and she smiles. She has a little pouty smile. She stays until I'm quiet, then she swims off."

"That's impressive." Beth whispered her response. "Have you shown anyone this?"

Gnat jerked, and her elbow knocked the glass over, spilling water. She stiffened. Her face clouded.

Beth grabbed napkins and soothe-talked to Gnat while vigorously blotting. Gnat's eyes brimmed. She twisted and turned, brushing water off the front of her dress long after it did any good.

"Please don't tell, please—"

Beth could barely hear her.

"It's our secret," Beth whispered back. "I promise."

"But if you do tell—"

"Gnat, listen to me. I don't break promises."

"Some die to keep others safe. I can't let the fisherman catch her, too." Gnat's bare feet constantly moved—quick shuffling back and forth, up on her toes, back down on her heels, back on her toes, with lots of jiggling. All this happened within a couple of seconds.

"Your secret place is still your secret. I'll never tell anyone about her. Please don't worry." Beth searched her own emotions to understand how to deal with this depth of pain in the child.

Gnat pulled the hem of her dress into a twisted knot.

Beth knelt.

"Gnat, may I give you a hug?"

Gnat nodded and moved into Beth's arms. This one moment of acceptance ended almost as soon as it started. The girl pulled away and stood stone still, her eyes dark as chimney soot.

Beth smiled at her, picked up the check, opened her purse, found her wallet, then put two dollars down for the tip.

When she looked up, Gnat was gone.

Never trouble trouble until trouble troubles you.

—ANONYMOUS

14

Beth walked down the street alert, search-ing, but she didn't see Gnat. She had been told to expect the disap-pearing and reappearing act from this child. Still, it filled her with an unfinished longing inside.

Anyone with common sense would be depressed when a child explains her intimate friendship with one of the most deadly neuro-toxic animals on earth. And Gnat even *sings* to this lethal sack of chemicals. One tiny dose, just the size of a pinhead, could be five-hun-dred times more potent than cyanide.

Gnat's secretive conversation with the fisherman worried Beth, because in Japan some consider her little puffer fish a delicacy. However, chefs have to undergo rigorous training before they can even serve fugu, and still some diners die. Yet Gnat would never buy this little fish to cook. Good grief—no. She loved her little crea-ture.

Gnat had said some die to protect others. She couldn't have been talking about people. She had to mean some fish die to protect other fish.

Beth shivered in spite of the afternoon heat.

Something terrible troubled that girl. Well, yes, her mother had disappeared—that's terrible enough. Who gave her hugs, who tucked her in at night, who listened to her stories without judgment?

Beth stood in front of a store that screamed tourist crap. She smiled, remembering those words coming from the little girl. Racks of scarves, hats, and sunglasses framed the door. She ignored these items.

Did the toxic little fish really recognize Gnat? Do they have facial recognizing abilities?

A fish who likes music, could that be?

Deer, elk, moose, and even elephants come out of the wilderness to listen to classical music, then retreat afterward. If they could be attracted to music, why couldn't fish?

Well, these creatures don't have higher-level brain functions, let alone the neocortex found in mammalian brains. Hold on. Everyone mistakenly discounts nurturing abilities in a reptilian brain. However crocodile mom builds a mound for her eggs, watches them until they hatch, helps them out of their shells, then carries them to the water in her mouth. And alligator moms do the same, but they stay with their hatchlings for several months of their lives. What about certain frogs who carry tadpoles on their backs to healthier locations? And studies are being conducted on human facial recognition by birds.

Maybe we scientists don't know as much about earth's little creatures as we thought.

Beth wished Gnat trusted her enough to allow her to see this phenomenon. She sighed. Embarrassing to admit even to herself, but she wanted to believed Gnat's story. The child wouldn't know how to lie.

We become fools when we only trust the hard, cold facts we think make up the truth of science.

Beth slipped into the coolness of the shaded store and wandered down the aisle. Next to a display of suntan lotion was a large basket of waterproof, disposable cameras.

After paying for her purchase, she strolled out onto the sidewalk. The *Dusky Angler* still bobbed in the water a hundred yards or so across the street.

Her stomach fluttered when she saw who was on the vessel this time—a bonus.

Beth ambled closer to the seafront, unwrapping the cellophane from her camera then stuffing it in her pocket. She pulled the camera lever, advancing the film to number one, and raised it to her eye. She framed not only the boat riding high in the water but the tall, lanky teen and one of younger boys with dark, curly hair. He was one of Missus Abu's attackers. She also recognized the tall one as the church-thieving teen because he sported a head of dark, wild locks that hung way below his shoulders.

Then another freckled-faced kid ducked out through the ship's cabin door and laughed at something. Beth could see he was missing both his front teeth.

This kid's way beyond the age of losing baby teeth. He must have been in some high-school brawl.

As she steadied the camera, the youngest boy, the one with the dreadlocks and the Maori necklace, stepped out on deck along with an extremely skinny boy with dirt-colored hair.

Heavens, how many boys hang out on this old boat?

She lowered the camera and watched. They scampered and scurried around on the *Dusky Angler* like spiders.

"Hey there—" She yelled and waved to them.

The Maori necklace child saw her, pointed, and hollered. They all froze.

She snapped their photos, not once but several times.

Take that you little poopholes.

The tallest one, with the wild-black dreadlocks, pulled a curved knife from his belt and slowly drew it in a wide arc in front of his neck.

Big egos, little brains.

Two of the other boys grabbed for the knives tucked in their belts.

She laughed at them, held up her camera, took a few more photos, then waved again and headed up the street to the library. She had something more important to do.

~

The library on Dronningens Gade was amazing in its organization and preservation, but for her desired information it was a bust.

They had no record of Kathleen McPherson. Since she thought Kathleen lived in Martin's home, there had to be records for him, but she didn't know Martin's last name. Besides, maybe he didn't own the home.

The woman at the Historical Preservation Society said their collection of photos had been relocated to Ft. Christian's depository.

She walked on down by the stalls of the vendors to Ft. Christian. Many of the photos here still needed to be dated and labeled.

One of a big sailing ship showed a group of people. Three swim-trunked men stood next to several swim-suited women. Beth guessed from the vintage styles the photo must be early forties.

She asked for a magnifying glass. Only the cigarettes and cocktails each held bore any resemblance to Kathleen.

Beth found no photos of the *Dusky Angler*. She checked for its name listed on a registry. USVI Planning and Natural Resources had jurisdiction over this type of income and didn't register boats using public or national park moorings during the day.

And to frustrate her further, the Port Authority had nothing to do with boats that docked or anchored in the harbor. No one had any paperwork on the *Dusky Angler*.

The locals would know about the current owner—but not about the owner of forty years ago.

Missus Abu might know.

Questions, questions, and Missus Abu's confusing conversation prompted even more. Why would Sylvia be associated with some man here, and why would he send for Sylvia's mother? Could the man be Martin? If Sylvia's mother knew Martin, then how did this connect to Kathleen?

Beth returned the materials and thanked the woman.

Kathleen ran away as a teen in 1923. So when she died she must have been around ninety. Women usually live longer than men. The chance that her father would still be alive seemed small. It was even less believable that he would still be here on this island.

On her way out the door, what she saw made her stop and hold her breath.

Off to the side, under a tree, sat the curly-haired boy from the boat. He looked a little older than the one who wore the Maori necklace.

She could hear him saying soothing words to something. He sat cross-legged, his back to her, paying no attention to anything except what he held in his lap.

His fingers worked fervently. He pulled one hand up high, then again, and then again.

She moved closer.

He had a tangle of fishing line dangling from his fingers.

Beth still couldn't figure out what captured his interest.

"There you go." Success filled his voice. "Now stay out of trouble you little butterscotch mouser."

He held up a scruffy, yellow kitten and rubbed it with his cheek. When he set it on the ground it scooted under a nearby pile of construction boards. The boy wound up and pocketed the knot of line. He stood, whistling some unrecognizable tune, and sauntered down the street.

Beth found herself gawking at the kid.

This boy, who now acted so loving to this kitten, was the same one who just a few hours ago threw rocks at old Missus Abu.

Let there be spaces in your togetherness.
—KAHLIL GIBRAN

15

On Beth's way across to the park, she let Missus Abu's words tumble around in her head. The old woman's tea, even though it made her feel refreshed and happier, must have permanently muddled her problem-solving abilities.

Missus Abu had mentioned something about a fine family she used to cook for—was that the grandfather, or Mister Davies, or are they the same? Years ago the grandfather employed her to be the nanny for his young daughter who grew up and then married poorly . . . the daughter had to be Gnat's missing mother, and what happened to Gnat's father?

Did Missus Abu call them a fine family because he had a grand piano and a large house? Didn't she ask Missus Abu about this? She couldn't remember what Missus Abu said.

Dammit, who's Martin, and who in the hell is Sylvia?

"My—hello, again."

Beth snapped to and saw Shalee standing in her path.

"Good grief, I almost walked into you."

"Usually when people come to St. Thomas, they don't walk around looking like they're solving world-peace problems," Shalee said. "What's troubling you?"

"Guess you could say I was doing a little genealogy research and ended up against a brick wall." Beth liked this woman. "Are you off work now?"

"My feet are happy to be headed home. Can't wait to put them up, enjoy a cup of soup, and read my mail."

"Shalee!" The voice came from behind them.

Beth spotted Malaka trudging up the walk.

Shalee took a few steps back. She glanced at Beth and then at Malaka.

"Don't you be running off now, Shalee," Malaka said. "I have something important to say, and you be listening to me, you hear?"

Shalee stood still and waited. Beth did the same.

"That silver candlestick—don't you be thinking my boy had anything to do with stealing it from that church. Tonight he be home packing his things cause he be helping on a fishing boat for a few days." Malaka gave a final triumphant nod to ward off any doubt.

"Your boy's on the edge of trouble." Shalee moved away from Malaka. "He may not have taken the candlestick, but one day he'll be in trouble so deep it'll scare you. Then it will be too late."

"He be a good boy. He's got a paying job and all." Malaka set her chin and squinted at Shalee. "You'll see."

"A boy his age should be in school, not sailing off on some boat." Shalee touched Beth's arm. "You're here for a good time, but you'll have to relax a little to enjoy it."

She brushed passed Malaka, crossed the street, and headed up the hill.

"She thinks she's too good 'cause she works in that bank over there." Malaka chewed her lip. "She don't work two jobs every day the way I do."

Missus Abu had said Shalee and Malaka needed to repair their friendship. Beth started to say something, then stopped. Harold would tell her to stay out of their personal tiffs.

"Working two jobs is impressive, Malaka," Beth said. "You sound quite proud of your boy."

"Shalee's right. He should be in school, but I can't make him go. What do a mother do if her kid hates school?" She shifted the woven-grass basket containing a few small grocery items to her other hand.

"Most kids his age would rather play around than go to school."

"That's not it. He used to be like he couldn't get out the door fast enough to go, but then the coach stopped coaching and quit teaching him things."

Beth didn't know what to say about this.

"I not home to check on him. That's why it be good he's got a job that pays him some money. He be out at sea, so he has to be staying out of trouble on that ship."

"Hard work at sea would keep the mischief down."

"Beautiful talking to you. G'day, ma'am."

Malaka trudged across the walk to the other side of the park and on up the hill, carrying a basket of burdens heavier than all her groceries.

My basket holds only questions.

Beth sighed. Perhaps a glass of Chardonnay back at the hotel would help.

～

Beth soaked in the quiet evening air on Hotel 1829's veranda with a glass of some kind of Italian white wine, studied the ocean, puzzled over her day, and watched each taxi as it passed. She waited for Harold's return and wondered how much to tell him.

When his taxi pulled up he climbed out, all smiles and jubilant. He paid the driver, patted the driver on the back, said some cheery words, then sprinted up the stairs. Before he pressed the button to unlock the gate, Beth opened it for him. His clothes were damp and he smelled of the sea's fishy creatures.

She held his face and kissed him on the lips. He pulled back and grinned even wider.

"Sit there and catch your breath." She pointed to her wine, then scooted into the bar area. She returned with a cuba libre and a dish of pretzels, placing both before him.

"I'm ready for your fish stories." She smiled. The longer he talked the less she would have to.

Harold glowed. "I wish you could have been with me—the thrill of it all."

He deserved this day. After he'd shared all his tales of fish that got away, fish he'd shipped home, and the fish too large to keep, he asked about her day.

She gave him a brief account of her friendship with Missus Abu then said, "Let's get a quick bite of dinner and make a cozy night of it—naturally, after you shower."

He grinned, sipped his drink, studied her, then spoke. "I've been nervous about this vacation since the moment we decided to come to the Caribbean."

"I hope today lowered your level of jitteriness." She gave him her lopsided smile.

He leaned in and wrapped his hands around his tumbler. "Here's something interesting I didn't know anything about. This morning the guys mentioned how South American drug runners, mainly from Columbia, drop cocaine in waterproof packages in the ocean. Then skinny cigarette boats with speeds up to 140 miles per hour pick the stuff up and unload it in Florida. I had thought of those speed boats as rich, conspicuous consumers having fun."

"Probably right on both accounts." Beth sipped. "Since they can't enjoy the scenery in those boats, they could go to a theme park for thrills, save their money, and be even richer."

"Damn Florida." Harold shook his head. "A large percentage of the cocaine traffic in the US originates in Florida, and here I was worried about St. Thomas."

Beth patted him on his knee. "I read the science journals, remember? Read that we've developed sophisticated radar detection systems in the US that can detect seagoing drug runners as they leave Columbia."

"Seriously? The distance must be over a thousand miles, at least."

She continued, "And the Coast Guard has some new tricks up their middy blouses too, causing Colombia and surrounding countries to shift their trade routes. Now they transport more and more cocaine and hard drugs by land, up through Central America and into Mexico."

"But still, Florida. It's such a tourist draw."

"Just like the Caribbean." She knuckle-punched him in the arm. "Tomorrow, Mr. Adventurer, we go snuba diving."

Harold set his jaw, then sighed.

"Just tell me what you mean by snuba. You say it isn't snorkeling and it isn't scuba diving. Since we don't know how to do either—" He stopped and let out a huff. "This doesn't sound like a good idea to me."

You can't cross the sea merely by standing and staring at the water.

—RABINDRANATH TAGORE

16

Early the next morning Harold and Beth stood at the dock at Red Hook waiting for the private boat to take them to St. John.

"Do you think we brought everything? Should we have brought longer fins?" Harold looked through his snorkel bag.

"If so, we're out of luck."

"Beth." Harold gave her a what-have-you-gotten-us-into look. "I think we should have gone to a swimming pool in Denver. We should have learned how to use our snorkel gear before this. We're going to look foolish."

"The snuba woman said we didn't need to have any experience. There's our boat."

"Do we need bug spray?"

"If we do we really are out of luck." She pushed him toward the dock. "Stop fussing. We're fine."

When they boarded, Jamie, the energetic snuba instructor, asked those who were snuba diving to move into the center cabin on the boat and sit on the floor for instructions.

Harold gave Beth his look again.

"Now what?"

"Our first trip to St. John, and we can't even see out."

They found spots on the teakwood floor where they could sit with their backs supported by the wall. They placed their snorkel-gear bags next to them.

"We'll see it all on the way back, cranky old man."

"Thank you all for choosing Blue Water Snuba Company," Jamie said.

Harold murmured, "If it's so safe, why do we need all these instructions?"

Beth gave him a squinty-eyed look.

"We're PADI-certified scuba divers, which is the world's largest diver training organization."

"Are we diving? I thought this was like advanced snorkeling—"

Beth put her finger to his lips.

"Once we get to the beach, Ron will get you in the water for more instructions while I get the equipment ready."

Harold gave a small groan and shook his head.

"Snuba's like snorkeling underwater, like scuba except we only go down fifteen feet, and you don't control your air tanks. Your tanks are secured on a floating raft that will stay above you while you enjoy the sites below."

Harold held up one finger. "How will we know if we go too deep?"

"The length of air tube from the oxygen tank to your mouth piece is only a little over fifteen feet." Jamie smiled at him and then continued on with instructions about equipment safety and how to equalize ear pressure and other procedures.

"When your hour under the sea is over, Ron will signal for you to rise to the surface. You'll be quite a distance from where you first started, so I'll motor over in the Bayliner, pick you all up, along with the equipment, and bring you back to shore."

Her instructions took up most of their travel time. When she finished, she handed out identification cards for fish and reef life. They had a few minutes to study them during the rest of the boat trip. Beth tingled with anticipation, excited about what she might see while underwater.

The boat docked, and everyone piled into a van. Jamie informed them Trunk Bay was a National Underwater Park, and St. Thomas and St. John were proud of their gains in protecting the environment. She spent the rest of the van trip pointing out scenes of interest as they headed over the mountain to the protected bay.

Beth could tell that Harold wasn't listening. Maybe she had pushed him too far. He never liked swimming. She owed him so much emotionally, and he was always there for her, even in her most awful, bitchy moments. Now Beth had dragged him into something totally outside his comfort zone, and she could tell he hated all of this. Heat flooded her face. She needed to do better.

When the van pulled into a parking area and stopped, they stepped out into the warm, humid air onto packed sand. Everyone wandered through the giant palms toward the beach.

Beth took Harold by the hand. "We'll be fine. I bet you'll love this once we get started."

He stopped and nodded, not at her—toward the bay. There before them stretched the brilliant white sands of the beach Kathleen had loved so much. The intense turquoise water of the bay gently lapped at its edges. The beauty of it all took Beth's breath away. All the times Kathleen had talked about this place—

"We're here," he said. "We're finally here."

She couldn't speak. Harold moved his arm around her waist and held her close. They stared. Beth doubted many of Kathleen's shocking stories, but the reality of this place gave a foundation of truth for all her tales.

"Harold . . . I still hear Kathleen's words about her lovely little bay with turquoise water where she laughed and drank and danced all night on the whitest of sands."

Did my father party and dance here with her? He must have.

The rest of the snuba group had moved past them and were gathered around Ron at the water's edge. Beth and Harold looked at each other and broke out in grins, running to catch up.

"Light acts differently in water than air," Ron said, "so if you don't have a mask, you can't see. You'll only feel pressure where you have air spaces in your body cavities, like your ears."

"Even swimming pools hurt my ears," Harold mumbled.

"When the air is compressed it changes volume. It expands if there is less pressure, compacts when there's more. You'll feel this as you go under the water, because water has a higher density than the ambient air on the surface. Keep your lungs equalized. Breathe constantly. Never hold your breath. I repeat, never hold your breath."

"God—" His face paled.

Beth reached over and squeezed his hand. *Poor Harold.*

[81]

"Next we'll practice buoyancy. Take a few minutes to put your gear on. Then lie face down in the water with your snorkel and mask. Fill your lungs with air, then exhale. Your body floats when your lungs are full of air and sinks when you expel."

At the water's edge the soft sand squished between their toes. They slipped their fins on and then their masks with snorkels and waded into the warm water. Here, the calm water couldn't have been more than two feet deep. They did as they were instructed. Beth guessed the warm water helped Harold to relax, because he soon had their lesson mastered.

"Line up with your partner," Ron said. "Jamie will hook you up to your air tanks on the floating rafts. Two to a tank."

Harold hung back in the knee-high water, making them the last two to head out into the deeper parts of the ocean.

"Remember, breathe at all times. Here we go—follow me."

Beth took Harold's hand and put her face in the water. She and Harold gently kicked their fins and skimmed along the shallow, white sand, marveling at the vegetation and silverside fish. Beth felt pressure, glanced around, and realized they were several feet under the window-clear liquid.

Harold, evidently enthralled, kept squeezing her hand and pointing at fish with his free hand. Surgeon fish, tang, and rasps meandered in and out of coral and around seaweed. Tiny creatures hiding in coral would pop out, see them, then flit back into the dark. Depending on their direction, the float with the air tank above them cast its square, green-gray shadow on the white sand below.

She noticed the blue fins of their next-in-line human companions some indeterminate distance ahead of them. She didn't care. They would eventually catch up.

Harold squeezed and pointed at one fish after another. His excitement energized her, and she forgot about the rest of the world. Beth cherished this time with him. His memory of this stunning experience would be one he would probably talk about for years.

A dark flicker sent chills through Beth's body. Then another dark shadow slid along the white sand. She rolled to her side to see above her and glimpsed something long—thin—maybe on or near the surface. Before she could comprehend its shape, it vanished.

Harold jerked her hand and pointed to a shark—a sand shark. He relaxed as he watched it lazily swim around some vegetation.

Maybe that's what she had seen. But, no, sand sharks weren't long and thin.

Perhaps it was a light-water refraction thing.

The sand shark continued to check out nearby coral. Harold seemed okay with the harmless creature swimming just beyond their reach and then disappearing into the darkening edges of her vision.

Her chest felt tight, the water thick like syrup. She sucked a deep breath in through her mouthpiece and then forced the air back out. The weight around her lungs stayed. Her esophagus—it didn't work. She couldn't breathe. She should swim, but her feet grew heavy, and she couldn't make them kick. She moved her eyes to the left, in Harold's direction. His fingers fiddled, one handed, with his mouthpiece. Then he looked wide-eyed into her eyes and let her hand slip out of his, and he leaned forward.

He curled into a ball.

She couldn't make sense of anything, but she needed to touch him. She snatched his hand and squeezed it hard.

He raised his head. He studied her.

Does he expect me to do something? Up—we must go up.

She jerked a thumbs-up toward the surface and tugged his hand at the same time.

Something important—something about ocean and too fast—nitrogen build up in the tissues—

She guided him to a stop to control their ascent, then continued, rising slowly. She refused to let Harold get ahead of her. Darkness crept further into the boundaries of her vision. Beth's energy drained toward empty. Her ears filled with noise . . . a rhythmic swooshing. . . sounds of struggled breathing against the pumping of a heart . . . her heart.

She might pass out. Then the regulator would fall from her mouth. Then she would drown.

He'll be so mad at me if we die.

The warm water swayed and pushed. She watched a flood of beautiful, tiny bubbles. The two of them rose, and so did the bubbles, caressing her cheeks and forehead. Sunlight glittered off these fragile little balls while warm, gentle waves rocked her.

She stopped fighting for air. She studied the phenomenon of the effervescence rising from their face masks. Mesmerized, her muscles relaxed. A calmness enveloped her body. She would stay here—be rocked to sleep in this lovely place—forever—

One meets his destiny often in the road he takes to avoid it.

—FRENCH PROVERB

17

Blinded by hot, sunlit air, the tranquility of submersion ended as Beth involuntarily sliced though the surface of the water. She gasped and floundered.

Looking around, she pulled her mouthpiece out.

"Har—?" He emerged a few feet from the float. She didn't have the energy to talk. She grabbed the oxygen-tank float, draped her arm over it, and pushed closer to him.

He took hold and rested his head against it. The other floats in the distance continued to move steadily away. Beth forced herself to open her eyes again and search all directions. She and Harold weren't far from the beach, but she knew they didn't have enough energy to swim the distance.

A Bayliner left shore and sped toward them. The boat slowed at some distance away and the engine cut. When the wake subsided, the boat glided up. Jamie dropped anchor.

"Hand up your fins, then climb aboard."

Beth grabbed the chrome ladder, enjoying the coolness of it in her hand.

We're safe. We didn't die.

With one hand she removed her fins and handed them up. Beth

now held the ladder with both hands and forced her leg muscles to cooperate. Still fighting to find enough air for her lungs, she managed to pull herself up and aboard.

Harold followed.

Beth sprawled on the deck, struggling to catch her breath. Harold, next to her, did the same.

Jamie tugged their float in, asking them questions the whole time. She checked the mouth regulators, the tubes, and then the tank gauges. Beth watched. She felt unsettled, hot and shivering cold. Her insides churned, and her head pulsed and ached. She rolled onto her knees, crawled over to the railing, pulled herself up, leaned over the side, and heaved.

Beth's head pounded. She looked at Harold, who stared at her.

A few seconds later he did the same thing.

Jamie waited until they both finished. She handed them tissues and plastic cups filled with fresh water. She wrapped sun-warm, dry towels over their shoulders.

"We were out of oxygen, weren't we?" The towels, heat, and the humidity didn't stop Beth from shivering. Cold descended on her, permeating her whole body.

"The gauge on the oxygen tank shows it's as good as empty." Jamie tapped on the gauge several times.

Beth had pushed Harold into doing this. He didn't want to—she had talked him into it. Her head—thumping pain behind her eyes. She might throw up again. Now it made sense. She felt a heat of anger.

"You gave us an empty tank?"

"We always check. Nothing's wrong with the tank. The oxygen tubes from the tank to your regulators are compromised."

"The connections are faulty?" Harold slid down onto the plastic seats.

"The tubes are split, I can't figure out—"

"They must be old." Beth took another drink and slumped next to Harold. *Damn irresponsible people. They only care about making a buck.*

"We replaced all of them two weeks ago. Feel them."

Beth picked one up and squeezed it. "They're still pliable."

Harold reached over and bent the tube in half. "Has this happened before?"

"We triple-check everything. We can't have accidents." Jamie chewed the inside of her lip and looked out where the others were. No other pair of snuba divers had surfaced.

"I think they've been cut." Beth handed one to Jamie. "Look at this long, clean cut, and then if you turn it over, there's a start of one on this side. Like a knife slipped."

Harold leaned over to see, then said, "How could that have happened out in the middle of the bay?"

"Was anyone swimming out there?" Beth squeezed Harold's arm, steadying her own emotions more than anything.

"I noticed some boys diving off an old fishing boat." Jamie pulled her bottom lip in and studied the bay. "They were swimming around not too far away. I was busy with paper work, getting ready for our next group. I didn't pay much attention. Just kids. I'm so sorry—"

"Kids—how many?" Beth shot a glance at Harold, but he gazed around the bay. His brow was furrowed.

Jamie shrugged. "Four or five. Maybe more."

"No fishing boat here now," Harold said. "Were there adults with them?"

Jamie shook her head. "I didn't see any."

"It must have been a small boat," Harold said. "Kids couldn't pilot a fishing boat without an adult."

"They do all the time around here," Jamie said.

"Did you notice the name on the boat?" Beth squinted. She shaded her eyes with her hands and kept looking out and around too. *Nothing.*

"Didn't give it a second notice. Just old—looked like it shouldn't even float. I don't think it could have anything to do with this."

"Harold, they tried to kill us." She leaned into him. He put his arms around her.

Jamie refilled their glasses. "I find it hard to believe someone on these islands would try to kill anyone, especially not a tourist. It doesn't happen."

"There's some other explanation," Harold said.

"Then explain to me what happened out there." Beth kept her voice even. "Some *person* purposely cut that tubing."

"You can't be sure about that, Mrs. Armstrong. All I can say is that this has never . . . Ron and I will have to . . ." She shook her head again and raised her palms up. "Of course I'll refund your money. Would you fill out some papers for us? We'll need to report this."

She fumbled around in a drawer then came up with a pad of papers.

She tore off one page and handed it with a pen to Harold. The form looked yellow with age.

Beth watched the remaining floats in the gentle waves. Two by two, little pairs of heads broke through the surface next to each float. They had enjoyed their full hour of oxygen.

~

The ocean did some pitching and rolling on their trip back. Beth's stomach needed her feet on solid ground. Outside of that, it seemed uneventful. She watched the small sail boats fight the waves while the yachts and the big fishing vessels sliced through it all. The sun, now low on the horizon, slipped in and out of clouds that dissipated only to gather again.

Neither talked.

Once again, no one really believed Beth, or that those boys had cut that tubing. The police assured Jamie her written reports with the Armstrongs' statement would be all they needed. When they had time the police would inspect the equipment. Beth silently fumed.

The boat pulled into Red Hook, docked, and everyone disembarked. Some took taxis back to Charlotte Amalie, while others went to the local pub.

Harold hailed a taxi and then turned to Beth and said, "When do we storm the pirate ships?"

They climbed into the back seat of the cab. Beth still felt she couldn't get enough air in her lungs. She found herself breathing short, shallow breaths. Her head might explode if the driver hit one more bump.

Harold chatted with the driver. She stared out the window. Her problem wasn't from lack of oxygen, but from guilt. She had caused what had happened out there.

However they were just boys—cowards—sneaking up when no one watched.

She had taken their photos, and she had goaded them. Naturally she should have expected them to strike back. How foolish of her.

Were deadly cobras cowards?

"Harold." She touched his arm.

He shut off his conversation with the driver, leaned back, and waited for her to speak.

"I have to talk to you. Let's eat early, get something light for dinner before we go back to the hotel."

"Are you even hungry?" he asked. "I still feel queasy."

"I know, but with what I have to tell you I need privacy."

"Isn't our hotel room private enough? It's more private than a restaurant."

"I need light. I need people around—noisy, talking, laughing people. I don't want dark and gloomy. Please, let's just go somewhere where we can talk for a few minutes."

"Will I need my kryptonite?"

She looked away, shaking her head.

"Hey there. What's—" He put his finger under her chin and lifted it so he could look into her eyes.

Her glance darted toward the driver.

He took his hand away and looked out at the passing scenery.

Of all the wild beasts, [boys are] the most difficult to handle.
—PLATO

18

At the cafe Harold found a table in the far corner. Beth waited until their sandwiches were served and the waiter was busy with others.

"I provoked those boys." She filled in what she had left out of her yesterday's events, starting with the rocks thrown at Missus Abu and ending with her arrogant photo taking of the delinquents.

He ate his fries in silence.

She moved her finger along a crack in the wooden table top.

"If it's only those boys," he said, "we're fine. Besides, do you really think they could sail that boat to St. John all by themselves?"

"They live with the ocean every day. Can Kansas kids drive tractors at twelve?" She snatched one of his fries. It was cold and greasy.

"Still, I don't know. They're kids."

"Kids who clobber an old woman and drown couples—I have no idea, and you don't either, about what they could do next." She dabbed the limp fry in his catsup.

"They're cowards. Cowards aren't clever."

"They were clever enough to kill us."

"We're still here. I'm breathing—aren't you?"

"Barely—and no one would have figured it out, Harold. We almost died out there, and it's all my doing." She dropped the uneaten fry on her plate and wiped her hands on her napkin.

"If we had an adult to suspect, not some dirty-feet urchins, then I'd worry."

"Some of those dirty feet belonged to teenagers."

"You're reaching, Beth. They are *children*." He studied her.

"Didn't you ever read *Lord of the Flies*?" She turned away and wouldn't look at him.

He held up another limp fry, moved it in front of her face.

She would not grin. She would not accept his peace offering.

He dipped it in catsup and held it up to her again.

"Gads," she said, "would you stop that? This is serious. If things hadn't worked out, we'd be at the bottom of Trunk Bay right now. Doesn't that scare you?"

"Makes me appreciate you and life all the more." He munched down on the fry.

"Missus Abu suggested someone might have killed a woman."

"What?"

"At least I think that's what Missus Abu implied."

"Who? What woman?"

"The mother of the young girl who gave me the nut I threw away. I think the girl thinks William killed her."

"William being—"

"The guy who stole my watch and—"

"What the—you're sure?"

"Not that he's a murderer. Missus Abu says he isn't. Yet the girl believes he's responsible somehow."

They both sat in silence for a few minutes.

"Don't we go to Virgin Gorda tomorrow?" Harold said. "It's not close to St. Thomas like St. John." He wiped his fingers and picked up the check.

"The brochures say it's a laid-back island with ultra-friendly people." Beth picked up her snorkel bag, stood, and slung it over her shoulder.

"You'll probably end up bored." He pulled out some bills. "No worries, mon, you'll find us some vampires or zombies to massacre." He wasn't smiling. He slapped the bills down and turned away from her.

"I—" She shut her mouth, not knowing what to say next.

This new quasi-humor undercurrent coming from him made her nervous. She couldn't evaluate his true level of hidden anger.

They paid and walked down the sidewalk, turned the corner, and saw Missus Abu purchasing some fresh fish from the same fishmonger Gnat had been talking with earlier.

Missus Abu waved to Beth.

"Good evening, Missus Armstrong. Did you and your husband enjoy your dinner?"

"We did." She introduced her to Harold.

"According to Beth," he said, "you're the book of knowledge for this island."

"I be here a long time. I know people, and I see things." She lowered her head, grinning.

"Have you been to a doctor?" Beth asked. "Your forehead is almost well." Only a thin red line showed.

"I be quick to heal. Your arm is better, right? Enjoy your walk back to the hotel this nice evening." She shuffled up toward the hill.

"Oh—Missus Abu, could you tell me who owns the *Dusky Angler*?"

Missus Abu stopped and faced her. Her head tilted slightly. She seemed to be sorting out her thoughts.

"Those two boys who threw those rocks were all over it yesterday," Beth said.

"I say he should not let them do that." Her brows pulled together, making her eyes even darker.

"Who?"

"William."

"You've told William about the boys on the boat?"

"I told him there be bad things happen today. He play deaf. Tomorrow you go to Virgin Gorda. You rest and be loving that island. Maybe we see each other when you return."

"We'd like that. Right, Beth?"

Beth agreed.

The elderly woman smiled, nodded good-bye, and trundled on toward her home.

"You picked a good friend there." Harold started up the steps to the hotel. Missus Abu was almost to Wimmelskafts Gade.

"Aren't you coming?" Harold asked.

"How does she know everything?" Beth caught up with Harold. "I never told anyone our plans."

They climbed the stairs and buzzed themselves in. Missus Abu's small interruption of their evening seemed to put Harold in a more open mood. She felt grateful toward the old woman and her wisdom.

He unlocked the door to their room and snapped on the lights. Beth walked over to open the shutters. She wanted to see the lights of the city.

He called her name. She looked at him, and he pointed. Something sparkled on the dresser top.

"My rings?"

She rushed over to be sure. Something else rested next to them. Something she'd discarded as useless.

The brown nut.

Regret is an appalling waste of energy; you can't build on it;
it's only good for wallowing in.

—KATHERINE MANSFIELD

19

Harold and Beth checked out of Hotel 1829 early the next morning and took a taxi back to Red Hook. Beth hated to leave St. Thomas, because she still wasn't any closer to identifying her father or Sylvia. Along with almost being murdered, she felt like a total failure. Correction—if she had actually died, then she would have been a total failure.

How awful to be incompetent even at failing.

"Did you check the bathroom?" Harold asked.

"I left all our toiletries along with my nightie for the maid." Beth used to be the controller, the planner, the worrier—not Harold. Her offhand remarks didn't cause her to feel any lighter. It didn't ease the darkness hanging in the back of her mind.

He shook his head. She could see he still carried the stress from the snuba incident too.

They boarded the ferry, which would first stop briefly at St. John, then go on to Tortola, and finally end at their destination on Virgin Gorda.

"We should have stuck with dancing and making love on that beach," he said.

"Maybe, or maybe this brown nut needed to be with us." She pulled it out of her pocket. "Why were my rings returned and this nut but not my watch? I'm not superstitious, but this is starting to make me wonder. How many more times will it be given to us?"

"To you—no one gave it to me." The corners of his mouth scrunched into his teasing look. "Keeping it close by for safety are you, Ms. Scientist?"

"It might be full of protein."

"Lame excuse."

The ferry turned into the wind. Ocean spray hit his face. He leaned away from the railing.

She sighed. "Guess I'll have to toss it into the sea to uphold my honor as a true woman of research who only embraces proven facts and scientific theory." She held it high, ready to toss it far out to sea. It seemed unusually shiny in the sunlight. She lowered her hand and turned it around. Its warmth increased. *Nonsense.* She studied its dark richness and the single light-tan spot on one side.

"What type of nut it is?" He wiped wet hair out of her eyes.

"I should have recognized it earlier. We have here the genus Aesculus, probably the species A. glabra, and it's not a nut. It's a seed. If you lived in Ohio you'd be quite familiar with this one. It's nothing special. It's the buckeye."

"Do you toss it, or do we eat it?"

"I'm not fond of tannic acid, but it can serve as my souvenir." She stuck it back in her pocket without looking at him. She stared out to sea at the profile of St. John Island.

He put his arm around her shoulders and watched with her.

When they arrived at the ferry dock on St. John, they caught another ferry that took them to Tortola's West End. There they boarded the final ferry, and within minutes they were docking in Spanish Town on the southern part of Virgin Gorda.

Beth pulled out her list and purchased groceries for the next few days. Then they signaled a taxi waiting outside the store and asked to be taken to Spring Bay.

The driver headed south out of Spanish Town and drove down a two-lane road past fields and homes and a few commercial buildings. Children, bicycles, dogs, and chickens seemed to be what tied this little community together.

Beth felt lulled by the slow passing of the scenery, but after taking a gentle curve, she bolted straight up and grabbed Harold's arm.

Holding tight to Harold's wrist, she pointed at a disheveled teen with dirt-blond hair who stood beside the road. Two older men handed the teen something small. He stuffed whatever it was in his short's pocket.

Harold said, "What about them?"

She held a finger to his lips, nodded toward the driver, and spoke in a whisper.

"That's one of the boys from the *Dusky Angler*."

"Can't be. We're on a different island miles away."

"I know it is. He's got a knife in his belt, too.

How would the boy know they were coming here? Yet, Missus Abu knew.

"Watch, we'll see lots of young guys with hair like that and machetes." Harold returned her whispers. "Machetes are a necessity here—you know—to cut open coconuts and threaten little Sunday schoolers."

Beth ignored his sarcasm and continued to study the people as they drove. She saw the usual assortment of men, women, children of various sizes and ages, and animals but no other teen boys with knives dealing drugs.

When they reached Spring Bay, Beth gave Harold the look he always gave her when he thought she was wrong.

He shrugged.

They signed in to their lodging and sauntered up the hill to find their cabin. The wooden, yurt-like bungalow held a combined kitchen and living area, a bedroom, a full bathroom, a wraparound porch, and an outside barbeque. They put the groceries away and unpacked their clothes. After they changed into swimming suits, they dashed down the sandy path, chatting the whole time. Beth couldn't wait to spend the rest of the day snorkeling in the bay's quiet, turquoise waters.

~

"I keep expecting jellyfish or man-eating sharks to get me." Harold toweled off and sat next to her. "If the bay stays this calm we might actually relax and survive."

Beth set her book aside. "Floating out there, in those gentle waves, I could actually study the annelida—"

"English please, professor."

"Different groups of sea worms." She shrugged. "They're segmented worms, like our common earth worms. I wanted you to see the

[95]

Christmas Tree one, about fifteen to twenty feet down, but before I could call you—poof—gone under the sand."

"If you don't get that promotion, let's sell the house and move here." He sifted the sand through his fingers.

She watched him a minute before she said, "Guess we could sell seashells down by the seashore." Maybe this wasn't such an outlandish idea. She could consider a career change, but definitely not connected to anything seashell-like, and certainly not in seashore sales.

"Serious thinking here." Harold slipped into his sandals. "Building island homes to withstand hurricanes and to be ecofriendly sort of intrigues me."

They both sat there on the sand for a few more minutes. Beth watched the catamarans sailing farther out on the sea.

Harold broke the silence. "Guess we'd first need to check the residency requirements and then what it takes for building permits and construction."

"You are actually giving this serious thought."

"Damn right. I'm exhausted. We could use some laid-back island life." He shook out his towel. "But then, almost drowning could be driving my current mood."

"Quite an adrenaline surge yesterday." She wiggled her toes into her sandals and wrapped her towel around her. "Fear of being murdered does wear one out."

She put her book in her beach bag, and they started back up the path to their cabin.

Harold said, "Read a study somewhere about a growing problem in today's world. Could explain why some teens live their young lives engaged in dangerous activities."

She stopped in the path to stare at him, not sure where his conversation would take her.

"Gang members show off by engaging in hazardous undertakings, which raises their adrenaline. Soon they're hooked on these rushes. Their thrill-seeking behaviors continue to escalate, which in turn increases adrenaline production. Now these kids continue their risk-taking just to feed their highs."

"Great, Harold. No more rest and relaxation for us. If the teen we saw dealing drugs is part of the *Dusky Angler*'s crew, then these kids *do* hop from island to island. Your unnerving information about dangerous teens has just fueled *my* adrenaline."

Friendship is one mind within two bodies.

—MENCIUS

20

After barbequing chicken for their dinner, Beth and Harold tossed a salad, ate, cleaned up, and hiked to the top of the hill above the bay to check out a local tavern called Mad Dog.

"Want to sit outside?" Harold pointed to the picnic tables under hanging flower baskets that lined the wooden porch.

"I'm too lobster-like for any more sun."

He held the door for her. The interior of the bar captured the light of the setting sun from windows on three sides. She caught a whiff of something mimicking squeaky freshness. Glass cleaner. They picked a table with the view of the ocean, spanning out far below.

A tan thirty-year-old with bouncy-blonde hair wearing sharply pressed white shorts and a red T-shirt placed water in front of them, handed each a menu, and indicated she would be right back. She sprinted out to the porch.

"Do you want anything to eat?" Harold pointed at the menu. Beth shook her head.

Only one other customer sat inside, seated at the bar. She went through odd periods where every stranger seemed to look like someone she knew, and his familiarity made him one of those. She wondered if this happened to others.

Beth took a long drink of water, looked away, then looked back and studied the man more carefully. He was tall, extremely old, and had dazzling white hair. It *was* him. The grandfather. He'd talked with Missus Abu and then walked off with Gnat back on their first day in St. Thomas.

The server came in and put the dirty glasses and dishes next to the sink. Beth nodded at Harold, stood, took her glass of water, and went over to the gentleman. Harold followed her.

"Excuse me, sir, I saw you on St. Thomas, and your granddaughter's dance captivated me."

"Aah." The man grinned ear to ear. "Pretty lady, what makes you think she's my granddaughter?"

"Missus Abu told me. She also told me you're Gnat's ice-cream supplier."

"Well—and so I am." He patted the barstools next to him. He wore frayed and holey cutoffs, sandals, and a baggy tank top, showing off his droopy, sun-cooked pectorals. Up close his skin looked like rumply brown elephant knees.

"May we buy you a drink?" Harold asked.

"Never one to pass on tha'. Jana, another one please."

"What would you two like?" Jana moved from the dishwashing sink over to the bar.

"Cuba libre for me. How about you, Beth?"

"Make it two." She gave the younger woman a smile.

"Three cuba libres coming up." Jana flashed a smile back.

"Aah—kindred spirits. Can't go wrong with a good rum in these islands. How long you staying?"

"We'll be here all week." Harold slipped into his social mode. His face relaxed, and a twinkle appeared in his eyes.

"Hell. You'll barely get your feet wet." The gentleman shook his head. "Shame, damn shame, you can't capture the rhythm in tha' short time. Ha, got it, you're tied to jobs. You must rush back—have to keep your life on track, right?" He downed the last of his drink. "No time to dally about unproductively. Damn shame."

"You're smacking us in the face with truths we don't want to hear." Beth gave Harold a wink. "Yet if we didn't, we'd not be able to pay the bills, and then—"

"We'd have to stay here and sell seashells." Harold grinned.

"'Fair is foul, and foul is fair: Hover through the fog and filthy air.'"

The man slapped Harold on the back, took a huge swig, then shoved his empty glass away.

"Excuse me?" Harold cocked his head, not sure what he was missing.

"Shakespeare," Beth said.

"Shakespeare, the ol' gentleman. His words clog up my mind and save me from my past."

Jana set three fresh tumblers with accompanying limes in front of them and went back to her sink duties.

"Or maybe not—maybe this is my savior." He held up his drink in a mock toast. "Maybe both are my reliable rescuers. What shall we toast? Ah, is there anything left in this goddamned world to cheer about?"

"Most certainly." Harold held his glass high. "Here's to new friendships."

"Aah, a good one. Hear-hear."

"We could toast," Beth said, "to your granddaughter and her future."

"Her future is her past, fair is foul, nothing there to last."

"Why would you say that? She's intelligent, compassionate, graceful, and exotic. She has the whole world before her."

"There you go, Salty. Listen to her since you won't listen to me." Jana set a dish of peanuts on the bar. "You should be ashamed. This lady knows her better than you."

"Hello, travelers." A plucky, suntanned gentleman with salt-and-pepper hair over his ears pushed through the door with a large basket of brilliant hibiscus blossoms. His age and his casualness of dress matched Salty's.

"Ah, Mad Dog, at last you and I have some interesting company."

"By all means, introduce me." Mad Dog handed Beth a blossom and kissed her cheek. He went over and set the basket on the bar then stuck out his hand to Harold.

"I can't," Salty said. "I don't have a clue who they are."

Harold laughed, offered his hand, and shook Mad Dog's.

"We're your typical tourists."

"Glad to meet you, Typical Tourist." He grinned and took Beth's hand, giving it a kiss. "Now, give me some short first names so I won't have to slur over a dozen matching syllables."

Beth and Harold obliged. Beth took a moment to tuck the scarlet hibiscus blossom in her hair. Something stirred inside her. Now she felt like she belonged on this island—here with these gentle people.

Salty studied her process of arranging strands of hair with the flower behind her ear. She found this amusing. Then he blinked his eyes a few times and lowered his gaze to his glass. Pervasive sadness seemed to overwhelm him.

She should say something, but she didn't know what.

Harold lifted his glass toward the owner. "Tell me why you and your bar are called Mad Dog?"

"Wasn't my doing. Friends started the name calling. You'll have to ask them."

"You, sir," Harold took a sip, then said, "don't look in the least mad."

"He's called Mad Dog because he is." Salty snorted, then said, "He's the original Mad Dog. Fifty-some years at sea makes anyone mad. Look at me. But then . . . he's also one ugly sonofabitch."

Mad Dog bolted from his stool and whacked his good pal up the back of his head. He stood there, with teeth clenched, and stared at Salty.

Salty jerked around, hefted himself off the stool, set his jaw, and glared eye to eye at Mad Dog.

Beth glanced at Harold. Harold sat frozen, his wide eyes locked on the two older men.

Mad Dog and Salty, even in their aging years, both stood close to six feet tall and each had the weathered-brown skin of island life. Salty sported a full head of white hair while the top of Mad Dog's head reflected lots of light. But Mad Dog had several pounds on Salty. They stood rigid, staring at each other, faces red and tight with anger.

Salty jutted his chin and pulled his hands up and into fists. Mad Dog tossed him a toothy sneer, swung his arm back, and smacked Salty's chest hard.

Salty growled. With two fingers and his thumb he vise-gripped one of Mad Dog's flappy biceps and shook it.

Mad Dog yelped. He swung again at Salty, but Salty ducked. Laughing, Salty yanked Mad Dog into a wobbly headlock.

Beth shot Jana a look. Jana, her back to everyone, continued to wash glasses.

The old men grunted and stumbled around, huffing, until Mad Dog, still bent in a headlock, managed to work them nearer the bar.

Cussing all the while, his fingers flailed out and around until he grabbed the basket of flowers. He flipped it, banging Salty on the back like a tambourine. Crimson hibiscus blossoms flew all around.

Beth needed to shut her mouth, but when she did it popped back open. She glanced at Harold. He looked horrified, still frozen on his barstool. Salty, emitting unnatural guttural noises, tightened the headlock. Harold gasped and stood. The cussing old men tottered around, bumping into chairs and stools. Jana continued her dishwashing. Beth could even hear her humming.

Desperate, Beth said, "Harold?" He shrugged and raised his palms up.

The men continued to stumble, growl, and gurgle their way back to the bar. Huffing, Salty, with one hand, worked an ice cube out of a glass. The glass crashed to the floor and shattered.

Mad Dog hollered, "Stop that you old fuzz nuts. Y'er breaking up the place. Y'er costing me money."

Salty grimaced and said, "You're a clumsy, hotheaded ass. I'll give you something to help you cool off." He maneuvered the ice cube down the back of Mad Dog's shorts.

Mad Dog yowled, reached behind him, and squeezed Salty's balls.

Salty gasped and bellowed, "You Bastard!"

Releasing Mad Dog, he crumpled to the floor.

Mad Dog lost his stability without Salty to hang on to. He crashed down on top.

Harold and Beth clutched each other. She gaped at the tangle of chicken elbows and knobby knees and wondered how many bones were broken.

The men's shrieking of cusswords diminished in volume until they both roared with laughter.

"I tell you, Salty," Mad Dog rolled onto his knees and said, "it's not the sea that done that to you ole boy. It's that shipping business that got to you."

A chill shot through Beth. She shut her eyes to recall a flash of memory from months ago.

Kathleen. Kathleen, with cigarette, studying one of her fingernails. She said something about her one true love . . . and . . . shipping business. Martin . . . was it Martin?

"Goddammit, someone help us up," Salty said.

He waved his arm out, flagging down any helper who might pass by. Beth lurched forward and grabbed an arm. Harold did the same.

"Aah, wrong, not shipping, you ole coot. It's the song. You know that old song."

Salty waggled his shoulders and shook out his arms. Then he stepped carefully, as if the floor rolled in uneven waves. He steadied the barstool, and with what seemed to be great consideration he finally settled back on top of it. He rested his elbows on the bar like he was concentrating on breathing normally.

"I'll drink to that. Jana." Mad Dog put his hands on his hips and arched his back. He rotated his head from shoulder to shoulder.

"You're drinking up all your profits, you know." She started sweeping up the hibiscus blossoms and broken glass.

"I'm not the one. It's the two of you who drain my profits." Mad Dog rubbed his neck. "His breaking the glassware, and you feeding all that ice cream to the young ones."

He walked behind the bar, picked up a clean glass, filled it with rum and Coke, and topped it off with a squeeze of lime.

Harold and Beth's glasses stood empty except for the ice.

"Give me those." Mad Dog filled each of them.

"What about my glass?" Salty squinted at his friend.

"You rich eccentric geezer, you broke it. Stop being such a freeloader." Mad Dog squirted Salty in the face with soda water.

"Stop that." Jana tossed the shards and blossoms in the trash. Then she reached over and took the nozzle away, handed Salty a towel, and fixed him a drink.

"If they're my profits, then I can do with them whatever the hell I like—" Mad Dog took his drink to the customer side of the bar and pulled his stool out so he could join their conversation.

"Like the two of you old tightwads could sponsor my private school." Jana shoved the broom in a closet.

"I'm not the rich one here, he is." Mad Dog pointed to Salty. "If I had half his coins, I'd hire some guys to finish that rock work I started years ago." He swigged most of his drink. "My true love, I promised her I'd get it done, then she up and left for the cemetery, leaving me with a broken heart, my broken promises, and her damned unruly flowers, and hell, it's all going to hell. Don't have enough handbaskets to even cart them in."

"And don't you believe a word of it," Jana said to Beth and Harold. Then she added, "Old man, the only reason you haven't hired anyone is because you're too tightfisted, drunk, and lazy to do anything productive. You need a life's project, and mine would make you proud."

Salty folded the wet towel and placed it on the bar. Then he stared at the menu on the chalkboard behind Jana.

"Tell us about your granddaughter," Beth said. "She's quite attached to you."

"She's . . ." He turned toward her. "She does what she wants. Even at nine she knows her own mind, if she even has one."

"That's an odd statement, and I'm sure not deserving." Beth looked at Jana for support.

"I was her teacher last year. Gnat's exceptionally bright, quite creative, and"—Jana bent over and put her face in Salty's face—"severely depressed."

"She's an odd one," he said, "shuttling herself hither and yon without any supervision. Pops up where you least expect her. Carries the ills of the world on her shoulder. Needs a mother. Goddamnit all to hell."

He appeared to stuff his remaining thoughts in the bottom of his glass.

"Do you know what happened to her—Gnat's mother?" Harold asked.

Beth looked away. She didn't want to tell the worrisome story about Gnat's visions of her mother calling to her from deep underwater.

Fear not—what is not real, never was, and never will be.

—BHAGAVAD GITA

21

"You're bringing Salty down," Mad Dog said. "Jana, put on some lively music. Look at that beautiful evening out there."

"Hear a twin engine?" Salty said.

"She's going to drop the diamonds." Mad Dog strode over to the windows.

"Not dark enough yet. Lucy's only scouting." Salty turned back to his drink.

"Diamonds?" Harold asked.

Beth heard the small plane too.

"Lucy in the Sky," Salty said. "Mad Dog, any vessels out there?"

"Not this evening."

"Good." Salty drank his drink.

"LSD?" Beth said.

"Not in this day's market," Salty said. "Meth from Mexico, cocaine and heroin from Columbia, but here it's only Mary Jane from Jamaica and Dominica, dressed in her watertight gown."

"Here's to the mystery of the night sea." Mad Dog collected his empty glass to refresh it. "Harold, have you ever played in the ocean at night? Not a good thing to do."

"What's the difference between day and night?" Harold asked.

"Light and dark." Salty slapped Mad Dog on the back. Both older men howled, shoving each other around for a few seconds over that one.

Warmth washed over Beth. These playful old guys were what she and Harold needed after yesterday's murder attempt.

Mad Dog went back to his bartending. He reached for Beth's glass. She put her hand over it.

"Do you know what the big predator fish hunt?" Mad Dog asked.

Beth looked at Harold, and he shrugged.

"Smaller, sleeping fish." Mad Dog gave a snort. "So don't swim after dark and be prey."

"Are you teasing?" Harold furrowed his brow.

"Hold it." Beth shook her head. "How do we know what's true? You two constantly play games."

"Aah, tha's rude of us," Salty said. "Tell you what, we'll play our favorite game. You pick any question that's popped into tha' pretty head, and we'll answer it."

"Our best game ever," Mad Dog said, "except he didn't tell you we may not answer with the truth."

The two men chuckled and worked to shove the other off the barstools. When Jana bellowed at them to stop, they both roared with laughter.

Harold grabbed Beth's hand, squeezed it, and grinned at her. She had hit the jackpot. Finally she could freely ask some questions.

When the geriatric kids finally settled down, Beth was ready with her question.

"My question is about a woman who's maybe a few years older than I am." Beth took time to select her words. "She's heavyset and sometimes plays the saxophone at Hotel 1829."

"Must be talking about Sylvia," Salty said.

Mad Dog agreed. "She's playing at that resort at the north end of the island. Is it Bitter End Yacht Club, or maybe it's Leverick Bay this time?" Mad Dog went over and pulled a flyer off the bulletin board announcing music at the bay.

"Bitter End it is." He handed it to Beth. Then he strode back to the window.

"That's her, Sylvia." Beth grinned at Harold. "But who is she? Who is Sylvia?"

Salty swigged his drink, set it down with a thud, then he looked at Beth and started singing.

> *Who is Sylvia? What is she,*
> *That all our swains commend her?*
> *Holy, fair, and wise is she."*

Salty's voice rang a true baritone, but the melody carried with it a hint of aged and crackly vocal cords.

"Shakespeare again, right?" Beth said.

"You've lost me." Harold glanced to see if Mad Dog understood.

Mad Dog wasn't interested. He was back by the windows, evidently searching for planes.

"Tell me about her." Beth felt she was about to turn a page in a new book.

"He just did. Shakespeare said it all." Mad Dog came back to the bar.

"But she was in Denver just last week."

"If you said you saw my granddaughter in Denver, I'd believe you. Don't know about Sylvia." Salty cradled his head in his hands.

"But why would Sylvia—?" She felt Harold's hand on her arm. He needed to stop being so nervous and give her one more minute.

"Don't think the twin engine is coming this evening."

"I think Sylvia knew my mother."

Harold patted her arm to get her attention. "We've enjoyed it, guys."

She ignored him. "One more question. Do you know anything about Sylvia's family, say her mother?"

Mad Dog whirled away from the window. "Sorry, most lovely lady." Mad Dog picked up her empty glass. "Game over. You have exceeded your number of questions."

No man needs a vacation so much as the man who has just had one.

—ELBERT HUBBARD

22

"Just listen to yourself." Harold guided her down the steps toward the darkened road.

"But it wasn't my game, it was theirs."

With no cars, houses, or streetlights, the road felt eerie. If they wanted to avoid cacti and other woody plants this road was their only choice. The night air hung warm and heavy around them.

"You're like an inquisitor, Beth. How do you think you make others feel?" He led her down the middle of the road.

"Happy." She let go of his hand to scratch a bug bite. "They enjoyed their little game. 'If my granddaughter showed up in Denver,' and that little song he sung about 'Who is Sylvia.'"

She stubbed her toe on something in the dark. *Where was the moon?* She hopped on her other foot until the pain stopped. Harold kept on walking, unaware. She bet the toe was bleeding.

"The bartender at the hotel, the waiter . . . Why do you think your camera was smashed? I can only guess at what you and Missus Abu discussed. Why did you ask about Sylvia's mother?"

She sprinted up to him. "Sylvia visited someone on St. Thomas with her mother when she was a little kid."

He stopped, turned, and looked at her. Then he resumed walking down the steep hill.

"If her mother came to see some man, and Kathleen lived around there somewhere, don't you think there could be a connection?"

"You don't even know when Kathleen lived here."

Beth sighed. She had no way of finding that out.

"Your imagination is running away—again."

Then he was silent.

"Sylvia being in two places where Kathleen lived that are thousands of miles apart isn't something I can ignore. There's a connection somewhere."

"And you're wrong about those men. They weren't happy about your questions."

"If I upset them, they wouldn't have told me about Sylvia's gig at the Bitter End Yacht Club."

"Don't you think if she wanted to talk with you she would have stuck around after the funeral?"

"Maybe she's shy." Beth's toe hurt, and she hated pretending to be cheerful when she fumed inside because of his questioning.

"Damn—now I get it. Shy saxophone players perform only at funerals for dead people. Are you going to spend the rest of our trip chasing her around this island?"

"There's no reason we can't go to Bitter End Yacht Club. Might be fun. We both like music."

"There are several reasons. One, I don't want to go. Two, you're being intrusive into other people's lives. Three, I don't think there are roads leading to Leverick Bay, let alone Bitter End."

"That can't be right." She walked in silence for a few minutes.

"I need a vacation from our vacation." He took her hand again.

"Water taxis. That's it." She chuckled. "Wouldn't that make an enchanting evening? So different. No water taxis in Denver." She punched him in the arm. "Who'd have thought?"

"Back to number one."

"What?"

"I don't want to go."

Beth knew she could come up with some way to convince him. He'd have fun at the north end. He just didn't know it yet. She made him stop and face her.

"Bet you would go if I offered to skinny dip with you tonight in the bay?"

"Woman, you're insane. Remember what they said—big predator fish."

~

Early the next morning Beth and Harold dashed down the sandy path to enjoy a full day of swimming, snorkeling, and reading on the beach. Beth stopped Harold before they reached the bay.

"Come see this." She took him a few steps off the path where she pointed to a tangled plant of prickly green.

"Good grief, I've never seen green-needled cables before." He grinned. "What type of cactus?"

"Night-blooming cereus." She knelt closer. "See here. This blossom looks ripe for opening. This type only blooms one night a year. Let's come back tonight with a flashlight."

"Wouldn't want to step on it in the dark. Hadn't thought we'd need to be careful because of dangerous plants."

"You wouldn't die, but you would feel miserable." She stood and scanned the area. "Closer to the beaches you might find something more lethal."

Harold held her arm. "Better point it all out, because I don't want any more surprises. I've had enough danger during this vacation."

She grinned and pushed him forward on down toward the bay.

"I haven't seen the manchineel tree here, so you're safe. Its leaves, bark, and little green apples are caustic. They call it *arbol de la muerte*, or the tree of death."

"Holy crap, you're talking about the whole tree, not just the apples?"

"The manchineel tree proudly holds the title of the most deadly tree in the world."

"And you're telling me it's here on Virgin Gorda."

"It's on all these islands, Harold. It's also found in Hawaii and Florida, too. The manchineel grows along the coastline. When their little apples fall off the tree, they're swept away in the currents to other beaches. There they settle and take root."

The beach, shaded in part by large palm trees, appealed to Beth because of its coziness. Big boulders defined and sheltered both ends of the little cove, protecting its water from rough waves. Beyond the boulders, the bay's sandy bottom plunged into the deeper ocean floor.

Except for the birds, sea life, and an occasional tourist couple, they had the whole place to themselves.

Private parties of boaters anchored a half mile or so off the bay. They could watch the passengers of the vessels snorkel and play around in the ocean. Beth became aware that many from the anchored boats were swimming toward the island south of their bay and disappearing behind the boulders.

"Harold, have you seen how many swimmers from those catamarans head over that direction? Shall we see what that beach has that this one doesn't?"

"Water looks sort of rough out there."

She had to agree. The water at the edge of the boulders showed a slight choppiness.

"You're right. Looks a bit rougher, but then we're used to no current in here. We should be fine with our fins. Are you okay with this?"

He shrugged.

They both clipped on their waterproof money belts and swam toward the boulders, circling the south edge of Spring Bay. She focused her attention on Harold. One more mishap and he'd more than likely be ready to give up this whole vacation thing.

He took long, strong stokes through the water, and when they reached the currents at the edge of the bay, his strokes didn't change much. He seemed to be enjoying this.

Beth's muscles let go of her tenseness, and she matched him stroke for stroke.

They had to swim against the current and be careful the waves didn't slam them into the rocks. They swam single file a little way out into the deeper water.

Once around the other side of the boulders, Beth caught up to Harold, and they treaded water.

"Where'd everyone go?" Beth scanned a boulder-laden hillside. Only three people sat on the beach, taking fins and snorkel masks out of their bags and putting their gear on.

"What the heck?" Harold looked at Beth. "Didn't we see dozens of swimmers come this way?"

He continued on toward the beach, and Beth followed. When they climbed up on the edge of the wave-whipped beach, they introduced themselves to the three who were preparing to swim back to their catamaran.

"We've watched several dozen people swim over here in the last hour," Harold said. "Where'd they go?"

The group all talked at once and pointed to a sign by an entrance near a myriad of large boulders. Harold and Beth took their fins off and walked over to read the plaque.

The Baths. The plaque told of how slave traders made the slaves bathe in the pools found within these rock structures.

"Let's explore." Beth took off her mask.

"Do you think our stuff is safe on the beach?" Harold pulled his mask off and looked back out to sea.

"Let's carry our gear. However the other beach—come on, we don't even lock our door at night. It's all good here."

Ancient volcanic action had piled up these hippopotamus-shaped granite boulders, where some tumbled down making tunnels, grottoes, and hidey-holes. Most of the rocklike rooms held pools of clear seawater, sparkling from shafts of sunlight.

Beth found herself searching for little secret places where the sea might let a small fish swim in to listen to the songs of a young girl. That had to be a place on St. Thomas. How would Gnat get here?

Maybe there were other formations like these on other islands. Beth caught herself regarding Gnat's story as true, not what it probably was, just a fantasy in the little girl's mind.

Harold and Beth waded through glasslike water of different depths and around other visitors taking photos. All were evidently enthralled by the photogenic qualities of these water, light, and rock spaces. Harold and Beth moved past the photographers, timing their moves to stay out of the pictures.

Other sightseers climbed and squeezed through passages ahead and behind them. Beth and Harold skirted around deeper pools of water. Hiking and crawling over these boulders harkened back to pleasant childhood days when Beth had gone on family outings in the Colorado Mountains.

All the while sunlight streamed through cracks above.

They smiled and nodded and heard their own "Good Afternoon" echoing to other tourists coming and going. Finally, Harold and Beth came to a short ladder and climbed out into brilliant sunshine.

Harold beamed. He held Beth's hand, and they started walking up the path, astounded by the three-hundred-sixty-degree view of this lovely island surround by a turquoise ocean.

At the top of the boulder- and cacti-strewn hill, two establishments greeted their hiking endeavors. A decent looking restaurant and bar named the Top of the Baths stood just north and east of the funky little joint where they met Jana and the crazy old men last night.

Harold nodded. "I vote for Mad Dog."

"Mad Dog for happy people." Glee engulfed Beth. For the first time in months she experienced a day they both could cherish. Even more wonderful would be its magical vacation memories.

"Wait, Beth. We left our stuff exposed on the beach. We have to go—"

"Geesh, it'll be fine. Seriously, would anyone other than Goodwill want our sandals, clothes, books, and towels?"

She continued her charge on up the path, and he followed.

"Hi, Jana." Beth waved at the young woman clearing glasses from the porch.

"Yay! Glad to see you two after all the others today. Come have one of our famous piña coladas."

"Water, water, everywhere—I need hydration." Beth pointed to the fresh lemonade advertised on a handmade poster. "Or that."

Harold pulled out a chair for her at one of the quieter inside tables.

"Aren't you famished?" Beth said when Harold finished his lemonade. "It's after one o'clock. Let's eat."

"Paninis sound good," he said, "but we left our things on the beach."

Jana shook her head. "It's all safe, trust me."

"See, I told you." Beth squeezed his arm. "Relax, guy. We have our cash." She unzipped her waterproof belt and pulled out a twenty. "No one wants the other stuff."

He shifted his weight to his other foot, glanced out the window, then said, "Thought you wanted to walk into Spanish Town."

"Dinner later tonight, okay?"

"You're up for another walk after dark?" He indicated her blackish-blue toe.

"Always. Unless you decide to lecture me more."

He tousled her wet, sandy hair.

They ate their panini sandwiches and watched the tourists leave in small groups. Then they were alone with Jana.

"Anything else for you two?" Her smile felt genuine.

"I'm good," Harold said. "If you're fine with leaving everything exposed on the beach we could explore some of those trails on the other side of this hill."

Mad Dog plowed into the room. "Jana, do you know where that

no-good Tony is? I paid him to help me with those blasted rocks, and he said he'd be here around noon."

"Seriously? He has the worst case of work avoidance I've ever seen. I don't understand why you're so attached to the kid."

"He's got no one to give a whit about him. Needs guidance. He'll be fine. Dammit, he promised he'd be here."

Jana shook her head.

Mad Dog rubbed his unshaven chin stubble, then said, "Saw him in Red Hook yesterday morning. He begged me to upfront him. Gave him a fifty and told him he'd get another after he finished my wall and terrace. Where in the hell is he?"

Jana laughed. "You'll be in your grave before he lifts even one rock. He's probably stolen what fast cash he needs by now. Better check your pockets."

"You're wrong, girl. He came yesterday—late yesterday. I told him to go back to St. Thomas. If he wanted to be paid, he'd have come back today. He's supposed to move stone, not be stoned." Mad Dog poured a glass of water and downed it.

The vision of the teen doing some dealing yesterday morning with two men flashed into Beth's mind. She shrugged it off. Many teens on these islands probably used drugs.

Harold nodded toward Mad Dog and whispered, "Beth, do you mind? This guy doesn't have the strength to move pillows, let alone rocks. I'd enjoy helping him with his project."

She poked him in the chest. "Go build. If it's okay with Jana, I'm sitting here and having some girl time."

Harold pointed at his feet. "I'll run back down and get my clothes. OSHA frowns on barefooted workers wearing swim trunks for construction work. Shall I bring your sandals and cover-up too?"

"OSHA doesn't have a presence here, guy." His thoughtfulness touched her. "Thanks. Guess I'm not acclimated to being a half-naked island person yet."

Harold gave her a kiss and bounced out the door, yelling, "Hey, Mad Dog, wait up."

"You have no idea how staved I am for woman talk." Jana poured herself some lemonade. "Riding herd on loudmouth tourists during the day and putting up with the geriatric romper room at night makes me wish summer vacation was over. I'm dying for a little estrogen-fueled conversation."

I am a part of all that I have met.

—ALFRED LORD TENNYSON

23

"This is a great place." Beth looked around the Mad Dog Saloon. "We feel safe up here."

"Not much happens except the nonsense you witnessed last night."

"Do you live on Virgin Gorda? Is this where you teach?"

"St. Thomas, I'm a US citizen. I teach at a private school. Excellent school but most can't afford the tuition." Jana looked relaxed and comfortable in her chair. "This is my summer income, and my touch with reality."

"Mad Dog and Salty?" Beth couldn't suppress a laugh.

"More like with normal tourist of all ages. On St. Thomas many kids lack ambition. They don't attend public schools regularly, and they lack any sense of entrepreneurship. They'll continue their family line of poverty." Jana shook the ice around in her empty glass.

"So you want to start a different type of school." Beth couldn't imagine what that would entail.

Jana bit her bottom lip, then said, "It seems hopeless. These kids have nothing to do in their spare time."

"My aunt used to say something like when kids become teens, they just sit around and listen to their organs change."

Jana glanced out the window. "They evidently have no idea how to plan for the long term. This vision of mine for education is a hands-on experience—basic educational and practical job skills. Teach them basic skills—how to interview for a job and how to maintain the attitudes necessary to hold a job."

"There's a challenge—shaping attitudes." Beth saw a small group of tourists heading up the hill from the Baths.

"If these children don't have something worthwhile to do, they hang around in small gangs looking for excitement and doing drugs. Last year we assembled a group of bright kids eager to play baseball. We didn't have a diamond, so we spent a month clearing trash, broken cinder blocks, and weeds from a vacant lot. You'd be astounded at how hard these kids worked. Coach got them a used bat, and a few had their own gloves. They picked teams and dug in for some serious competition."

"What a great project." Beth gave Jana a thumbs-up.

Jana shook her head. "One month later, big earth-moving machines showed up and started digging up the diamond for the basement of a new apartment building."

"Are these the same kids I see hanging around on leaky boats or doing drugs?" Beth emptied her glass. "I swear I saw one of the boat delinquents here yesterday making a deal."

"Could have been Tony—messy looking kid with no ambition."

"Light-colored hair, rather tall?"

"Sounds like him."

"I'm worried about Gnat." Beth played with her straw.

"Me too." Jana checked out the window, again.

Beth shook her head. "I can't figure out where she lives or who takes care of her."

Jana got up and waited on the arriving group of tourists. When she finished, she filled a pitcher with lemonade, set it on Beth's table, then sat.

"Tell me more about Gnat." Beth watched her.

"These islands aren't like the harsh climates you experience. We don't have high mountains or hot deserts. Here it's warm year round and in some ways nurturing. Without too much work a person could make a shelter, or find nourishment, even catch rainwater to drink. Gnat's an island child. She won't let anyone take care of her."

"Did her mother care for her?"

"When she was here."

"Do you think she's dead?"

"Gnat does. I don't know what to think." Jana leaned back in her chair to wait for the next question.

"Is that the real problem here?"

"It's part of it. The difficult situation is Gnat's father. He decided to change his lifestyle by adopting a new religion. He became verbally abusive to Gnat's mother and practically kept the mother a prisoner in her own home."

Beth's mind went back to something Missus Abu had told her. She couldn't bring it forward enough to make a connection.

Jana traced a crack in the table with her finger. "His religion requires wives to always be at their husband's beck and call. And this is supposed to be a peace-loving religion. Deceitfully sad."

"Rastafarian, I bet." *Like William.* "Where's Gnat's home?"

"Above Charlotte Amalie. Haven't you seen it? Gnat's grandfather's home."

"Missus Abu says he mostly lives here, now."

"His legal residence is in St. Thomas."

"Am I annoying you with my questions?" Beth shifted a little from embarrassment. She forced herself to sip lemonade.

"Beth, unfortunately no one talks about this. It makes the problem worse. Gnat's anger won't go away, Salty won't find peace and happiness, and Gnat's father's a loose cannon."

"Why doesn't Gnat's father do something about her? Or does he abuse her too? I'm sorry for all the questions, Jana. I just can't sort any of this out. Why would the grandfather allow his daughter to be abused? Why didn't he throw the guy out? It's Gnat's grandparent's home, but Salty chooses to live here."

"First, it's not her grandparent's home, just the grandfather's— Salty. According to those close to him, he never married the grandmother. After Gnat's grandmother died, Salty walked out of that house, leaving his daughter to live there with her husband and Gnat. Salty never returned. Gnat's family lived there until a few months after Gnat's mother disappeared. When her mother went missing, Gnat's father got deeper into using marijuana and transporting illegal substances for some scary dude in Dominica." Jana stopped and took a deep breath.

"Did her father kill her mother?"

Gads, sounds like drug dealers swarm all over these islands.

The door burst open and Harold charged in with Beth's clothes. "Beth, I hate to interrupt, but I need some help with Mad Dog's project."

Every man is guilty of all the good he did not do.
—VOLTAIRE

24

"Jana, thanks for the lemonade. We'll chat another time." Beth slipped into her sandals and pulled on her swimsuit cover-up.

Harold led the way past the road and along the hillside to Mad Dog's home.

"Hated dragging you away. You've never been one to do girl-time stuff, and you seemed to be enjoying yourself. Honestly, Beth, I thought Mad Dog and I could get it all done. He just doesn't seem capable of doing any type of physical work. Jeez, Beth, he's upside down in some emotional state. There's not much work left to do. It will take a while, and I can't get it done today unless I have some help."

Beth couldn't figure out if Harold's uncharacteristic chatter came from nerves about Mad Dog's condition or his own anticipation of getting involved in construction.

"Mad Dog needs some repairs to his stone wall. He'd like to complete the last few feet of his stone terrace, too. Honestly, Beth, he's in bad shape."

By the time Beth and Harold got there Salty had arrived. His soft voice worked to comfort his friend, who was sitting dejected on his rock wall. Mad Dog moaned and waved everyone away with one hand, covering his eyes with the other.

Harold mentioned an emotional state, but I certainly didn't expect this.

Beth looked away out of courtesy, but like a magnet the breathtaking scene beyond the men trapped her attention. Mad Dog's dark sorrow seemed incongruous against this showy display of nature.

A cacophony of tropical colors—flaming orange, pink, royal purple, and crimson—blazed from the unruly and massive oleander, bougainvillea, and hibiscus bushes. Each species paraded its own shade of green leaves, from emerald to lime green. This riot of flowers personified a living coloring book—a parade of vivid hues set against a deep-cerulean sky.

Far below, the tranquil turquoise sea completed Beth's view.

She snapped back to the men when she heard Salty's voice say, "Twasn't your fault, you know tha'."

Mad Dog shook his head. "I'm the one who sent him off in his godawful deteriorated condition. I should have kept him here—safe."

"It'd make no difference. Have another pull." Salty handed him a flask and watched him drink. "Come on, then, let's go to your kitchen and have a real nip. You'll feel better after."

Salty helped Mad Dog up and herded him into the house.

Beth tugged at Harold's arm. "What sent him over the edge? He already knew Tony wouldn't show today."

"Salty brought news to him that Tony's missing. One of Tony's friends suspects he tumbled off the boat and drowned."

More likely someone probably murdered him in a double-crossed drug deal.

A slight breeze tumbled by, bringing an aroma reminiscent of sweet, flowering apricots. She moved nearer the oleander bush and sniffed.

Another island example of deadly but beautiful.

She stepped away and said, "I pointed this boy out to you when we first got here. We saw him dealing drugs."

"We saw a kid that might have looked like him talking to two other guys. You have this tendency to jump to conclusions, my love."

"No matter." She shrugged. Harold didn't need to know her thoughts on this. "He's probably wandered somewhere to sleep off his high."

Harold picked up a shovel. "I read somewhere young teen boys think about sex every few seconds, and teens as a group need about ten hours of sleep. If this kid spends his time smoking pot, fantasizing about sex, and sleeping, you're probably right."

Beth didn't get Harold's connection there. Because he liked to espouse trivia, so she let it pass. She squinted at the rock wall.

"Your work looks finished."

"Not quite, and the terrace needs more sand in this corner and more cobbles on top. Poor old guy has no strength. He depends on the muscle power of youth. Do you mind?"

"I'm being categorized in the youth department. How could I resist. Tell me what to do."

The screen door banged, and Salty came up to them. "He's snoring like the drunken sailor he is. Worry about his unfinished work does ruin him. He can't finish these little projects by himself, and my help is worse than nothing."

Harold patted him on the back. "Hey, guy, I get into building things. Hated to drag Beth away from her chat with Jana, but with two of us, we might be able to finish before dark."

"Jana. The girl needs some outside time, and I pour a mean drink." Salty sauntered off toward Mad Dog.

Harold handed Beth the shovel.

"You can level out the sand over there, then embed the cobbles in the sand so their tops are level with the rest of the terrace. I'll finish patching up the wall."

Beth filled her mind with Jimmy Buffet's "Margaretville" and slid the tip of the shovel deep into the mound of sand. She heaved the contents onto the designated area. It didn't take long for her biceps to start burning. She still had half the pile to move.

"Hi," Jana called out. "Salty said you could use some more muscle." She approached with a spring in her step. "I'm so happy to get to do something physical in the fresh air. The tourists will just have to suffer Salty's incompetence."

Beth grinned, handed her the shovel, and explained their assignment.

"Jana, tell me, do you think Gnat's father killed her mother?" Beth picked up the rake and started smoothing out her labors.

"Her mother, Frangi," Jana said, "took his abuse for a few months, then became fed up and started fighting with him. She called him a

[119]

control freak. He said she wasn't maintaining her place according to their chosen culture. She reminded him she didn't choose it. He chose it years after she got knocked up, and her mother made them get married."

Beth wiped beads of sweat off her forehead then rested her arm on the handle of the rake.

"Gee whiz," Jana said, "this shoveling makes muscles I haven't used in a long time cuss me out. I always thought Gnat's mother to be a logical and strong-minded woman."

"So that's where Gnat gets her stubbornness. Let's trade. You're almost finished there anyway." Beth handed her the rake and started shoveling what was left of the remaining pile of sand.

Jana took up the leveling challenge. "Since the grandmother never married Salty, guess she hoped marriage would make life different for her daughter, Frangi. You have to understand, the home sits on two or three acres of land, so neighbors aren't that geographically close. But even they could hear the fighting going on in that house."

"No wonder Gnat's so tenacious. Who's living in the house now?"

"The house is unoccupied. Except her father might sleep there on occasion."

"Is Gnat living there?"

"Second thought, he probably doesn't even live there now." Jana rubbed her shoulder. "And Gnat refuses to be anywhere close to him or all the other Rastafarians."

She sure hates William and some of those boys.

"If Gnat heard those horrific fights," Beth said, "it makes sense why she put her father on the list of people who might have drowned her mother."

"The police suspected foul play and questioned him, but he had a steel-trap alibi. When Frangi disappeared he was still employed—as a history teacher and head coach. The night she disappeared he was coaching a baseball practice. Afterward he took his baseball kids out for ice cream."

"If she's dead, I'd think they'd have found a body by now."

"None found, but think of where we are. Miles of island coastlines, at times unpredictable currents, miles and miles of ocean, and the hungry predators with bone-breaking jaws."

"Could she have left to stay with relatives? Or maybe she ran away."

"Everyone says she hiding somewhere, but no one believes it."

"You don't believe it either. I can see it in your face." Beth wiped her forehead with the back of her hand. She hated sweating.

"Frangi would never leave voluntarily, because she's a good and loving mother."

Beth didn't know what to say about that. She finished moving the last shovel of sand, thinking about little Gnat. She studied the cobbles, then picked up some, knelt, and started positioning them.

"Here's another sad part of this tale about self-destruction. Gnat's father, when he first married her mother, taught at the same school where I teach. He got to those boys like no other teacher I've known. He knew how to talk to them, motivate them, but not so much with the girls. These kids who wanted to laze around and do nothing actually started achieving."

Before Beth continued with more cobbles she asked, "Do these look level to you?"

Jana had finished leveling the sand. She studied the work. "Looks good to me. She dropped to her knees, too, and helped position cobbles.

"This sure gets to your back after a few minutes." Beth stood and stretched. "I'd like to have seen how he reacted when Frangi disappeared."

"Trust me, he was devastated—absolutely a ruined man. His ganja usage escalated."

"Does he love Gnat?" Beth asked.

"He does."

"I'm guessing here, like some dads," Beth said, "he didn't understand emotional female children. He related better to boys."

"When he taught those boys or coached them, they showed aspirations and energy. Such a beautiful thing to watch."

Harold, glistening with sweat, hollered over to them. "How're you fine ladies doing?"

Beth dropped back down and picked up more stones. "Well, sir, fine ladies don't muck around in sand, playing with stones."

Jana grinned. "We should be finished in a few more minutes. Tell us how we're doing."

"After the first rain settles it all, it'll look terrific. I'm headed back down the hill. I need a shower. Do you want me to wait for you, Beth?"

Beth waved him on.

Jana stood and said, "Wait a minute. I have an idea. I'm off tomorrow morning. If you're flexible about your time, I have a friend with a neat little skiff who might take us out beyond the reef east of Little Dix Bay. She can drop us off there, and then we'll snorkel back. You can't begin to imagine the beauty you'll experience."

"We wouldn't want to be an imposition." This idea thrilled Beth.

"She lives close to Little Dix, and every day she heads out to sea somewhere on her skiff. She just has to drop us off, and we simply swim back to shore."

Harold cocked his head, then said, "She'll drop us of in the middle of the ocean and leave us to swim back to land?"

He'll never go for something this crazy. Dang it.

Beth glanced at Harold. "We better pass on this—"

"Nonsense, Beth. Let's do it." He gave a thumbs up.

The swim from Spring Bay, around those rocks, to the beach in front of the Baths must have built his confidence.

This guy loves his island life.

Beth tingled with expectations of a new adventure. She watched Harold stride off down the hill, then turned back to her previous conversation.

"Gnat's father seemed to have discovered how to make more money than any teaching job would pay. Guess dealing drugs cost him his educational career."

"His absences did him in as well as too much Ganja. He took too many trips to places like Jamaica and farther west."

They both worked quietly. Beth considered the ramifications of his drug dealings while she silently counted the number of stones left to finish their job.

"The men in Gnat's life are useless," Beth said. "Missus Abu and you seem to be the only ones who care. She deserves more."

Jana held her palms up to correct Beth's thoughts. "Salty loves that child. He wouldn't let you know, but he dotes on her every whim."

Harold always wanted children, and this brilliant little girl needs a mother.

Jana said, "When her mother disappeared last year, Gnat was brought here to live, screaming and kicking. You can guess how long that lasted. She's pretty much on her own. Have you seen her drawings? She's obsessed with puffer fish."

Beth bit her lip. The image of Gnat with puffer fish gave her the chills.

"Gnat uses crayons and presses the wax into the paper until the colors glow. Her drawings are quite good."

"Do you know the significance of puffer fish?" If Jana didn't, Beth wasn't going to tell her.

"Pretty scary stuff. She's so angry with her father. If I were him, I'd worry."

"She seems to have several people she's ready to shove off a cliff." Beth chuckled. "She calls them poopholes."

Jana glanced at Beth and said, "Can you imagine in a few years, as a young adult, what a force this little girl will be? Bet she'll make everyone sit up and listen to her. I suspect Gnat won't be a fitting name."

"Jana, speaking of this, do you know Salty's or Mad Dog's real names?"

Did either of them know Kathleen? They both seemed touchy about answering questions concerning Sylvia's mother.

"Do you mind telling me why before I answer?"

"Missus Abu told me an interesting story. It may have some connection to a mystery in my life. There's a woman who plays the saxophone, Sylvia, and someone she called Mister Davies. He seems to know something about someone in Sylvia's family. And Sylvia seems to know something about someone in my family. If this Mister Davies and Sylvia knew my biological mother, they could know something important about my life."

Jana didn't say anything. She kept her head down and maneuvered another stone into place.

Beth studied her new friend and knew these half-truths she told Jana were the cause of her own growing uneasiness inside. Beth sighed and said, "I didn't know until last week, just before she died—my mother gave me to her sister for adoption. My mother lived on St. Thomas with a man named Martin. I think that man might have been my father. Sylvia and this Mister Davies guy may know who he is. I'm wondering if Salty might even be Martin. He's about the right age."

Jana stared at Beth for a few moments, then shook her head.

"Beth, I don't know anyone named Martin, but Salty's name *is* Jim Davies."

Silence is foolish if we are wise, but wise if we are foolish.
—CHARLES C. COLTON

25

Beth hid her disappointment in learning Salty's true name. She liked the eccentric old guy and secretly hoped he might have been Kathleen's lover and maybe her own biological father. She mentally scratched Mad Dog off her list too, since Jana said she didn't know anyone named Martin. She had asked Jana about Mad Dog's name just to see if she'd heard if from Kathleen's stories, but his real name, Patrick O'Dell, struck a big zero in her memory banks.

She waved good-bye to Jana and headed back down the hill.

Dang it all anyway.

She liked Mad Dog, too, but he didn't have the same—maybe call it depths of emotions—*la passion pour la vie.* Wrong. His bringing flowers to the tavern for the ladies, and his anguish over Tony—he had abundant passion. She continued to puzzle over their differences.

Shadows spread out over the landscape. The birds' songs softened, preparing for the night.

If the wind is right you can sail away. Music started in her head. *Sailing takes me away to where I've always heard it could—sailing—*

What the—? Beth stopped. *First the Jimmy Buffet song, and now this?*

Her mind always echoed music from symphonies or operas, not

[124]

pop songs with lyrics. Geesh, she didn't even know the name of this song, or who wrote it, or who sang it.

Sailing . . .

Still, the soothing melody fit the scenery.

Yacht silhouettes moved in front of the setting sun far out on this tranquil, Caribbean Sea. Being here wrapped her in pure joy. She practically skipped downhill to their cabin.

Harold was stretched out on the couch reading one of the paperback mysteries he'd bought at the airport. He looked so damned handsome with his hair tousled, and she loved the slight smile he always gave her whenever she entered the room.

And comfortable. He'd look even more comfortable in their king-size bed with the remains of the afternoon sun dancing over them.

"I knew it, I knew it." She danced around him, clapping her hands.

He laid the book down on the floor and sat up. She plunked down on his lap and ran her fingers through his mess of gray-black hair.

God, she loved him.

"First, I thought that either Salty or Mad Dog might be Martin. They're both about Kathleen's age." She took a moment to catch her breath. "She said she liked men who made her laugh. And do they ever make a person laugh. Right? Then Jana said she didn't know anyone named Martin." She nibbled his earlobe and ran her fingers down the back of his neck.

"Beth—"

She hopped up, leaned over, and put her face in his. Freshness of aftershave—she inhaled deeply.

"Jana admitted that Salty *is* a Mister Jim Davies. He *is* the one who lived in a large home on St. Thomas. I know he's not only Gnat's Grandfather, but he's the one who Sylvia's mother visited. How cool is that?

"Missus Abu had me terribly confused, but I bet Sylvia's mother not only knew Jim Davies, but she also knew Kathleen. I just need to find out why Jim Davies, aka Salty, wanted to talk with Sylvia's mother thirty or forty years ago. I'm closing in, Harold."

"Beth, please—" He put his head in his hands.

She continued to smile at him, her feet tapping out little dance steps.

He stood, strode to the refrigerator, took out a beer, popped the top, and guzzled.

"Well, aren't you excited?" Why wasn't he? He was acting like he didn't care. Heat rose to her cheeks.

He turned the can around several times, guzzled some more, then walked out on their balcony and gazed out toward the seascape and setting sun.

"Harold?" She joined him. "I'm worried. You're usually happy for me when something good happens." She slid her arms around him, scrunched between his body and the railing, and put her chin up toward his face. "Hey, guy, put yourself in my place. If you didn't know your biological father, you'd be excited if you found clues."

She stood still—waiting. She wasn't going to give in until he admitted why he was acting like this. They needed to resolve this little tiff. She wouldn't let it ruin the rest of their vacation.

Neither spoke until Harold broke the silence a few seconds later.

"Of course I'm pleased." He crushed the can, turned, and banked it into the trash. He studied her for a moment, then pulled her in close.

She had goofed. She had not only interrupted his reading, she had disturbed his comfort, and she had expected him to be over his snit about her looking for her father. Now, since he'd decided to be a sport about it, she decided she had better reward his capitulation.

"Let's stay home tonight and have grilled hamburgers later. We'll have dinner in Spanish Town tomorrow evening." His warmth, a living magnet, drew her close. She nuzzled his neck, inhaling mandarin, sandalwood, and maybe a hint of lavender aftershave. Beth planted a long, yearning kiss on his mouth.

She hated him being mad at her.

There is no little enemy.

—BENJAMIN FRANKLIN

26

Beth and Harold planned to meet Jana at the junction of Spring Bay and the Spanish Town road early the next morning, where they would wait for their taxi. Beth wiped up the short kitchen counter top and folded the dishcloth over the edge of the sink.

"Harold, my builder of walls, you're not moving very fast this morning." Beth's muscles had complained all night about yesterday's labor at Mad Dog's home, too. "If it's a comfort, I've found some muscles I didn't know existed."

"A few days of no hard labor, and it all tightens up." Harold rinsed out his coffee cup. "I can't imagine how out of shape I'll be when we get home. Are you ready?"

"It's not as warm as a sauna, but playing in the ocean should help relax all those knots."

They picked up their snorkeling gear, grabbed their hats, and headed out the door for another day of sand, sun, and island fun.

Jana waved to them from down below at the intersection just as the taxi arrived. They stowed their snorkeling gear in the trunk. In their excitement the three of them talked over each other.

This tickled Beth. Harold's enthusiasm about today's adventure became contagious.

Once in the taxi they drove up the coastal road toward Spanish Town while Harold quizzed Jana about the types of fish near the reef at Little Dix bay.

Jana, in turn, started ticking off a list of what they could expect to see, some fish Beth and Harold had already identified during their ill-fated snuba dive on St. John.

Their driver slowed for some traffic ahead in the road.

"What's that about?" Jana asked the driver.

"D'oan know, ma'am." He skirted around two cars, several people, and a police vehicle before speeding up again.

"Any guesses?" Beth asked Jana.

"I suspect it's somethum way over there, down on the beach, or maybe somethum happened at one of those bed and breakfast places."

Beth studied the landscape. "I don't see any roads to a beach."

Jana answered, "It's pretty isolated in this area. Not many direct roads."

The taxi drove past Spanish Town and a few minutes later pulled into Little Dix Bay. The driver helped them unload their gear and asked if he should wait. They waved him on, saying they'd just call when they were ready to return.

"My friend with the skiff said she would meet us in front of the Rosewood restaurant." Jana led the way down the path where they met a tall, attractive woman with smooth, latte skin.

Jana made the introductions.

"Follow me to the dock and on to a spectacular day of snorkeling." Karen strode out and across the beach to the wooden pier where dinghies, zodiacs, and small boats moored.

She called to them, "Just leave your snorkel bags here on the beach. No one will bother them."

Jana, Beth, and Harold collected their gear from the bags, removed their sandals and outer wear, and stowed them in their bags with their hats. Then they followed Karen onto the wet, wooden dock. Jana and Karen stopped before climbing into the skiff and rinsed sand off their feet.

Harold nodded at Beth. Beth took the hose and squirted cool water on her feet, using her fingers to help brush gritty sand from between her toes. More boat etiquette, like asking permission to board.

She followed Karen and Harold onto the boat. Jana stood on the dock next to the piling where the rope tethered the boat. Beth and Harold found their seats in the stern of the little boat. Their sitting in this little vessel on the crystal-blue water, bobbing up and down, erased all desire to face another of Denver's frigid winters. Island-life magnetism grew stronger.

"You're super to do this for us," Beth said. "We hate the thought of inconveniencing you."

Karen fiddled with some papers, then stuffed them in her bag.

"Jana and I get a kick out of introducing tourist to our little secret treasures. Besides, I'm meeting a friend who's been staying at the upper end. It'll only take a few minutes to drop you three off, then I'm on my way." Karen started the motor.

Wouldn't be a coincidence if her friend happened to be Sylvia? Beth started to ask, but she stopped when Harold called out to Jana, asking if there would be any jellyfish to worry about.

If Beth asked any questions about Sylvia, it would kill Harold's enthusiasm. She wouldn't ruin today's most excellent adventure for Harold. Besides, Sylvia being Karen's friend stretched possibilities anyway. She could live without knowing.

Jana assured him no one would be stung. She unwound the rope from the post, tossed the rope into the boat, hopped in, and Karen backed the boat out from the dock then headed across the bay.

Karen pointed ahead to their left and said, "I'm going through a break in the coral reef right there. Sometimes reefs grow across the opening of bays, but here we have a passageway for boat traffic. You'll be swimming back through here. Let the current guide you. This is probably the only place where you'll be bothered with boat traffic. However, when you're out there beyond the reef, look around every few minutes to be sure. Don't want you run down by a fast mover."

Beth noticed Harold furrowing his forehead. She jumped in to ask, "How far out will you take us?"

"You'll only be short of a half mile from shore. On the far side of this reef, the coral beds extend for almost a quarter of a mile, making this a little-known paradise for snorkelers."

Karen cut the engine, fussed with a few other things, then said, "Snorkel up. Ride's over."

They scrambled to put on their gear. They had already stowed their few necessities, like money and IDs, in waterproof belts.

One by one they slipped over the side of the small vessel and down into the water. They treaded water, waved, and shouted thanks and good-byes to Karen.

Jana said, "Buddy system here. We each keep our eyes on the other two every few minutes. Remember what Karen said. Watch for possible boat traffic. Right now we're the only ones out here, but that could change."

Harold took his mouthpiece out and asked Jana, "Do we worry about sharks?"

"They told me you don't taste at all like chicken, so no worries, guy. Forgot to mention the best part. You really don't need to swim much. See how we're drifting. You can pretty much just float. A natural current will take us from here and guide us right through the reef opening onto the beach. Let's go."

Harold adjusted his mouthpiece, lowered his head, and stretched out in the warm water, following Jana.

Beth put her mouthpiece in and slipped her face into the water. Her mask started filling with water.

Dang it.

She raised her head, slowly treading again, and lifted the bottom of her mask to drain out the water. After repositioning it, she put her face back into the water and floated—astounded at the colorful corals and abundant sea life below.

Water rose in her mask again.

Geesh.

This time it was up to eye level. She popped into an upright position, treaded water, and fiddled with the bottom of her mask in an effort to empty it.

Harold, back at her side, took his mouthpiece out and asked, "Are you all right?"

She removed her mouthpiece and said, "My mask keeps filling with water."

"Is there anything I can do to help?"

She shook her head.

Dang it, so frustrating.

Harold looked at her mask. "Hey, sweetie, there's a lock of hair under the seal by your temple."

She took the whole thing off, brushed her hair aside, and pulled the mask back on over her eyes and nose. Then she put her mouthpiece in and plunged her face under the water again. She could see Harold treading next to her.

Her mask stayed free of water. She raised her head and gave him the divers' okay sign, a circle made with thumb and finger.

Beth couldn't even guess how long they floated along with the warm current, because she lost herself in the enchanting world of dark sea urchins, corals, and swaying sea fans, while a school of sea bream with their yellow-horizontal stripes swam up to and around her—even close to her face—curious and unconcerned.

She lifted her face from the water and looked around for Harold and Jana. They floated, heads down, nearby.

Her eyes adjusted to the strong morning light. The sunshine helped illuminated the wonderful creatures who lived underwater. She moved back into the magical world below.

A large, solitary gray grunt peeked out from under a ledge while a blue, yellow-mouthed parrot fish cleaned algae from the rock above it. Lady Parrot Fish had found her tasty morning meal.

Studying the tangs, rasps, and jacks, Beth discovered herself in the middle of hundreds of tiny, thin silversides. They flowed around her and darted everywhere as if all of one mind, like they were repeatedly telling her they didn't have time to play. These silversides just had to figure out how to catch the right current that would take them to nowhere.

What an enchanted world.

Harold, swimming next to her, grabbed her hand and pointed over at a silvery, three-foot-long fish with a large underslung jaw.

She tensed—did she imagine she could see teeth? Its mouth opened and closed.

Needle-sharp teeth. . . many of them.

Beth studied it for a moment, then prickles of terror swept through her. She wanted to get away.

She jerked Harold's hand, pulling and motioning to him to come with her. She started kicking, pulling him along.

He began swimming next to her without question.

She slowed and studied the space around and below them. It still followed but lagged several feet back and stayed less than half a dozen feet below them. She could hear herself breathing hard.

Silly. They'd never be able to out-swim this sleek swimming machine of a barracuda.

She stopped kicking and quieted her breathing, keeping the predator in her sight.

Even though the fish kept pace with the two snorkelers, it seemed passive. When she slowed and signaled to Harold to copy her movements, it had slowed. She and Harold floated, bobbing facedown in the gentle waves, watching it.

After a few seconds the skillful predator turned and drifted off. Beth caught sight of the lone barracuda slipping into a school of silversides and swimming away with the group.

She lifted her head out of the water.

Harold did the same and asked, "What in the hell was that?"

"A barracuda."

"Jeez! Fish with sharp-pointed teeth. It kept opening and closing its mouth."

Beth gave Jana a visual check, then put her head back into the water.

When she remembered to look up again, Jana and Harold swam close beside her.

Feathery ripples of contentment drifted through her. Anyone would be mesmerized by this community of living creatures hunting and hiding below.

Beth scanned the surface across the gentle waves. A catamaran approached. The waves grew, sharpened, and radiated out from the wake. She hated snorkeling when she had to look over the little hills of waves to see her buddies. The three of them had worn yellow vests in order to be more visible to the boat traffic. Still, out in this open expanse of deep-blue water, Beth needed to keep Jana and Harold in her sight.

The catamaran stopped and lowered a zodiac, then people climbed in and they motored off toward Little Dix.

Harold now looked around too. Beth pointed to a dingy approaching, probably from some other part of the island, motoring into the bay area.

The three of them were almost to the reef. She glanced around but didn't see any other vessels.

Jana raised up, treaded water, and turned in all directions. Then she indicated it was okay for them to swim on through to the bay.

The strong current swept them through the channel and across the bay, then gently washed them up on the warm, white sands, as predicted.

They removed their fins and gear, attempted to brush some of the sand off, stored it all in their snorkel bags, and trudged up the beach to the restaurant, chatting the whole time.

"You were right, Jana." Harold grinned. "I saw a shark, about a foot long, and I have no bite marks."

"The barracuda must prefer chicken, too." Beth said.

"Did you see the ray?" Jana asked.

"You saw a stingray?' Beth longed to go back.

After they finished their crab sandwiches and had downed the rest of their beers, Jana called the taxi service. They walked up the path to meet their ride—excitement still high.

Beth didn't want this morning to end.

How long had it been since she had seen Harold so happy? His excitement over what he had seen even infected Jana. He kept asking Jana about fish he couldn't identify, and Jana gave him possible names.

Again, after they passed Spanish Town, the driver slowed, then stopped. "Quite a crowd here."

Several cars, the police car, and now an emergency vehicle were parked alongside the road. A group of islanders mingled around, talking.

Harold asked, "What do you think—?"

"Hold on, sir. Lemme go see what's up." The driver climbed out and sauntered over to some man he obviously knew. The man patted him on the back, shook his hand, then gestured toward the sea, shaking his head."

Beth watched.

Jana started to get out, then stopped. "He's coming back."

The driver got back in, started the car, and a path cleared in front. He drove slowly past the crowd.

"Seems they've found a body of a young man on the rocks down from a ledge over there."

Jana glanced at Harold and Beth, then asked, "Do they know who?"

"Some kid from another island. He comes here to deal drugs. Guess he won' be doing that no more. We happy people here. Don' need no drugs."

Maybe they had found Tony.

Logic is the art of going wrong with confidence.

—JOSEPH WOOD KRUTCH

27

Harold and Beth spent the afternoon lounging on their deck. They snoozed, read, and took turns interrupting each other when they remembered something exciting about the morning's snorkeling adventure.

Beth pointed at the sun heading lower in the west and grinned. She jumped up and strode into the cabin, coming out a few seconds later with two glasses of merlot.

Harold clinked his glass with hers and said, "Here's to our most fantastic vacation."

A wash of relief spread over Beth. "We've collected quite an assortment of stories to share when we get home." She and Harold had found a happiness too great not to share.

Harold sipped his wine and set his book aside, staring out at the ocean. His face, relaxed, showed a twinkle in his eyes, and his mouth had a hint of a grin.

Everyone should know this joy. Perhaps all the islanders felt this way all the time.

Malaka's frustration and Gnat's anger invalidated that thought. She and Harold couldn't do anything about Malaka, but they should share their life with little Natalie Bowman. Such a precious young girl needed a happy family.

"Beth, let's send Jana something special from Colorado when we get home. Let her know how grateful we are about today's outing."

She nodded, sipping her merlot. Sitting here on this deck with Harold filled her with contentment. Silent in her thoughts, she sipped her wine and relished her own gratefulness in sharing her life with Harold. If they did adopt Gnat, Beth would have to figure out all the legalities and logistics. Maybe if she had all the answers before mentioning it to Harold, then he couldn't really object. Actually, he'd be delighted to have such a little charmer around.

Missus Abu would be the one to talk with about how to make the arrangements.

"Here's something I'd like to do." Beth ran her finger around the rim of her empty glass, then said, "When we leave Virgin Gorda, could we go a little earlier than necessary? I'd like to say good-bye to Missus Abu. She's been kind and, well, I'm fond of her."

"Let's. But now I'm starving. Time to get ready if we're going to eat in town."

After showering and putting on going-to-town clothes of clean shorts, colorful shirts, and sandals, Harold said, "I could get used to dressing up for dinner like this."

"Could you really live here—like year round?"

"Wouldn't take much in retirement money. Could do some renovations or small building jobs if we needed cash." He held the door open for her. "What about you?"

"Nice place to visit—"

"So, why not?" He took her hand and they strolled down the narrow road leading into Spanish town.

"I love my work."

"Do you ever."

She pulled him to a stop. "Your statement has disagreeable undertones. Why?"

He ran his fingers through his unruly hair, then said, "Think about all you did and all you went through this last year to save the institute from financial ruin."

"I agree—I do work hard." She squatted to check a wildflower then continued walking. "Why is that disagreeable to you?"

Harold pointed off to the side of the road. "Look, prickly pear cactus. Guess cacti are ubiquitous."

Their mile walk to Spanish Town took them through a landscape that could have been in southern Colorado or New Mexico—sandy soil, cactus, scrubby-looking bushes of various sorts.

"Feels that way, but it's pretty much confined to the Americas," she said. "It's one of the more recent plants to evolve."

Then she awoke to why he'd changed their conversation to prickly pear cacti. He had developed an art of not answering questions.

He's right, because now he's given me a chance to drop this and let it be a win-win situation.

The cars, police, and signs of the commotion on this road they passed earlier in the day had disappeared.

The sun slipped below the clouds, hugging the ocean's horizon. She listened and then touched Harold's arm. He waited for her to speak.

"Do I hear a twin-engine plane like Mad Dog and Salty watched for the other night?"

"Could be. Bet there are many twin engines around. The airport's over to the east of us."

"Virgin Gorda has an airport but no highway to Bitter End Yacht Club?"

He laughed. "They may. I didn't check the map."

This narrow thoroughfare took them past homes set back off the main road. Harold smiled and nodded at a woman standing at her gate. Beth gave her a wave, and the woman returned the gesture.

"Good evening to you. You're on your way to dinner. Enjoy your evening on our lovely island."

"Why thank you," Beth said. She looked up at Harold. He grinned and tugged Beth over to the side of the road.

A school boy on a bicycle yelled to them as he sped past. "Hello. I hope you are having a good time on our island."

"We are, and a good afternoon to you," Harold called over his shoulder.

"What friendly people." Beth looped her arm through his and relished their closeness.

"I'm still thinking this could be a great place to live compared to our chaotic life in Denver." He squeezed her hand.

"You never answered my first question, but to finish answering yours, I also have an affection for snow and mountains."

"Agreed. Colorado's four seasons beats them all."

"Harold, what do you do when someone doesn't answer your questions?" she asked.

He shrugged.

After this perfect day, she didn't want to drag ill-feeling baggage home. Certainly enough nastiness had been conjured up between them these last few months. Yesterday his helping Mad Dog went beyond what most tourists would do on their vacation, and this morning's snorkeling adventure surpassed everything. Yet this afternoon relaxing, reveling together in the island's ambiance . . .

He's such a decent man.

"Good evening." School girls waved to them from the front drive of a house on the outskirts of Spanish Town.

"And a very good evening to you three charming ladies," Harold said.

"Do you like Virgin Gorda?" one girl said.

"It's better than chocolate cake," Beth said.

The girls giggled.

After several blocks Harold pointed to an open-air restaurant. "How about that one?"

"Yay, it's not a McDonalds. If this happens to be an island chain, we'd never know."

They walked over and waited to be seated. The waiter waved them on to select their own table. She sat where they could see the road and picked up the menu. Harold did the same.

He put the menu down, and when the waiter came over he ordered a beer. He looked at Beth.

"Water, please."

"Damned if I do, damned if I don't," Harold said.

Beth tilted her head and stared at him. He must think she only ordered water because she blamed him for something. She raised her hand to signal the waiter.

"I'd also like a cuba libre, please." She smirked at him.

Harold looked around the establishment.

"Guess if you're so damned damned," she said, "I might as well drown my sorrows with rum. However, I'm feeling dehydrated, hence the water. I did plan to order wine later."

"You're saying I didn't need to damn your ill attempt to punish me?"

She loved him. He'd be a good father.

He studied her, then softly said, "It seems no matter what I say, I make you mad."

"Give me another chance." She reached over and squeezed his hand and grinned. "I actually don't think I'm *that* much of a bitch. You see, I already know your answer. What we need to do is to clarify how we feel. When you don't like something, but you don't say anything, it's like giving me a pass. If I'd known all those overtime hours—"

"If you'd known, Beth? Come on, you wouldn't have changed anything. It isn't overtime that matters, it's whatever strikes your fancy at the moment."

"Strikes my fancy? That's a bit whimsical for my line of work, don't you think?"

She interrupted him with a touch on his arm again. "Look, out there on the street."

"The little kid and the two men?" Two men leaned against a building, listening to what the young boy said.

"He's one of the kids I told you about. On the boat. He's the smallest." Her heart skipped beats.

He's too young. If someone killed Tony for dealing drugs—but this one's not dealing. He's just talking.

She watched Harold barely glance at the boy. He studied his menu. Her cheeks flushed over his dismissiveness.

She tapped his hand and gave him her squinty-eye look.

"What? You keep seeing kids doing business with older guys. Kids are kids." He studied the menu again. "Must be a bunch his age all over this island with dreadlocks."

"How many kids in these islands wear a New Zealand Maori carving around their neck? He wore it when I took his photo. He's wearing it now."

She hated feeling defensive.

"But this is Virgin Gorda," he said. "This isn't part of the states anymore, like St. Thomas. For the kid you saw to be here, he'd need a passport. This is the British Virgin Isles, remember?"

"The Mad Dog group pretty much said Gnat hops all over these islands whenever she pleases. Bet she doesn't have a passport. Besides, I bet St. Thomas is only thirty miles away." She tilted her chin up.

He glanced at her, then looked more closely at the boy.

"You're little delinquent may be doing some dealing."

"Dealing what?" she said. "Nothing exchanged hands."

One of the men pointed to his watch, patted him on the back, then they walked down the street toward the middle of town. The boy turned and headed the other way.

"Guess just words. They evidently liked what he told them," he said. "And speaking of words, if you're sure it's him—" Harold pushed his chair back and stood.

"Let him go," she said. "You'll scare him."

"Beth, they almost killed us."

"Not the little one. The group needs scaring and more. It's obvious these young ones mimic the older boys. They'll do anything to be accepted by them."

Harold continued to look out and down the way they had walked from their Spring Bay cabin.

"What's happening?" she asked.

"I'm not sure. People seem to be gathering for something."

Beth glanced at the cashier and the waiter. The noise of their conversations escalated. Someone who had just walked into the restaurant had stirred them all up about something.

Now everyone talked fast and seemed concerned about what was going on to the south of the place.

More people gathered down the street and headed quickly up the road toward Spring Bay.

The waiter came with their drinks.

"Do you know what's happening?" Beth asked.

"Not sure if it's true, but they say a ship's on fire somewhere out off of Spring Bay."

A mob is a group of persons with heads, but no brains.
—THOMAS FULLER

28

Beth gasped, jumped up, and bolted out into the street.

Harold slapped a twenty-dollar bill on the table and waved off the drinks. He caught up with Beth a half block away.

"Whoa! What do you think's going on?"

"The boy with the dreadlocks helped fix up the *Dusky Angler*. He hung around and played with the other kids there."

"It's an old boat, Beth. It couldn't sail far."

"Made it to St. John. You know they were the ones who sliced our air hose."

"The difference in miles," he said, "to St. John and to Virgin Gorda makes sailing to this island unlikely."

"There's the boy again." Beth's adrenalin added urgency to her words. "He's in front of the woman in the yellow dress carrying the baby."

Harold clutched Beth's hand as they jogged south toward Spring Bay.

He spoke again. "If you're thinking the boy has something to do with the ship's fire, then I'm mourning my drink left untouched on the table back there. I've got this bad feeling I'm going to need a stiff one before tonight ends."

They slowed when they approached the moving crowd of islanders. Tones of excitement embellished their murmurs.

Children demanded answers from parents. The parents didn't know what to say. Many speculated about which boat burned or how the fire started.

"He's making time." Harold pointed at the bouncing head of dreadlocks disappearing toward the front of the crowd. "Should I run and catch him?"

"We're all going to the same place. No need." Beth occasionally glimpsed the lad pushing between and around others. He seemed panicked. Her mind sorted the events she observed with those boys on the boat. She couldn't make any connection to them being here or to a fire.

Harold's face looked intense, more than a tourist's curiosity.

"Beth, I'm beginning to believe—"

"That it's the *Dusky Angler* on fire," she said. "The boy does too, I bet." She swiped a strand of hair out of her eyes. They were both breathing hard, more from the excitement than the exercise.

"I get it," he said. "No passport needed if you anchor off shore and swim to the beach."

Missus Abu had talked about Gnat's anger toward William and doing something soon with fire. Her heart skipped a beat.

Gnat couldn't be responsible for torching a ship, could she?

They both picked up their pace. The sky ahead glowed in the grayness of the coming night. She smelled burning wood. A few yards farther up the road, they saw flames with black smoke billowing up, spreading a veil over the early-evening stars. The prevailing night breeze off the ocean now brought the smoke toward the crowd.

"Ganja," Beth whispered. There was no mistaking the skunky, rope-burn smell.

"Ganja?" He stopped and looked at her.

"Marijuana." She tugged at him, and they continued.

"First we face trial by water, now fire. Do you know how to ward off the plague?"

"This fire has nothing to do with us." The hard edges in his words annoyed her.

"Hell, we both know that won't last." He picked up his pace.

"You're not making sense." She wanted to stick her fingers in her ears.

[141]

"You'll quickly find a way to make this our problem," he called back.

"Why are you so negative—and hurtful?" She caught up to him. "This isn't like you, Harold."

"Hurtful? What makes things hurtful, and deadly, is when you never leave anything alone."

"I didn't mind leaving our drinks alone. You're joining in on this excitement, too. You can't throw all the blame on me this time."

She didn't like his attitude or the current look of defeat now on his face.

They turned off the main road and headed down the path through the palm trees leading to the beach.

"Ha!" he said. "This is going to be one mellow crowd with all that gana smoke."

"Ganja. The breeze will shift soon, carrying it and the smoke out to sea."

The crowd noises increased, and so did the darkness of night. A few minutes later the smoke changed directions.

"Did you really know it would do that?" Harold asked.

"Sunshine. Land heats and cools faster than water. The temperature differences cause breezes. Cooler air flows in when warmer air rises. In the day, when the land is warm, cool breezes move in from the sea. At night the land cools faster than the water, and the breezes flow back out to the warmer sea."

"I suppose everyone knows that but me." His voice held an edge.

"Probably only those who live by the ocean—or care."

When they reached the beach she saw flames eating away at the vessel anchored out beyond the cove. The boat sat low in the water— must have a full cargo. The reflections of the flames flickered and danced among the black waves of deep water.

The crowd became silent, watching. She and Harold also stood silent next to each other—enveloped in the cover of night—not touching.

"Do you see Jana or anyone from the Mad Dog?" She hoped maybe he'd loosen up a little. "I'd think they'd be here."

"It's difficult to know who's in this crowd."

The ship looked like the *Dusky Angler*, but she couldn't identify it for sure in the dark and with the distance. What caused the ship to burn? Missus Abu's words about Gnat and fire tumbled like ice chips inside her. The little girl's safety could be at stake, but there was no way those boys would let her be on the ship.

Beth needed to do something. Just sorting it all out—the fire, Harold's frustration with her. Her mind became a smorgasbord of thoughts.

Flames shot high and burned brighter. She glanced at Harold. He stood ridged with his jaw set tight. A coldness grew between the two of them . . . He didn't understand, or maybe he didn't want to understand. She stood straighter and breathed deeper.

They would have to have a heart-to-heart discussion. She would listen, really listen to what he wanted. He had to understand what mattered to her, too.

The ship now listed sharply to one side. It was about to roll.

Please don't let Gnat or those boys be on board.

She thought she saw figures dive off the high side of the boat, but maybe her eyes were playing tricks in this light.

She heard the surf compete with the full, clear tones of something quite primitive. She looked around. Harold grabbed her and pointed toward the huge rounded rocks at the southern edge of the bay. They worked their way through the islanders.

Gnat, standing—no, moving—slowly back and forth. She was singing, chanting—maybe making small animal calls.

With the voices of the crowd and the noise of the water lapping on shore, the sounds were difficult to distinguish. Beth pushed in closer. She broke free of the crush of people and found herself standing in the wet sand next to the boulders at the water's edge.

Three shapes emerged from the dark water in front of her. She flinched, sucking in her breath.

One plowed through the thigh-high water. She skittered aside as they rushed on toward the beach. A tall boy yelled at the villagers. He begged them to swim out to save the boat. A skinny teen, followed by a smaller kid, emerged from the water and joined in to holler and plead with the villagers.

The crowd moved back closer to the trees, mumbling to each other. No one came forward to help. Beth couldn't see how to help such a hopeless situation, because the ship burned like straw.

The boy with the Maori necklace who'd been in town burst out of the crowd jabbering something. He grabbed the taller one's hand.

Now Beth recognized this thieving teen. He had thrown the church object into the ocean. The delinquent cussed and gave the younger boy a powerful backhand in the face, which sent him flying into the beach sand.

[143]

A stab of astonishment hit Beth. She clinched her fist, then heard Harold's voice off somewhere yelling at the guy.

Boiling adrenaline rushed through her.

Bullies! Cowards! Enough!

Gnat continued to prance adroitly about on the slippery, wet rocks. She pointed and shouted gibberish in the teen's direction.

The teen swiveled toward her.

Gnat shook her fist at the *Dusky Angler* and kept shouting. Then something caused her to stop her yelling. She remained quiet, dropped her arms to her sides, and stared out to sea.

Her silence eroded into wailing and sobs.

The teen charged in her direction.

Beth, full of heated anger, stood resolute. She would not let this ruffian hurt Gnat. He swerved to bypass Beth.

She swung her foot out, tripping him. He stumbled and skidded in wet sand, face forward. He sprang up, growling, and lunged toward her. Beth shoved her palms up in front of her and smacked them hard on his sandy chest.

"Stop it." Beth did not recognize the insane furry growing within her.

His mouth curled. He threw his head back and laughed. Then his arm shot out and pain seared the side of her face. Blackness engulfed her.

Sharp jabbing, throbbing sensations filled her cheek. Beth's nose ached. It filled with pressure. She lifted her head up off the coarse wet sand. Had he broken her nose? She touched it gently.

No blood yet, but Gnat—

"Beth!" Harold helped her up and examined her.

"Stop him. Don't let him—" It hurt her to move her jaw.

"It's okay," he said. "The little girl's gone. I don't think he can catch her."

Beth brushed sand off, touched her face again, and wondered about the quietness.

She looked out to sea and knew. She and everyone else stared mesmerized. The *Dusky Angler* had rolled completely over, quietly slipped down under the surface of the water, and extinguished all visible firelight.

She leaned into Harold.

Singularly and in small groups the villagers silently disappeared, making their way back to the places they'd left. The sea held no more interest for them.

Harold cradled Beth around her shoulders. He studied her face, but the darkness kept most of the damage hidden.

"Tomorrow morning we leave this place." He took her arm and guided her up and toward the path.

"We've paid for two more nights." She panicked. What if he meant it? What if she couldn't talk him out of going? She couldn't leave yet. She had to find out what happened to Gnat. Why did Gnat change from singing to hysteria? And what about her questions for Salty—why did he invite Sylvia's mother to St. Thomas? She couldn't leave yet—she *couldn't*.

"Let's pack, Beth." He took her arm.

"Listen—" She jerked away.

"Don't even bother to argue. You know we have to go."

"Not that, listen . . ."

They stood quiet.

Nothing.

"Won't work, Beth—"

"Shhh—" This time she grabbed his arm and stood firm.

The whimpering started up again. It came from somewhere to their left, then stopped.

Whoever profits by the crime is guilty of it.

—ANONYMOUS

29

Beth held her breath but heard only the surf breaking.

Harold started to speak, but Beth put her finger to his lips.

She moved quietly toward where she thought the sound came from. She heard a muffled sob, then silence.

From the light of the rising moon she made out a silhouette. It wasn't Gnat, but the boy who wore the necklace. He sat on one of the boulders of the cove's northern edge. Beth took her sandals off, waded into the water, then climbed up on the adjoining rocks.

"Let us help," Beth said as quietly as the surf would allow.

"Go away, lady. I don't need anyone's help."

"Maybe not." Harold joined Beth. "Did you know your friend practically broke this lady's jaw? She's really hurting. Now let me see how much damage he did to you."

Harold made his way over to the boy. The boy held his face up, but again the darkness didn't reveal much.

"Hard to see," Harold said. "Come up to our cabin where it's light."

"I'm fine." The boy turned his face. "Leave me alone."

"Was that ship your home?" Beth asked.

No answer.

Harold said, "Those two boys were your friends. Seems like you've lost everything now."

The boy made a quiet but agonizing sound.

"I need some ice on my face," Beth said. "Our cabin's up this path. Come with us, and we'll get you some ice too. Helps with the swelling and pain."

The boy didn't answer.

"Hey, guy. You're not in trouble," Harold said. "Your friends are, but you're not."

"Told you, I don't need your help."

Harold started to take Beth's hand and move away, but Beth made him stop, because now the boy was sliding off the rock. He stood, waiting to follow them, while Beth slipped back into her sandals.

The three walked in silence. Earlier Harold said it would be dark when they returned from dinner, so he had switched on the deck light before they had left.

When they started to climb the stairs to the deck, the boy held back.

"Come on," Harold said. "Let's clean up some of that blood and see if anything's broken."

The boy must have been used to following orders. Beth felt rather proud of Harold right now. Maybe his investment in this incident would change his mind about leaving. She found some towels and washcloths while Harold made baggies of ice.

They took turns using the hand mirror and cleaning their wounds. Harold pulled out a package of oatmeal cookies for them to eat while Beth and the boy held their ice packs in place. The boy's nose kept bleeding off and on.

"Will you tell us your name?" Harold asked.

"Jack."

"Would you like some milk with those cookies?" Harold brought over a glass and poured milk in it without waiting for an answer.

Jack guzzled it down. Harold offered more cookies.

Beth wiped a crumb from her damaged chin. "Your nose seems to have stopped bleeding. What do you plan to do now?"

The boy's face clouded. He put the ice pack down, glanced at the door, then picked up two more cookies. He slid off the chair and stuffed one in his mouth and the other in the pocket of his shorts.

"Guess it's too early to have a plan," Harold said. He glanced at Beth. "Would you like to stay here for a while?"

Jack pulled the cookie out of his mouth. "Got to go." Then, like someone told him to remember his manners, he said, "Thanks."

Beth furrowed her brow and nodded for Harold to do something.

Harold shrugged.

Jack sprinted to the door and scuttled down the steps out into the night.

"Nothing more to do, Beth." Harold started cleaning up the ice, cookies, and washcloths.

"I suppose not, but it feels inadequate. I wish he'd told us more about his life. I wonder where he'll go. I've only seen him on that boat." Her face felt swollen and hot. She picked up a bottle of water and took a swig. Soon, she suspected the throbbing would turn into a headache too.

"Here's an example of you not wanting to leave things alone. If he'd been at all cooperative you'd have bombarded him with a hundred questions, annoying the hell out of me and him."

"Yet I didn't." Her insides flared hot, making her pain more intense.

"Goddammit! Look at you. You'll be a mess tomorrow with your swollen cheek, puffy eye, and the side of your face all black and blue. We almost drowned, you were mugged—your watch is still missing—we're going, Beth. We're getting the hell out of this miserable place." He stopped cleaning and dropped back down into the chair, resting his elbows on the table.

"Yesterday you said you could live here."

Harold's shoulders slumped. He put his head in his hands.

"Let's not change our plans. Think of how much joy this island's brought us. The friendships, all the welcoming people, and yesterday—the best snorkel adventure ever. Seriously, what else could happen?"

He didn't respond.

She stared at him, then said, "I'm going to take some aspirin, shower, and go to bed. Thank you for taking care of Jack and me."

Harold rose from the table, walked around it, leaned over, and gave her a kiss. Then he walked out the door and down the steps and disappeared into the dark.

Fear follows crime, and is its punishment.

—VOLTAIRE

30

He could leave. She didn't care—but she did. Her face grew hotter. She blinked, closed her eyes, and swallowed.

She hated crying.

Damned hormonal differences.

Dammit.

He didn't care enough about her to stay.

Bull—He loved her.

Down deep she knew it. It had to be his ego.

Dammit, anyway.

She stormed to the bathroom, pulled out some tissue, and blew her nose. Pain shot threw her face. Tears leaked out. She wadded up the tissue and flushed it away.

After all, she had planned this vacation for him—for him to travel. This was supposed to make up for all she made him suffer through this last year: the chaos at her work, her mother dying, then Kathleen—Kathleen, her other mother, dying too.

He loved the deep-sea fishing, enjoyed Spring Bay, exploring the Baths, working with Mad Dog, and yesterday's snorkeling.

It didn't make sense for him to shove the last few days of their vacation overboard because of a few unfortunate incidences.

She needed to remember to breathe.

None of it had caused much harm, really—it could have been much worse. Yet her watch—the watch Kathleen gave to her mother, and then her mother gave to her.

Breathe . . . breathe . . . deep breath.

And they did almost drown because of her. Totally her fault. She let her knees fold. She sank onto the edge of the bed, staring at their luggage.

Beth gazed at it, neatly stacked in the corner. He'd be back. She stood, picked her largest suitcase up, put it on the bed, and started packing.

Her stomach hurt. She needed more than a cookie.

That's where he went. He went to Mad Dog's for dinner.

She closed the suitcase, stuck a flashlight in her purse, and headed up the hill. The moon actually made the flashlight unnecessary as soon as her eyes adjusted. The slight breeze felt invigorating—good for the spirit.

Beth would surprise him and apologize. He'd be his normal self and put all this dissention behind. Kathleen had been right. She said Harold only wanted to protect Beth. That he needed to keep her safe. That's what men do. Kathleen scolded Beth, saying she had to at least give him that.

After climbing the steps to the porch of Mad Dog, she pulled open the screen door. Jana sat at a table with her back to Beth. The rest of the tables were empty.

Where was Harold?

"Hi, Jana. Are you busy?"

Jana shifted sideways and gave a slight wave. Beth could see Gnat sitting across from Jana, a plate of cookies and a glass of milk in front of her. Gnat, too busy sobbing, didn't seem to care.

Her face, red and wet, with her black hair plastered to her skin and her eyes skimming and darting all about the room—she had a wild-child look.

Beth, confused because she had expected to see Harold, stood in the doorway. Now she didn't know where he'd gone, and she didn't want to intrude. Jana and Gnat might need privacy.

Jana jutted her chin toward Beth, knitted her brow, and beckoned her toward the chair next to Gnat. Beth scooted over as quietly as she could and sat with her hands folded in her lap.

Jana pointed to Beth's cheek and winced. Beth shrugged.

The girl's anguish grew louder.

Jana inched the coconut cookies closer to Gnat. Gnat arched away, her hands flying over her eyes, and she cried a long, loud wail.

Jana shook her head and sighed.

"Evidently, Jana, these cookies upset Gnat." Beth removed the cookies and took them over to the bar area. She returned, sat, and waited until Gnat peeked through her fingers, choking back sobs. She quieted and rubbed at her eyes with her fists.

"Gnat, at least drink some milk," Jana said. "You'll feel better."

Finally, Gnat did as Jana suggested, but she was shaking so hard she dribbled milk all over. Beth got up again, found a dish towel, and handed it to Gnat to wipe her neck and chin. When the child finished, she set it on the table and sniffed. Her shoulders trembled.

"Take a deep breath," Jana said.

Gnat again did as she was told. Then she took another big breath.

"Feel any better?" Jana picked up the towel and wiped milk off the table.

Gnat shook her head.

"You're certainly upset." Beth rubbed Gnat's back. "Will you tell us why?"

"I—" She broke down in muffled sobs again.

"Deep breath," Jana repeated.

"Do it with me." Beth took Gnat's hand, and she started deep breathing. Gnat copied her, looking in Beth's eyes the whole time.

"Gnat," Jana said, "you're in control of whatever awful thing has you so upset. Let's make it better. Tell us what happened."

"My father . . . I killed him." Tears flooded her sideways glances accompanied by more wailing and kicking of her bare feet. "I did, I did. He didn't swim to shore. He's dead, Missus Jana. He died on the *Angler* because of me."

"Gnat, why on earth would you think you killed him?" Beth said.

"Because when I set the boat on fire—"

Good lord, Missus Abu said Gnat might do something like this.

More sobs.

"Go on, tell us," Jana said.

"He didn't jump off. He didn't swim to shore. He ate the boys' soup, so he didn't know the boat was on fire. I killed him—my own father."

Missus Abu had talked about the boys playing on the boat and about Gnat's propensity for fire activities.

[151]

Ganja. Gnat's father quit teaching because of ganja, according to Jana. Gnat's father and William must be friends or brothers or partners in crime. They had to be, or he wouldn't have a reason to be on the *Dusky Angler.* The *Dusky Angler,* loaded full of something, probably carried a fresh supply of Ganja.

Beth should have asked Missus Abu more questions about Gnat's father.

"What soup?" Jana asked.

"The soup with those cookies—the fish soup he ate. The soup to get rid of those poopholes." Gnat sucked in a big sob.

"Jana, I'm worried this may be true." Beth recalled the vision of Gnat, and then Missus Abu, talking to the fisherman. The two of them might have made puffer-fish soup.

"I didn't want him dead. I only wanted to get rid of all the ganja, those mean boys, and that horrid boat. I didn't want him smoking stuff anymore. He never used to be mean."

The girl sniffed, wiping her nose with the back of her hand.

"Your father doesn't eat soup with fish," Jana said. "You know it's against his religion."

Gnat put her head down on her arms on the table. The sobbing continued, but now more quietly.

"Jana, no one should eat those cookies." Beth searched her memory for tests on toxic substances.

Jana's eyes opened wide.

Beth knew there had to be some way to settle this mess. "Can you think of how we could find out and verify what happened to her father?"

"Not really. However we have to do something." Jana looked at Gnat, who now seemed to have fallen asleep. "When Mad Dog or Salty get here maybe they can tap into the island grapevine. Someone will know something. They always do."

She couldn't disagree with Jana, because Beth saw how the island grapevine worked in St. Thomas. Her rings had appeared, and Missus Abu had known exactly where she and Harold were going . . .

Beth's temples throbbed. She needed to find out where in the world Harold went. And what legal ramifications the girl faced if she had set the boat on fire and poisoned her father, and if he had in fact died?

"Jana, Harold and I didn't see you or Mad Dog or Salty on the beach tonight. I'm surprised you would miss the hottest event of the season."

"We have the best seats in the house without having to walk down the hill in the dark." Jana pointed to the windows overlooking the ocean.

"Of course, but where is everyone?"

Especially, where's Harold.

"We'll be swamped with a new group of tourists tomorrow night, so after the *Dusky Angler* sank, Mad Dog decided he'd check the pantry stock and take care of some dreaded repairs. Not sure where Salty is, unless he's helping Mad Dog. I'm starving. How about some grilled-cheese sandwiches."

"Actually, I'm famished. Have you seen Harold?"

"The two of you . . . I'm shocked." Jana put some bread slices on the cutting board, not looking at Beth.

"I only asked because he might have come up here to for dinner, but now I don't know where he went."

"I see." Jana set the butter and cheese next to the bread. "I've always been a good judge of men. This totally unnerves me. Harold didn't seem the violent type. What happened, Beth? You're a mess."

Dang it. She had forgotten how she looked. Being reminded of the incident made her aware of how raw her face still felt.

"Nicest thing anyone's said to me all day." Beth touched her cheek. "Harold would never do anything like this."

The door swung open and slammed shut. Salty escorted Jack in, holding him by his biceps. Neither looked pleased.

Gnat raised her head. She let out a curdling squeal, knocked over a chair, and flew into them.

Jack, flailing his hands in defense, backed into Salty.

Gnat, screaming, clawed at Jack's face. She kicked at his legs with her bare feet.

"Lily Jack, you poophole, you'll all burn in *hell*—you're murderers!"

Beth leaped over a chair, grabbed the wild child, and pinned her arms to her sides. The girl continued screaming and kicking.

Salty pulled Jack away and held out his arm toward the screaming child.

"Shush, now." Beth smoothed Gnat's hair away from the girl's eyes. "Calm down. You don't know that your father's dead."

"He is, he is, and they killed our mother, Missus Beth. He's wearing her necklace. See it? I thought Sam did it, but Lily Jack—"

Beth dropped to her knees and wrapped her arms tight around the girl. The girl crumpled into her and started sobbing again.

Jack touched the carved Maori necklace and looked up at Salty.

"Now what do you think that was all about, son?" Salty said.

"You brought Mother one just like it when you came back from New Zealand. That's why I wanted this one. I didn't steal it. Honest." Jack looked frightened. "I asked Sam. He said I could keep it."

"Mother?" Beth said. "Are Jack and Gnat brother and sister?"

"And I have the wee misfortune to be their grandfather." Salty sighed and looked to Jana for support.

"I'm fixing us all something to eat, but I think the two young ones need to be kept across the room from each other." Jana started setting out plates and chips.

"Gnat, listen to me," Beth said. "We should help Jana, but you can't fight with Jack anymore, okay?"

"Lily Jack." Gnat sneered at him.

"Stop calling me that." He balled up his fists.

"It's your name, Lily Jack. Why not?" She twisted her face into an ugly smirk.

Beth turned Gnat to face her. "Because it makes him angry for no good reason, Gnat. You're a better person than that. Now set out the plates and napkins, and let's all act civilized, okay?"

"Lily Jack, I hate you. I hate you, I hate you. You murdered our mother. You're evil, Lily Jack." Gnat pulled away from Beth and bolted out the door.

Both Jack and Beth started after her, but Salty grabbed Jack's tank top and pulled him back. Beth stood on the porch staring out into the silent, dark night.

She felt Jana's hand on her arm.

"You'll never find her. She'll wander back later tonight for something to eat after she's calmed down."

They went back inside. Jana grabbed Jack and studied his face.

"Good grief, everyone's been punched in the face tonight. Who was on that ship when the fire started?"

Jack gently covered his damaged nose with his hand.

Jana shook her head.

"Just Sam, Joman, and maybe the new kid, Bucky." Jack studied his bare feet.

Buttering bread, Jana said, "Jack, if you weren't on the ship, where were you?"

"In town, lining up buyers. When I got back to the bay, Sam punched me and then her." He nodded toward Beth.

"You mean lining up buyers for the night's drop," Salty said. "You'll find yourself behind bars before you reach manhood, boy."

"It was all coming to an end, anyway," Jack said. He looked miserable.

"Why would that be?" Salty asked.

"Dad went over to West End tonight. He thought he had a buyer."

"But—" Jana paused with her hand on the refrigerator door. "Then he wasn't on the ship? Jack, you said you were the one lining up buyers."

"Not those buyers. Dad wanted the *Dusky Angler* fixed up so he could sell it. Sam kept saying it was up to me to stop him 'cause he was my dad."

"So Sam and Joman blamed you for all the things that happened tonight, considering your sister set the fire." Beth shook her head at the craziness.

"Guess so. They didn't want to go back to small-time stuff if dad was out of the business."

"Jack, watching the ship burn had to be hard," Jana said. "All your beautiful renovations ruined and buried underwater. Your dad has to be quite proud of all your sanding and varnishing."

"Yeah, well, now I have no home, no friends, and no work. Fuck it all."

Salty grabbed his shoulder. "You'll not be using that language in here, not around these ladies. Now apologize or get your worthless behind out the door before I whack you a good one."

Jack sat and stared at nothing

Salty stood over Jack, his arms folded and his jaw twitching back and forth.

Jack shrugged, looked up, and mumbled something.

"What's this?" Jana held up a large container she had taken from the refrigerator. She opened it, her brow raised.

"It's the fish soup." Beth's heart quickened.

"Wonderful, love a good chowder." Salty sat on a bar stool to watch the food prep.

Beth picked up the lid, saying, "Afraid there's no soup tonight, Salty. Don't let anyone eat this soup—nor those cookies. I think they're contaminated." She slid the cookies into a plastic Ziploc and put the lid back on the soup.

"Contaminated?" Salty waited for an answer.

"How did they get here?" Jana said. "Do you think Gnat brought them?"

Beth said, "Or her father. Throw the cookies away, but let me take the soup. I'd like to know if it's poisonous." She might have a way to test the toxicity of the soup in her little kitchen

"Hah, these young ones make me tired. What to do? I don't have the energy for all their nonsense anymore."

All Salty and Mad Dog did was thrive on nonsense, but deep inside Beth felt queasy. Not about the soup but about Harold. His disappearance worried her, and she found she questioned the safety of everyone tonight.

This wasn't the time to ask Salty any personal family questions or pester him about Sylvia. She decided to forgo the sandwich, too. She needed to find Harold.

"It's time, Salty." Jana interrupted Beth's thoughts. "Let me turn your place into the school. Jack can spend the summer helping renovate it, and maybe if your son-in-law is serious about giving up weed, he'll come back to teaching. Your grandkids will have a decent home there and a good education. If you say no, I won't bother you anymore, and you'll be stuck with this problem until you're in your grave. It'll be someone else's problem then, but not mine. I'll be long gone—back to the states."

Skepticism's slow suicide.

—RALPH WALDO EMERSON

31

The moon hidden behind clouds made the flashlight a welcome tool. Beth hurried down the path to the road. No headlights indicated a lack of traffic on the road tonight. She would own the middle of it.

Squinting, she saw their deck light way down the hill. He's probably home. She quickened her pace, overflowing with things to tell him. She would leave with him tomorrow, whatever time he wanted. She couldn't bear another evening like this, worrying about his safety or where he was.

Tonight, right after she tested the soup, she would finish packing. He'd be so relieved. She owed it to him. Gads, this vacation had turned into a dreadful gift for him, not at all what she expected. These last few horrid hours—the pain of his leaving, his anger, her face . . .

She could give up asking Salty her questions, but she would never give up Harold.

Beth stopped, closed her eyes, and took a deep breath of moist tropical-night air. A life without Harold—his humor, his wit, his love—was unimaginable.

She refocused on their deck light, her beacon, drawing her back to normal. She needed to unwind her tangled thoughts about the soup she carried.

Gnat probably didn't make the lethal soup, considering how she panicked about her little puffer fish not being safe. She would never turn around and make a deadly soup out of the same family of fish.

Back in St. Thomas, Gnat had said something about, *Some needed to die to protect others.* Did she mean fish or people?

Yet, Gnat didn't want her father to die. Well, tetrodotoxin didn't always kill. Sometimes it created a coma state where it just appeared the person was dead—like a zombie. She remembered reading about someone—some man—in Jamaica who supposedly died then came to life again. This *zombie,* just by his existence, terrified some people. He'd been an intentional victim of tetrodotoxin poisoning.

However, Gnat wouldn't know the strength of the toxin in the fish she used. It varied among different fish and in different conditions. She'd never know the right dosage to put her father in a zombie state, and she had no reason to do so.

Besides, what would her motivation be if she had already decided to torch the ship?

Hold on. Gnat obviously loved—loves—her father, or she wouldn't have been so upset. And she did adore the little fish.

Gnat did not make this soup.

So how did she know about it? She was convinced her father ate some this afternoon.

Missus Abu.

Missus Abu gave it to Gnat to take to her father. Wrong. Probably not. Missus Abu would be the one to give it to the father, not Gnat. Missus Abu would have given him the cookies too. Why?

Yet, Missus Abu adored Gnat. She wouldn't want the father to share contaminated food with Gnat.

Beth couldn't think of even one reason why the soup or cookies might be deadly or why Gnat would think they were.

Gnat seemed certain the soup was the reason her father didn't leave the ship. Or did Gnat know her father had the soup and only suspected it was poisonous when she didn't see her father jump off the ship and swim to shore?

Jana said the father wouldn't eat fish soup.

Hunger and the violent events of the evening made Beth's head throb.

This makes no sense. I need food and sleep.

She climbed the steps of the deck, opened the screen door, and snapped on the overhead light. With the deck lights on, she thought Harold would be home. She must have left them on when she left. She didn't even know where to look for him.

She turned on the table lamp.

He must have gone back to Spanish Town.

She set the soup container next to the stove and opened the cabinet above the sink. She needed diluted acetic acid—vinegar would work.

First she would separate a piece of the fish from the broth and heat it to—where was the vinegar?

She opened one kitchen cabinet door after another. She didn't even know if her experiment would work, but it sure as hell wouldn't if she didn't have vinegar. The cabin came stocked with salt, pepper, mustard—why not vinegar?

She banged open the screen door, dashed down the deck steps, turned on her flashlight, and trotted along the path. She swept the flashlight along the edge of the path, on the lookout for the tangle of the night-blooming cerus. She didn't need to damage herself further.

The commissary for Spring Bay was always open—honor system. Somewhere between candy bars, chips, tuna cans, flour, and refrigerated TV dinners she found a glass bottle of cider vinegar. She signed her name to the sheet. She would pay for it when they checked out tomorrow. Even though she fought fatigue she hurried.

She sprinted around the cactus and back up the path to the cabin, taking the steps two at a time. Beth stopped at the top to catch her breath. The glaring overhead light inside was off. Did it burn out?

Only the soft table lamp illuminated the cabin. The hairs on her neck and arms stiffened. Something moved. She caught it out of the corner of her eye—a shadow, a person.

Harold. Yet something didn't feel right. She glanced at the window next to the door. Everything seemed still, too still.

She tiptoed over and peered through the screened doorway. No one.

"Harold?" She held quiet and listened. She smelled something—an odd combination of odors.

She waited. No response. She had only been gone maybe less than ten minutes. Everything was fine when she left.

Nerves from the days' events—nothing more.

Besides, this island exuded friendship. No need to lock doors here. Bath and bed would be so welcomed. She pulled open the screen door and let it again bang shut as she hurried over to the soup.

It wasn't on the counter. How could—?

She glanced behind the box of crackers and bread, moved the dish towels, then looked around and shrieked.

The noise filled the room. All her muscles twitched—the bottle of vinegar slipped from her grip and shattered on the floor.

Sam stood between her and the door with a spoon in one hand and the soup container in the other. His wiry, muscular frame with his long, black dreadlocks made him appear more adult than teen.

Beth held her breath. Sam stared at her, then slung the empty soup container and the spoon aside. They clattered to the floor. His eyes were bloodshot, and he jittered around, moving toward her.

He slowly pulled his long knife out of his belt and grinned.

"Where's the little shit?"

There's nothing I'm afraid of like scared people.

—ROBERT FROST

32

She regretted her startled scream. He wouldn't see fear from her again.

"Who, the girl?" She had to stop shivering.

Her muscles didn't seem to get the message. Sam carried one huge knife.

"Naw, Joman will take care of her. Jack—your little best friend—I heard you talking with him on the beach. You and your helpful husband being all nice and all."

He moved around the couch and glanced into the bedroom, twitching his blade in her direction.

Think. Run? No. Sling something at him.

"Where is he?"

"He's up at Mad Dog's having dinner. Why?" Then her brain took in the meaning of the empty soup carton.

She studied his pupils, searching for symptoms.

"Jack's a loser. Need to get something from him. First I'm going to take care of a bigger problem." Sam grinned and strode closer. He waved his knife blade up in front of her face.

She stared at his eyes. His dilated pupils stared back, but he didn't move the knife. Eye dilation meant nothing here. Yet he didn't seem to be losing muscle control as she watched him hold his knife steady in front of her.

"You're mad at them because the boat's gone." She smiled at him, a dangerous thing to do because he twitched. "Are you blaming Jack because of his relationship with his father and Gnat?"

"Shut up." He shoved the knife under her nose.

"Ouch, be careful." She pushed the blade away without thinking. She surprised herself. "I think you broke it earlier."

Her body reacted to her stupidity with profuse sweating.

Still she must have rattled him. He didn't know quite what to do with the knife, so he now jiggled it around the vicinity of her chin. She wanted to wipe her face, but she knew she dare not make any more movements.

Taunting a testosterone-driven teen with poor decision-making skills, one who thrived on adrenaline-producing activities, would not work in her favor.

His jitters looked worse. The athletic smell of unwashed armpits, burning-ship smoke, and musky marijuana oozed from his pores.

"You're a clever guy, Sam. I'd have enjoyed your giving me a tour of the *Dusky Angler.*"

Speaking of poor decisions—she quickly shut her mouth.

His gaze skimmed the counter top and settled on the loaf of unopened bread.

He stabbed at the loaf of bread with his knife.

"Bitches on board—bad luck." He gave a loud snort. "Hear you invaded my territory by climbing on deck without my permission."

"I didn't know women weren't allowed. I didn't see any signs." She put an earnest look on her face, forcing herself not to tremble.

"Yeah, Jack's mom did the same thing—a real bitch. She kept nagging to sell it, always nagging, nagging, nagging. Made him crazy—made us all crazy. Boss man didn't have the guts to put her in her place."

Sam slit the cellophane open and grabbed a couple of slices, then stuffed both of them in his mouth.

He waved the knife toward her and mumbled, "If he can't control his damned woman, how can he control his business?"

Beth didn't move.

"And you—you screwed everything up with your prying and snooping. Maybe you're the one to blame you for all of this." He glared at her.

"I had nothing to do with the boat." Rivulets of sweat stung as they inched down her damaged cheek.

His lips pulled back over his teeth. Beth was surprised at how white and straight they were.

"I don't mess around like the boss man." He touched the tip of his knife.

"Hold it, guy. I didn't set fire to it," she said. This man-kid was like a lizard, his moves unpredictable. She had inched as far away from him as she could, but it wasn't far enough. Now her back pressed into the inside corner of the counter.

"You put a curse on her, coming on board with all your questions and picture-taking—made boss man nervous. Kept saying he should have sold her earlier, now it was past time, had to sell now, had to get out."

Sam shoved the bread aside, found the cookies, tore off most of one with his teeth, and chewed with his mouth open while he talked.

"Come on, Sam. He probably decided to sell after you guys cut our air hoses. He didn't want to be blamed for your attempted double murder."

Sam burst out with a laugh.

"Almost worked. No one would have guessed."

He spied the jar of Nutella. He set his knife on the table, opened the jar, sniffed, and smiled. "Hello, what's this?"

He scooped out a huge glob and sucked it off his soot-covered fingers.

She visually measured the distance from her to him and then his knife.

Trapped. Nothing would help her.

Earlier she had washed all the dishes and put the cabin's large kitchen knife in the drawer behind him. He probably was no Johnny Depp, but her knife-wielding skills left her vulnerable. The value of fencing lessons never occurred to her. She searched her brain for something—anything.

Nothing.

"Hot damn. Whatever this is, it's good stuff." He continued shoving Nutella in his mouth with his fingers.

She swept her gaze around the room. A heavy-looking lamp stood on the end table, and there underneath it laid the soup carton and spoon.

"Sam, you ate that soup."

"So." He'd pretty much cleaned out the Nutella jar.

"I bought the vinegar to test the soup for poison. You've heard about puffer fish and how toxic they are, I'm sure."

He let the jar slip from his fingers down to the counter, studying her. Then he swung his knife up again and glared.

"You're lying."

"I think you're in for more bad luck."

He held the knife out in front of him with a scowl on his face. *Like the knife could save him.*

He didn't move. He must have been processing what she said.

"Don't believe you." He studied the vinegar on the floor, then glanced over at the empty carton by the door. "I ate it. Feel fine."

"Great," she said. "It's your problem, not mine. It's actually a delicacy in Japan. They have a saying. 'Those who eat fugu are stupid. Those who don't eat fugu are stupid.'"

"You're calling me stupid." The blade swung up close to her ear.

"No, no, it's just a saying." She flinched, talking faster. "You see, in Japan chefs study and practice long hours before they're allowed to prepare puffer fish for human consumption. Those who eat it obviously like it, or maybe it's the thrill of eating something that could be 160,000 times more potent than cocaine. One mistake in the food preparation could make fugu deadly. Sam, you have a problem because a master chef didn't make the soup you ate."

"You said test. Test means it might not be poison, right?" He stepped closer and slowly raised his blade to her neck. He pushed the tip of it a fraction of an inch into her skin just under her chin. "Huh?"

His hot breath smelled of fish and sweet, chocolate hazelnuts. With his free hand Sam used the bottom of his muscle shirt to wipe at the sweat on his forehead, which caused his knife to press deeper.

One slip, one jab, one angry push, and she would be—Harold would never forgive her. Getting murdered on their vacation . . . she would never again feel his warmth or watch happy crinkles appear at the corners of his eyes. She wouldn't be there to scowl at his corny jokes. Her muscles turned syrupy.

Please, Harold, walk through the door. I need you.

Sam clenched his teeth while his impatient eyes studied hers.

"Maybe it was poisoned, but then maybe not." Her voice sounded shaky, but she continued talking. "We'll know if you develop symptoms."

He pulled his weapon away and waggled it at the wall clock. "I ate it at least five minutes ago. I'm fine."

"Then you're probably okay." With the sharp blade flapping around elsewhere, she took a deep breath. With Sam's worthless ability to concentrate, Beth found she could almost relax.

"How long?"

"How long what?" Beth squinted at him.

"Before symptoms happen, woman, how much time?" More beads of sweat appeared on his face. He *had* the liberty to wipe them off.

"Anytime now. I suspect maybe fifteen minutes to an hour. If you're still feeling well, then maybe you've nothing to worry about."

His eyes darted to the clock. He licked his lips, then ran his finger over his bottom one.

"Did you hear what the Chinese said about fugu? Probably not. They say, 'To throw life away, eat a blowfish.'"

He didn't look amused.

"What happens? What should I expect first?"

Beth searched her memory.

"Not much. It's like an anesthetic. The tetrodotoxin reduces voltage of dependent sodium channels, or you could just say it inhibits sodium influx through membranes."

"Cut the crap, woman." He swung the blade up next to her nose. "What's gonna happen? What'll I feel?" His breath was coming hard and fast. Muscles in his neck pulled taunt.

Careful . . .

"You might experience tingling in the lips and in your extremities." She took a shallow breath. She feared what he'd do if he saw her make the slightest move. "Maybe you'll feel other sensory phenomena in your tongue. You might find it difficult to swallow."

He stood frozen, glaring.

"Are you still feeling all right?"

"Yeah." He ran his fingers over his lips again. His face and shirt were wet from sweat. His face grew pink and then seemed to turn cherry red.

Temperature? She'd not seen that listed as a symptom. She studied him and watched, realizing the redness of his face came from raised, rosy ink blotches. These blotches now spread over his arms and face.

He scratched at his arm and wrist.

"Listen, Sam," she said. "This is serious. Even though you threatened me and have probably done worse to others, I don't want you to die. You're having a reaction. I can see it all over your face and arms. Look in that mirror over there."

He darted over to the decorator mirror above the sofa.

"See? Tell me, do your lips or mouth feel different."

He nodded. His eyes grew wide and wild. She could see he was terrified.

"You may start to drool. Do you feel nauseated? You may have trouble walking and not be able to catch your breath."

She found it curious. He had hives, and he was scratching them— again. Hives were allergy symptoms.

"My chest won't work. I can't breathe." His knife clattered on the floor. He bent over, picked it up, and put it back in his belt. "Ya got to help me."

She could hear a wheeze when he breathed.

"I think not breathing is understandable. Often a paralysis sets in; the person is fully alert but can't move. Sort of like you become a zombie, a living-dead thing. When the lungs become involved, breathing stops, and you'll go into cardiac dysfunction—that means heart problems if you don't get care within the next hour."

His discomfort didn't come from poison. He *was* having an allergic reaction. He must be allergic to the Nutella. Still, if he's having problems breathing, this allergic reaction could be life threatening.

"Lady, do something. You know how to help me. Do it."

She took a second to gather her thoughts.

"Well, toward the end you're muscles become paralyzed." She made the tone of her voice sound like she was reading an encyclopedia. "If you go into a coma, your lungs won't work, and you'll die, unless we can get you to a medical facility quickly. Maybe intubation, some charcoal, I'm thinking a gastric lavage might do the trick. Or, in your case, a large dose of antihistamines."

His eyelids were swelling. She might have some Benadryl in her overnight bag.

"I could give you a pill that would help."

"Hell no. You must think I'm stupid. Call someone. Where's the goddamn phone?" he sprinted over to the phone on the end table next to the couch and dialed a phone number.

"Too bad," she said. "The nearest hospital is on Tortola, and the St. Thomas one is forty-five minutes away. Will there be anyone at the health clinic on this island at this time of night?"

"Hello? Yeah, I've—I've been poisoned. Hurry. Dammit, I don't have much time. Meet me at the road intersection by Spring Bay."

"Who did you call?"

"999—fire station. They work with the Health Service Authority." He sprinted out the door and down the steps. She followed.

Interesting. No one had poisoned the soup. She hadn't needed the vinegar after all.

The less we know the more we suspect.

—JOSH BILLINGS

33

Harold's absence worried her. She glanced at her bare wrist and immediately felt a wash of sadness. Her mother's watch meant more to her than she had ever realized. She couldn't imagine never seeing it again. Without it she felt hollow and incomplete. *Wrong.* The missing watch didn't cause this. Harold's absence did. Devastation settled over her.

In the past Beth manipulated all the controls over her life, keeping them tight in her grasp. Tonight that power disappeared when Sam's knife pressed into her throat. Only Harold mattered to her. Nothing else.

Beth carefully washed her face and hands, drank some milk, shook out two aspirin in her palm, then swallowed them. Her headache may have been from the trauma, or the emotional impact of Sam's behaviors, but she suspected it was more a result of her conflict with Harold.

She put their dirty laundry in a plastic bag then packed all her other clothes. Finally, she zipped her large suitcase closed and rolled it over next to Harold's luggage. She would finish with her cosmetics and her overnight bag tomorrow morning before they left.

The cabin still reeked of vinegar. Beth trashed the broken glass with the empty soup carton and tidied the room as much as she could.

Sam must have cut his foot on a sliver of glass. She wiped the streaks of blood off the wooden floorboards. She would clean out the refrigerator in the morning.

What had triggered Sam's allergic reaction? It may have been the nuts in the Nutella or something in the fish soup.

When the firemen had arrived to take Sam, she told them of his confessions about cutting the snuba hoses along with tonight's threat on her life. She mentioned he may have been responsible for Mrs. Bowman's disappearance. They promised her he'd be under tight security until they contacted their local law enforcement. One of them took down the information of where she could be reached.

The wall clock read 12:45. She paced around the small cabin. She didn't want to turn out the lights and go to bed without Harold.

The cabin screamed empty at her. It wormed its way into her mind, reminding Beth of her vulnerability. With Harold next to her, she never experienced not being in control. However after the exhaustion of the day combined with the lateness of the hour, she couldn't muster much in the way of positive thoughts.

Harold must have gone into Spanish Town. Where would he go there? If she hiked into Spanish Town, she might miss him.

She slid open the deck door and wandered out under the starlight. Night sounds surrounded her. Croaking frogs, the ocean gently sliding up on the beach then splashing on the boulders before it retreated, the breeze of the palm fronds above her head, and then a person way down the road singing off tune. Someone—Harold—singing Zippity-do-da, Zippity-day.

Beth sprinted down the deck stairs and tore down the road to meet him. She stumbled, caught her stride, then plowed into his chest, breathing hard. She held on to him with a fierce grip.

"Whoa, lovely lady," he said. "I missed you too."

She turned her face up to his, and he bent over to plant a kiss on her lips. He missed. Her cheek momentarily smarted, but his kiss turned into more of something she might expect from a Labrador puppy.

"Whew, Harold, your breath—I'm getting drunk from inhaling secondhand rum."

She took his arm, and they trudged toward their cabin. When they got to the stairs she steadied him with one hand on his back.

He laughed.

"I can manage, my sweet one," he said. "You needn't worry about me falling."

"Not so sure. Don't want you to split your head open."

When he reached the top, he turned and grabbed her hand and pulled her up close. He nuzzled her hair, then lead her into the cabin.

"Been thinkin' and drinkin'—" He smiled at her. "Come sit, I have something to tell you."

"And I you. You go first." She snuggled up next to him.

"Tonight, in town, the only thing missing was you." He tilted her chin up and looked into her eyes. "Steel drums, dancing, laughing, and jokes—these people are great, Beth. They made me feel—like I belonged here. They didn't treat me like just another tourist."

"Well, then I'm happy for you. When you were gone for so long, I—"

"I know. But I'm not angry anymore. I've been wrong. We'll stay here like we planned."

She flushed. She needed to tell him her decision.

"What's wrong? I can see by your face you have other plans."

"I've finished packing," she said. "I couldn't stay without you here." She looked around the room. Harold always made everything different—safe.

"But your heart's not in it is it?"

"I'd rather stay—but only with you."

"I've another little tidbit of a surprise for you." He grinned and held up one finger.

She couldn't imagine what. She waited.

"Guess who I had a little chat with tonight."

"Mad Dog?"

He shook his head.

"Salty?"

"Your mysterious woman, Sylvia."

Was he teasing—he wouldn't, not about something this important to her.

"You what? How? Was she there in the bar with you? What'd she say?"

"Slow down," he said. "She saw me come in and motioned for me to join her at her table. There were two other guys there—the steel-drum players. When they went up to play, we talked."

"Did she know who you were? What is she like?" Beth grabbed his hand. He pulled it away and put his finger across her lips. She shut her mouth and bit her tongue. If she rushed him, she would only slow him down.

"She knows about us. She asked where you were."

"She did? She wanted to talk with me?"

"Shhh. She said you were annoying the hell out of her and everyone else." He burst out laughing.

Beth's mouth opened. She didn't know if she should be hurt or angry, but whatever she was, she wasn't happy. She crossed her arms and sat back against the cushion.

"She thought we'd trailed her here. I explained to her this was supposed to be a vacation. We didn't know she would be here in the Caribbean. Then I asked her why she was at the cemetery with her sax."

"Did she tell you?" Her insides fluttered.

"Calm down, okay?" he said. "She said it was no one's business but her own. She had completed an obligation, but before she left Denver she decided why not play a little saxophone music in the cemetery as her final note, so to speak. Then she laughed at her own private joke."

"You're confusing me. Did she know Kathleen, or did she only want to play jazz in a cemetery?"

"You'd be proud of me. I asked her. She said, again, it was no one's business but her own." He stood and stretched. "She refused to discuss it anymore."

"Is she still there?" She could take her flashlight and be in town in less than fifteen minutes.

"The place was closing down. Let's go to bed. I'm actually looking forward to spending one more day at our little beach, burned ship and all." He got a drink of water from the sink.

"I can't wait for tomorrow. How perfect." She would use the day to look for Sylvia. First, she would ask Jana or Salty if they were expecting a visit from Sylvia. If not, she would go back into town and check out hotels or places where she might be staying. She knew she could find her. She felt it deep down in her bones—and she knew she would get some answers from the woman. Saying it was none of her business wouldn't stand up, because Kathleen *was* Beth's business. Tomorrow would be the day.

"Why in the hell does this place reek of vinegar?" He looked around.

"Oh—well, I dropped the bottle and it broke." She flushed again and looked away.

"And you needed vinegar for . . . There's something else going on here." He moved to her and touched her shoulder to study her face. "I don't think I'm going to like whatever you say, either."

"You might find it amusing." She brushed at something on her shorts. "Only I don't want you mad."

"Why would I be mad?"

"Because the oldest boy on the *Dusky Angler*, Sam is his name, surprised me tonight. He waited in here with his knife." She might as well tell him the worst first. Next she would tell him about the poisoned soup not really being poisoned, but Sam's allergic reaction making him think it was, and maybe—

She now studied his face and could tell he wouldn't think any of this the least bit humorous.

She sank deeper into the couch and waited for him to join her. When she finished he sat in silence.

"I'm exhausted. Let's go to bed," she said.

He stood, turned off the table lamp, and reached for her hand, saying, "In a few hours, it will be morning. We're catching the first ferry out of here."

A wise man cares not for what he cannot have.

—JACK HERBERT

34

"You can't ask me to leave now." Her voice sounded strong but surprisingly quiet. "You know how much I need to talk to Sylvia, and now she is *here*. I'll find her, and she'll talk to me. Please don't deny me this."

He looked away.

"Sylvia has answers about Kathleen, and I know she'll tell me." She took a deep breath. "You're not the kind of person to drag me away when I'm so close."

He pulled back the coverlet on the bed, climbed in, and turned out his table-side light. She prepared for bed, then went to her side and took one last look at him. His face seemed resolute with his gaze fixed on her as she studied him.

"Harold, if the flights aren't full, and you can actually book your seats, the price at this short notice will be extravagant. We're scheduled to fly out in thirty-some hours anyway. Let's spend this one last day here, please."

He didn't respond.

She turned off her light. She could be stubborn too. If he wanted to leave—she shuddered—maybe he would leave, thinking she would never stay behind on her own.

Wrong.

He knew she had packed tonight. She told him she only wanted to stay if he stayed. The pull of unanswered questions about Kathleen and maybe even her biological father—the force of needing to know felt stronger than ever since Harold had mentioned earlier they could stay one more day. And he had actually talked with Sylvia.

He could no longer use danger as an excuse. Sam was in custody. She hadn't seen William since their first day in St. Thomas. And this happy island welcomed them with friendly greetings wherever they went. Harold reveled in his night out, being accepted as an islander in Spanish Town.

This vigilance of his was nothing more than a façade.

Beth wouldn't leave until she had her answers. She rolled over on her other side with her back to him. He didn't reach out or put his arms around her. Sadness swept over her. She waited for him to give in and cuddle.

He didn't.

Maybe she should turn over and apologize. Her mind filled with a replay of the day's events and then went on to imagine how she might locate Sylvia. If she actually met Sylvia, face to face, she should figure out what she would say to her. Beth didn't remember when she fell asleep.

～

When she woke Beth found Harold dressed, sitting on the deck in the sunshine with his coffee, the phone book, a notepad, and a pen in front of him. Their packed luggage stood by the door to the deck. He glanced up, then back to the phone book.

"Made coffee," he said. "How long will it be before your cosmetic bag is ready?" He ran his finger down the page.

"Tomorrow morning." She jutted her chin out, leaned against the door jamb, and crossed her arms. She couldn't wait to know what he'd say next.

"Last night you said you would leave with me today." He put his finger on the page and looked up.

"And you said you wanted to stay for one more day." This was silly. They knew what the real issue was here.

He went into the kitchen, poured her a mug of coffee, and returned to the sunlit deck. "Come join me." He patted the back of the chair next to his. "Your face doesn't look as bruised as I thought it would this morning. Does it hurt?"

He placed her cup on the teakwood table.

"I'm fine—I should dress." She'd slept in a large cotton-knit tee. "Just in case someone stops by."

Now she was the silly one. No one ever stopped by. She moved to the chair, sat, and sipped her coffee. She glanced at the phone-book page—taxi services. She bristled and put her cup down.

He wrote a number down, closed the book, then leaned back in his chair with his cup and stared at her.

"If you're waiting for me to blink first, you're a jerk," she said.

He laughed.

"What?" she said.

"You're so damned inconsistent, yet predicable." He leaned toward her, picked up her hand, and covered it with his other. "You say you don't want to go, then you say you'll go because you don't want to stay without me. Then you change your mind and say you won't go even if I do."

"The original situation has transformed into other, more unique situations, so my responses adapt. Inconsistencies do not play a part in this." Her cheeks burned.

"And if I agree to stay—here's the predictable part—you'll finagle another way to put our lives in danger." He let go of her hand and picked up the paper with the phone number.

The muscles in his jaw grew taut. "We're going, Beth. I can't let it be any other way." He pushed back his chair. "Time to get ready so we can catch the ferry and then the plane."

He left her on the deck and entered the cabin.

"You're now going to call a cab," she called after him, "and leave this morning."

"You got it. *We* leave this morning."

"I'm going to go shower. Looks like I'll see you back in Denver in a couple of days." She stood and strode into the bedroom, pulled off her nightshirt, and turned on the shower. She blinked back frustration while waiting for the water to warm. Yet it seemed to stream down her cheeks.

Damn him, anyway.

When she finished her shower, dressed, and left the bedroom she saw only her suitcases. No note. No Harold.

[175]

She sort of expected this. His pride wouldn't let him back down, but she felt strange about it just the same.

He wouldn't really leave without her.

Kathleen would have chewed her out, if she were still alive.

Sure, Harold only wanted to protect her.

Dammit, Kathleen, I don't need protection.

No one was left to threaten her. Harold understood this. Pretending to be upset put him in control.

This said a lot about their marriage, but she couldn't figure out just what.

He'd left, and now there was nothing she could do about anything involving their marriage. She shoved it all into the steel vault in the back of her mind, slammed the door, spun the lock, and started humming a happy, made-up tune.

She picked up the phone, dialed 999, and asked about Sam. He'd been taken to the hospital on Tortola and dismissed after they injected him with antihistamines. The law-enforcement officers placed him under arrest for assault with a deadly weapon.

Harold.

Beth shoved the thought of him toward the back of her mind, where he could no longer make her angry or sad.

She decided to hike up to Mad Dog's. They should know about Sam, and with Sylvia nearby, maybe Salty or Mad Dog would give Beth more answers about her own life.

Hear reason or she'll make you feel her.

—BENJAMIN FRANKLIN

35

Groups of tourists ate breakfast at the tables on the cafe's deck. Beth nodded to them and went inside. Jana stood at the grill cooking. Jack, holding catsup and syrup, sprinted from behind the counter over to the few inside customers.

"Hi, Jana." She looked around for Harold but didn't see him. Salty and Mad Dog hadn't arrived either.

I can't believe this. He did go catch that ferry.

Her world tilted. Weak-kneed, she managed to say, "Do you need a hand?"

"Could you refill coffee and water? Soon as I finish these pancakes I'll have a free moment." Jana seemed pale. Her eyes bore the dark circles of no sleep.

"Miss Jana, they want some Tabasco sauce outside." Jack looked under the counter.

"Check the fridge—inside the door."

He found it and scurried out. Beth took the coffee pot and the water pitcher around to each table. Jack seemed to be enjoying his new line of work.

Finally Jana motioned for Beth and Jack to join her at the counter. She pushed orange juice over to Jack and filled a cup of coffee for both Beth and herself.

"I'd hoped to catch Salty here," Beth said. "Any idea of where he is?"

"Unfortunately, I do. He, Mad Dog, and Gnat's father have rounded up some of the neighbors. They're searching the Baths and some of the bays for Gnat. She never returned last night."

"Everyone says she often disappears. If it's normal, why worry?" Beth's emptiness from Harold's departure now grew larger.

"Gnat's never been utterly out of control like you saw last night." Jana glanced around the room, checking the customers.

"Boy-oh-boy," Jack said. "When she gets mad she's something else, but last night she was like nonstop wild, you know. She even scared me." He downed his juice.

Beth liked seeing this new side of Jack. "I've never met anyone with such uncontrollable anger. Gnat must feel terribly hurt."

Jana pointed to the clock on the wall and said, "I'm concerned someone out on the porch might need something."

"I got this." Jack slid off the stool and disappeared out the door.

"Honestly, we're all worried," Jana said. "We've never seen her at this level of uncontrolled hysteria."

Jack loped back in, grabbed the water pitcher, and headed back outside.

Beth watched him smile and chat with the tourists as he filled their glasses. This would give her time to talk with Jana.

"I don't know how much of this you or Salty will want Jack to know. It's not my decision." Beth told Jana an abbreviated version of her encounter with Sam.

"My God, did he admit he killed the children's mother?"

"Sam complained their father couldn't control her but implied he knew how to stop her nagging. That's all."

Jana's mouth hung open for a couple of seconds. "He could have killed you. He could have died from poison. I don't know what to say."

"The soup wasn't poisoned. Nonetheless Sam might have died from an anaphylactic reaction. He seemed severely allergic to something." Beth finished her coffee. "However why did Gnat believe the cookies and soup were poisoned?"

"I want to know how they got in this kitchen. More coffee?"

Beth shook her head. Jack bounced back through the door with an armload of dirty dishes.

"Jana, with Jack around you have yourself some first-class help." She felt an urgency to get to Spanish Town.

"Wait a minute." Jack carefully dumped the dishes next to the sink. "Wait 'til I show you something a guy gave me."

He scraped the dishes, stacked them in the sink, rinsed his hands, then plunged his fist into his pocket and pulled out a five-dollar US bill.

He handed it to Jana.

"Why are you giving it to me?" Jana tousled his hair.

"Aren't I supposed to give you the tips?"

"It's yours. You waited on them. I didn't."

Jack plunked down on the stool and studied both sides of the bill, now grinning ear to ear.

Maybe she could catch up with Harold. Beth glanced at the clock but realized the ferry would leave before she got there. Her heart sank.

Still, if she went to Spanish Town she could look around for Sylvia. Then again if Sylvia wasn't in Spanish Town, she probably had gone back to St. Thomas. Beth reasoned she wouldn't have gone back to the north part of this island, because her gig was over a couple of nights ago.

"We're not very busy yet." Jana picked up the dirty glass and mugs. "I'll appreciate Jack's help when we get hit with the next boatload of tourists. It's good he's getting some decent tips." She filled the sink with hot, sudsy water.

Beth stood. "Heard Sylvia spent time on the island last night and wondered if she planned to visit Salty."

"She never schedules anything with him." Jana finished her coffee. "She'll just pop in for a few drinks, some laughs, and leave. He never knows when she'll show up."

"Got to go, but I'm sick about Gnat. They have to find her, and she has to be okay." Beth started toward the door, stopped, and looked at Jana.

"They will. She'll be fine." Jana glanced over at Jack, who now refilled the water pitcher.

"An idea, probably not a good one," Beth said, "but do you think Gnat could have gone back to St. Thomas? She seems quite attached to Missus Abu." Beth waved her hand in the air. "Silly idea. How would she get there?"

"Not silly at all—she has ways to get back and forth. I suspect the easiest and fastest is to swim out and sneak on board some fisherman's boat. If he's not a friendly person, then stow away."

Jack grinned.

"Have you traveled that way too?" Beth studied him.

He glanced sideways at Jana, then shrugged.

These children belong to the islands, not to her or Harold or anyone. They wouldn't survive in a world of high-rise buildings, street crowds, traffic, pavement, and snowy winters.

Heaviness overtook Beth. Her throat started to tighten.

"Harold and I are leaving the island today. I hate saying good-bye." She searched for her voice. "You've made me feel so welcome." Beth took a pen from her purse and scribble on a napkin. "Here's my contact information. Would you let me know about Gnat?"

Jana nodded. She couldn't seem to speak either.

Beth again took a few more steps toward the door, then slowed. Without looking at Jana, she said, "This idea for a school...I'm keeping my fingers crossed Salty comes through for you. The children need it."

It takes all sorts of people to make the underworld.
—DON MARQUIS

36

Beth faltered and stumbled on her hike back down the hill. She couldn't pay attention to anything around her. She didn't want her last few hours on this beautiful island to be filled with such sorrow. She trodded up the steps to the cabin and opened the door.

"Harold?"

No answer.

He actually *had* left without her. Beth spun around, letting the door slam, and looked down the road. Her arms clutched around her waist. A moment later heat flared through her.

His annoying overprotectiveness seems to be one big theatrical sham.

What if she needed help now? She smirked.

On the other hand then, he probably couldn't believe she'd stay behind either. She sighed and entered the cabin. Nothing seemed right, especially knowing he might have actually left without her. A kernel of emotion deep down inside would not allow her to believe this.

Beth's luggage stood where he left it, making his conspicuously absent. Her throat closed. She crumpled into a chair, not able to find sense in what they had done to their marriage.

After a few minutes, with only silence instead of music in her mind, she stood, looked around, and wondered what would happen next.

She couldn't just do nothing.

Beth phoned for a taxi to pick her up in thirty minutes. Then she packed her cosmetics, cleaned out the refrigerator, wiped up the counter tops, and checked the rest of the cabin to be sure no forgotten items stayed behind. Finally, Beth opened the safe.

As she suspected, only her passport remained. She wrapped her fingers around it and tucked it inside her shoulder bag. Their dream vacation had turned into a whole pile of accusations and regrets.

While she signed the office documents and paid their bill, the taxi arrived and waited to collect her and her luggage. The hunt for Sylvia in Spanish Town wouldn't happen.

Sylvia had labeled her as some sort of nut. Beth's motivation for the pursuit faded with her increasing sorrow over Harold and fell even more when she visualized herself dragging her luggage all around the village.

A thought brightened her mood. Harold probably waited for her on the dock. Seriously, he wouldn't leave with her.

The taxi dropped her off in Spanish Town close to the ferry terminal. She craned around ticket buyers, looking for Harold. He'd be easy to spot because of his height. She scanned the benches, the outdoor vendors, even the parking lot.

He's actually gone.

~

Beth pulled out her passport to purchase the ferry ticket. The ticket seller took it, studied it, then looked at her like he was about to say something. Then he shut it, gave it back to her, took her money, and handed her the ticket.

"Is something wrong?"

"A man asked about you this morning. He wanted to know if you had purchased a ticket."

Harold.

Beth gave the area a quick visual search. She didn't see him.

"Probably my husband. Do you know what time?"

"Just before the last ferry left, about an hour ago."

Harold said we had to catch the first ferry of the morning if we were to make our airplane fight. This must be about the third ferry trip. Who—maybe Salty? Maybe they found Gnat.

"Would you tell me what he looked like?" No one else waited behind her to purchase tickets. She didn't need to hurry.

"Real tall, dark, with long dreadlocks—I've seen him around here many times, but he never takes the ferry, so I don't know his name."

William.

There wasn't enough air for her. She couldn't say anything. Beth nodded thanks and made her way out and up the gangplank, scanning everywhere. She didn't see him.

Beth found a place to sit, shut out the murmur of conversations, and stared at the water. Every few seconds she looked up and around. Taking stock of what she knew about William didn't give her comfort. He stole, he bullied, and he had turned Gnat into the angriest of all, according to Missus Abu. She also said William shouldn't let the boys be playing on the *Dusky Angler,* and that William uses too much ganja.

Beth shivered and searched her brain about why William would bother to look for her.

Sam. He accused me of causing Lily Jack's father to sell the Dusky Angler. *William must believe it too. Damn. More likely, he's found out about what happened to Sam and blames me.*

She studied each passenger as she boarded the ferry. Her stomach churned. She slipped her hand in her pocket and closed it over the nut. Harold would tease her, but just in case.

What had Missus Abu meant for this little nut to do?

By now Harold would be flying somewhere over the ocean toward Puerto Rico. Beth let go of the nut and wrapped her arms around her middle, hoping to ease the ache. She never had emotions like this before. This world, without Harold close by to share it, became meaningless. She shut out these thoughts. They weren't helping her stomach.

The ferry pulled away from the dock, bringing back memories of when she and Harold first took the ferry from St. Thomas to Virgin Gorda a few days ago. Harold had teased her about the nut.

Silly. This common seed couldn't protect her or bring her safety. It wasn't with her when Sam attacked her on the beach, or, for that matter, when William attacked her in the park. Yet when Sam invaded their cabin with his humongous knife, the nut lay on her bedside table in the next room. His blade poking into her skin—he could have murdered her, but he didn't.

[183]

She didn't have the nut when they snuba dived or snorkeled, but she had it in her possession on the boat. Gads, the nut wasn't even a nut. The stupid seed was nothing more than that.

No more magical thoughts.

It was only a shell full of nothing important—like herself.

She watched the docks of Tortola loom into view. Next they'd stop at St. John, then St. Thomas. St. Thomas hung tight to all Kathleen's secrets.

If Kathleen still lived, she'd be furious with Beth. Harold—Kathleen's best drinking buddy. Those two whooped it up over drinks and stories night after night. Now Beth needed Kathleen, not so much for her stories but for her common sense. Kathleen would tell her what to do next. Beth hated feeling lost and empty and couldn't imagine a tomorrow like today.

Yet human nature expects another tomorrow.

Mist anointed her face. She started to move to avoid it, but the cool dampness kept her thoughts anchored in the moment. If she had left all thoughts of Sylvia and her real father back in Denver, this vacation would have a different ending.

Beth stared out to sea, watching the wake left by the ferry, and admired the yachts in the distance.

Kathleen, in her own sneaky way, connived and pushed Harold and Beth toward a happy-ever-after path. Her voice echoed in Beth's head, but this morning Beth couldn't understand a word of what she said.

Couldn't understand, or didn't want to understand?

In less than an hour the ferry docked at Red Hook. Beth hailed a taxi to Charlotte Amalie and asked to be dropped off in front of Hotel 1829.

She climbed up the red-brick steps, dragging her luggage behind, and swung open the grillwork gate. She crossed the rosy-pink and green veranda and entered the bar. Her stomach tumbled at the thought of staying in an empty hotel room. She forced her voice not to quiver and asked the desk-clerk bartender for a room.

"We do have rooms, Ms. Armstrong, but they aren't ready yet."

Beth couldn't pull her luggage around all day. She needed something to eat, and she wanted to find out if Gnat stayed at Missus Abu's last night. She tucked in her lips and looked around, uncertain of what to do next.

"We could store your luggage for you, and we'll take it up when your room is ready. Sign here, please. Just stop by the desk when you return, and we'll give you your key."

"You've read my mind." Beth signed the reservation document and headed back through the veranda and down the steep steps.

She scanned the park, looking for Harold. She held out hope he might decide to stay and wait for her here on St. Thomas. Neither of their bluffs had worked.

Beth detested the lump forming in the pit of her stomach. Eating might make it go away, but she shuddered at the thought of food.

Here she stood, getting what she deserved. She couldn't even guess what her actions would do to their marriage.

What was Harold thinking now?

Her mule-headed stubbornness had put her in quite a fix this time. She examined her choices. She could call the airport and see if another flight was leaving today to Puerto Rico in time for her to make the connecting flight to Denver.

Silly.

Beth knew the only flight to Denver would leave in an hour. It would take her longer than that to get to Puerto Rico.

If she had a room she would go to bed and hide under the covers. She grimaced at engaging in such a blatant act of depression. However, her burning desire to hunt for Sylvia and her father had fizzled out.

Trash it all. They didn't matter. They weren't a part of her life, and they would never be. A folly, that's what Kathleen would have called this whole trip. A dangerous, emotionally costly folly.

Strange how these things worked. Harold stole her ability to care about anything but him.

Deep down, her words about not caring niggled at her, because she did care about Gnat. Not knowing what had happened to the little girl who sang to toxic fish, ran around in the dark, and hid from dangerous people gnawed at Beth's insides.

I can't stand here in the park forever. There must be something I can do to salvage part of this day.

Sorrow makes men sincere.

—HENRY WARD BEECHER

37

Gnat might be with Missus Abu. Beth shut her eyes, envisioning the wall with the gate to the hounfour. A rumpled cement sidewalk led to the emerald, leaf-covered wall. She suspected there were many broken sidewalks and dense, foliage-covered walls on this island.

On the south side of the park, tourists meandered through the vendors' stalls. Beth joined them, hoping to see if Missus Abu was shopping. Then she surveyed the main street along the waterfront. She didn't catch sight of the familiar calico-dressed woman.

Shalee strolled up the walk.

Beth waved, catching her attention. "Hi, you must be off work today."

"And you must be doing much on your vacation. I haven't seen you for a while."

"It's been like a carnival—surprises and delights. Are you enjoying your Saturday?" Beth asked.

"A day off to shop and plan. I'm headed to buy fresh vegetables and fruit over there. Come walk with me." Shalee guided Beth toward an open-air farmers' market.

"I'd hoped for a chance to ask you some questions," Beth said. "I'm almost afraid it will sound like gossip."

Shalee didn't miss a step, but she looked over at Beth.

"It has to do with those boys on the *Dusky Angler*, doesn't it?"

"Everyone on this island seems to be psychic." Beth's feet stuck as if glued to the path.

"I see your ties with Gnat and Missus Abu—" They stood next to the fruit and vegetable vendors' temporary wooden stall.

"Do you know where Gnat is?"

"No one does, until she appears." Shalee selected three bananas and a mango.

"I'm worried about her—we're all worried."

Shalee glanced up at Beth and shook her head. She placed a cabbage and some carrots in her cloth tote bag and replaced her fruit on top of them.

"You think she'll show up on her own schedule."

"I've heard the boat burned last night."

"Virgin Gorda's an hour away . . . How did you—"

"Your concern about being out of line with gossiping isn't an issue here." Shalee smiled and pointed toward a park bench. She sat and placed her purse, a package, and her farmers' market bag on the ground next to her feet.

Beth followed, sat, and internally struggled with how rapidly island news traveled.

"What is it you want to know about those boys?"

Beth sighed. She looked around to be sure no one else listened. Then she told the story about the boat burning, about Sam's attack, and how he later appeared in her cottage.

Shalee nodded when Beth told of his being taken away for treatment and questioning.

The woman had kept quiet, making no attempt to interrupt, until Beth sat back and folded her hands in her lap.

"Did Sam say anything about Joman?" Shalee asked.

"He mentioned Joman would take care of Gnat. I worry what he'll do to her if he finds her."

"Those boys live in an imaginary world, and Malaka doesn't help. She insists Joman's hired on as a mate on a fishing boat. If anyone told her the truth, she'd deny it. With the boat gone and Sam being locked up, there's no venue for their antics. Maybe there's hope for Joman." Shalee smoothed down her skirt. "He's been a good kid, studied hard in school, always polite, but once he became Sam's loyal puppy dog—"

"Missus Abu," Beth said, "told me you shouldn't end your friendship with Malaka."

Beth waited to give Shalee time for all the new information to settle.

Shalee picked an imaginary something off her blouse. She glanced out to sea.

"I heard Malaka tell you on the plane you've been friends since childhood."

"This hurts. After Joman desecrated my church, I had no other course to take."

"I saw Sam toss something like a silver candlestick into the sea. I didn't see Joman."

"He and Joman interrupted mass a month ago when they burst through the doors waving their machetes." Shalee stood, gathered her package and purse, and smiled at Beth. "This isn't your problem. You're here to enjoy our paradise."

~

Beth worried she'd not be able to find Missus Abu's home again. She took a deep breath and decided the best chance of finding the walled courtyard behind the little home would be to walk up the alley where Lily Jack and Joman attacked Missus Abu with rocks.

Beth watched the street signs and the buildings. Some people seem to have an internal global-positioning system. Hers had always served her well. She touched the brown nut.

William. He had asked about her this morning. Maybe she should worry about being mugged again.

She turned on Wimmelskafts Gade and continued. Beth stopped and looked around and behind. None of the islanders paid any attention to her. She followed the sidewalk around a curve and paused to study the view below, causing a few neighborhood dogs to bark. Walking farther up the hill, her directions felt right. Down below, the shopping district spread along the waterfront. The sun glinted off the azure sea, making the boats and ships look like toys floating in someone's bathtub.

She relaxed. She knew why she didn't need to worry about William. He had talked to the ferry ticket master on Virgin Gorda, thirty miles away.

Beth rounded a corner and continued up the hill. This had to be the right street. Large vines covered fences and walls. A few steps later she stopped and pulled aside large emerald leaves and knocked gently on the gate.

Birds chittered and wheezed in the nearby foliage. She strained to hear if these sounds covered up a young girl's voice. Occasional soft clucks from the hens punctuated the continuous chirping.

Should she enter and knock on the door of the house? She waited. She couldn't bring herself to invade Missus Abu's little walled-off refuge.

Except maybe Missus Abu and Gnat were inside the home.

This walled yard—Missus Abu had called it an hounfour. Beth felt this private space possessed a higher ranking than the usual courtyard. Right now, Gnat's well-being overtook any unknown etiquette breach.

Beth knocked louder and called out, "Missus Abu?"

The rooster crowed.

She waited. Then she heard a door softly close and a shuffling of feet. The latch on the gate rose, and Missus Abu smiled up at Beth, holding the gate wide open.

Beth stepped onto the flat stones and took in the smells with a sense of welcome.

"I be expecting you," Missus Abu said.

Beth tilted her head.

"You not be leaving our island without saying good-bye." Missus Abu moved a hen off a chair and nodded to Beth. The hen clucked and started to peck between stones.

Then the rooster fluffed his neck feathers, strutted over toward the wall, scratched a place under the frangipanis, and began to settle himself down in the dust. He stood again, repositioned his rear end, and then lowered his body into comfort. His white eyelids closed.

"I like your animals." Beth settled into the vacated chair.

"I make us tea."

Time and the world ceased to exist in this little gardened yard. Missus Abu returned and poured their tea. They savored the hot liquid for a while, with no rush to enter into conversation.

Gnat was not here.

Beth's urgent quest for information faded. She watched butterflies flutter around and the hens peck. Something also fluttered deep within her, just under her rib cage, and something pecked at her mind. She sipped, working to recognize the flavors of this new tea.

Gnat.

She needed to discuss Gnat with Missus Abu. Missus Abu cared about the girl.

The tea tasted sweet with berries and another flavor Beth couldn't identify, and it bore a pinkish tinge. Its aroma reminded her of something from her childhood. She couldn't figure out what evoked this smell from her youth, either. Still, sorting through her little-girl thoughts, she lingered on a memory of when her father would come into her room and read her stories at night.

The warm April air hung onto the fragrance born from the lilac bushes below her opened window. Sometimes her father would talk and talk—special times—especially when something troubled her, and she'd storm off to her room, slamming the door. Those moments showed everyone she wanted to be alone, but she desperately needed someone to care. So he did.

She sat up straight. She had come to Missus Abu for a reason. For Gnat, not for her mind to wander all over.

"Missus Abu," she said, "I believe you have an alarm rooster."

Missus Abu chuckled and gazed at her handsome sleeping bird.

"His crowing told you I was here, right?"

"He tells me many things. We be good friends."

"Tell me how you've been since I last saw you," Beth said. "I hope those boys are leaving you alone."

Something inside tugged at Beth. She hadn't even bothered to ask Missus Abu about Gnat yet.

"You're kind to ask, but I be thinking you're the one having problems with those boys." Missus Abu pointed to Beth's bruised cheek.

"Sam. Everything's under control now, nothing to worry about." Except it wasn't, and William was looking for her. "Where is Gnat?"

Beth blinked at her own outspokenness. What had happened to her manners?

"She be searching for herself." Missus Abu set her cup down and folded her hands in her lap.

"Last night," Beth forced herself to concentrate before she continued, "she ran away from her grandfather, terribly upset. She kept saying she killed her father."

"What made her think he be dead?"

Beth inhaled, then took time to exhale while she organized her thoughts. She told Missus Abu about Gnat burning the ship, her father not swimming ashore, and the worrisome soup.

Beth continued with the story about Sam's allergic reaction.

"I don't understand what happened," Beth said. "Gnat seemed to think the soup and maybe the cookies were poisoned. And why would she think her father had eaten some?"

"She heard me tell him they were for the boys," Missus Abu said. "He lets them climb all over that boat. They want to be like him, so they do not ask for money. But they be so skinny all the time. They be hungry, growing boys. If they eat good food, maybe they calm down and not be so angry. He said he be going to Virgin Gorda for business, and he'd give the food to the boys when he sees them."

"Then Gnat knew you'd cooked and baked—?"

"She asked me why, and I told her soup and cookies were my way of taking care of those bad boys."

"If you were good to them, maybe they'd be nicer to you and Gnat." Beth set her tea aside. "Your words—Gnat put her own different meaning on 'taking care of them.'"

Missus Abu sipped her tea.

My important questions—ask her now.

"Mister Davies," Beth said, "may let Jana turn his home into a school."

"We will hope this be so."

Beth covered her eyes with her hand. She needed to concentrate. "Was his home where you worked?"

"I worked for Mister Davies before he be here in St. Thomas. Then he moved here and asked if I wanted to be his cook. Some of us came to work for him. He be a good man."

Missus Abu stared off into some long-ago time. Beth remembered another question.

"If Gnat's mother's been gone for almost a year now, then I'm guessing Gnat's been running around on her own for several months." The rooster opened his eyes and watched one of the hens scratching for bugs nearby. "What condition is his house in after all this time?"

"At first I go there to keep the spider webs away, vacuum, dust, but my ankle bones and arms don't want me to go up there to do that anymore." She held her arthritic fingers in the sunshine for Beth to see.

"Is the home far from here?"

"You go back one street over and turn up the hill and keep walking until your feet hurt and you can't breathe." Missus Abu smiled at Beth. "Mister Davies' home be the large white one with upstairs balconies—the long veranda overlooks the sea. When he lived there he had two housekeepers and a gardener. Now there are other houses all around his. Everything changes."

Kathleen had lived with Martin in a large white house, high on a hill. She mentioned the house had a second-floor veranda overlooking the ocean. This house Missus Abu talks about belongs to Jim Davies, not Martin.

"What was Gnat's mother like?" Beth poured Missus Abu more tea, but she decided not to finish what Missus Abu had poured for her.

"A sweet woman, beautiful creamy skin, dark hair. She liked to draw and paint. She taught art at the school. Then she and Gnat's father—"

"Was it always a bad marriage?" Now Beth knew she was prying into none-of-her-business territory.

"I could see they be in love. She'd do anything for him. They both do anything for their children. A few years ago she quit teaching because he wanted her to be home. Then he didn't want her to leave the house unless she asked permission. Oh my, the screaming, cussing, and breaking things kept poor Gnat and her brother hiding in their rooms."

Missus Abu unwrapped her turban and let her gray-streaked locks tumble to her shoulders.

"We all wanted out of there."

She shook her head, then ran her fingers, comblike, through the dark and light strands, untangling them.

"What did Mister Davies do?"

"He went away after Gnat's mother died. He found a little shack to stay in on Virgin Gorda."

"If her father's a heavy ganja user, I suspect the house might be trashed."

"He took many things from the home to sell," she said. "He makes big money now. He only takes things when ganja makes him angry or crazy."

"Missus Abu, I'm very worried about Gnat. Jana said they've never seen her so hysterical. Everyone over there is searching for her. Do you think she could be around here?"

"Where would you be if you were her?" Missus Abu reached over and poured out Beth's cold tea and refilled her cup with hot tea from her little cast-iron pot.

"I haven't a clue. Gnat's life is so different from anything I've experienced."

"When you shut your mind to the possible, you find no answers." Missus Abu held her cup toward Beth and nodded.

Beth picked up the cup and sipped. She smiled as she became aware of the liquid sliding down her throat . . . a mellow flavor with a hint of how she'd expect nectar from a flower to taste. A hen wandered by, stopped, and nestled in the sun next to her sandal. She watched it until the hen's eyes closed.

"Missus Abu, I don't think my mind is closed, but I can't even begin to imagine where Gnat would go."

"Listen to you. You be wanting answers from everyone when deep inside you be knowing."

Beth studied the old woman's face. Why would Missus Abu think—Beth really didn't know. She sipped and worried over this.

"When something be handed to you, you throw it away. You be not knowing the value unless you seek for yourself, but when you find what you look for in your own mind, then you be giving yourself the power."

"But what—" Beth stopped herself. Missus Abu had just told her not to ask questions. She took another sip of tea, buying herself some sorting-out time. She didn't have a clue what Missus Abu was telling her.

But then she remembered what was in her pocket. She felt the outside, and it was there. The nut. Beth had thrown it away. She didn't understand what worth Missus Abu found in this common seed. Beth still didn't, but when Gnat returned it to her she decided she had better keep it.

What we think we know shuts out the possibilities of what might be.

Missus Abu refilled both cups, saying, "Sometimes the value of something for one person may be only in a lesson learned." Missus Abu put her cup to her lips and stared at Beth.

Beth's inner being felt gentle, calm with a childlike carelessness about time. She closed her eyes, and that's when she heard her father's voice, deep, soft, reassuring. She smelled his shampoo, his aftershave.

What was he saying?

Then she heard a little lullaby. He'd always listened to her. He'd tucked her in. A harpsichord—Brahms—the lullaby. Her room was her sanctuary. Her father was her protector. Beth's inner being felt vibrant. She opened her eyes.

Missus Abu smiled.

"Missus Abu, could Gnat enter her old home?"

"All the doors be locked. One sees much crime against valuables on this island. Ganja be not the worst thing here."

"Missus Abu, I know where to find Gnat."

Missus Abu stood, held out her hand for Beth's cup, and said, "Gnat be only part of what be lost."

Among mortals, second thoughts are the wisest.

—EURIPIDES

38

Beth thanked Missus Abu and let herself out the gate. Stepping out into the neighborhood erased all feelings of comfort, and her gaze darted to the sky, searching for a plane long gone on its way to Puerto Rico.

She went to the corner, and when she was one street over, she walked up the steep hill, stepping over buckled and broken pieces of sidewalk. Missus Abu's directions left much to the imagination.

Stopping every few minutes and staring at the homes above her, Beth found that many were partially hidden because of foliage. None had second-story verandas. She came to a street filled with two-lane traffic and no sidewalks or roadway shoulders.

She squirmed and tugged at her T-shirt and bra, soaked with sweat. This wasn't working out. Beth retraced her steps and went back to Missus Abu's block, found another street that might be called the next street over, and headed back up the hill from there.

This street became another, and then another, and soon Beth was high above the city of Charlotte Amalie. She could only catch glimpses of the ocean below because of all the buildings and trees.

She paused at an alleyway and checked out the structures above and around her. A large white house at the far end of the alley, partially hidden by neglected hibiscus bushes beside other smaller homes, caught her attention.

Beth tramped through the weedy, graveled path dappled in sun and shade. She ignored barking dogs and chickens scurrying out of the way but squeaked when something furtive and black darted out in front of her from under a vine—a cat. It disappeared over a fence.

The large white house was snuggled in an overgrowth of greenery. She expected a fence or something to define its property, but there wasn't any. A limestone building the size of a single-car garage stood in the expansive, jungle-filled backyard. Evidently she was at the rear of this home. Cement steps, not a driveway, connected this building to the house.

The neglected appearance of this home gave it an abandoned feel. Occupied or not, it intrigued her. There'd be no harm in taking a quick look—since there wasn't any fence or such.

Beth peered into the stone building's window. It was all dust and dark. Counter tops and a huge marble-top table reminded her that many large estates used to have kitchens detached from the house in case of fire. She went down the steps to the house. The door opened into a screened-in porch, but she decided it wasn't good form to knock on the back door. Besides, what would she say if someone answered?

Beth ambled toward the front of the home through the uncut grass and overgrown vines.

In spite of the neglect, hibiscus, bougainvillea, and red ginger bloomed everywhere. She pushed through their scraggly branches.

The house stood three stories high at least and faced out toward the bay. She held her breath and took in the expansive ocean view far below.

She glanced back at the front of the house. Her heart skipped a beat. Large verandas spread across the face of the whole second floor.

Oh, Harold.

He'd love this. The thought brought an ache. She needed him with her. This house fit the stories Kathleen had told. Her bedroom had opened out onto a large veranda, and she watched ships and storms far out to sea.

Weeds had reclaimed the circle driveway, which lead to the street below, making the whole place look vacated. She wouldn't have been surprised to see plywood nailed over the windows—but there was none, and the glass appeared unbroken. A fleeting thought of Gnat's Rastafarian father lurking about made Beth pause.

She had enough grief from the other Rastafarian, William.

Except both were still on Virgin Gorda. She shivered because William was there searching for her, and Jana said Gnat's father was with Salty, hunting for the child.

Beth decided not to let some remote fear of danger stop her after coming this far. She sprinted up the stairs of the front porch and shielded reflections from the sun by cupping her hands around her face. She peered in the large window next to the big front door. She couldn't see much, just draperies, rugs, and some furniture. She pulled back and wondered if the front door was locked. She gripped the door knob but then decided she should knock before she turned the handle.

Beth grabbed the knocker and gasped. She gawked at a brass plate fastened in the center of the massive front door. The tarnished initials in the metal read, *J. M. Davies.*

Not Jim, but J. M.

The image of a photograph from Kathleen's trunk swept through her mind, the one with the silhouette of the man on a veranda with the ocean behind. Beth slid her fingers over the initials.

Could this be the home—the home of a J. Martin Davies?

She knocked. No response. She pressed down on the door handle. It didn't budge. Her mind leaped into a bog of questions. If Martin and Mister Davies—Salty—are one and the same, and he's Gnat's grandfather, how could he be Beth's father?

This house is like the one Kathleen described, and Gnat is a child of another woman whom Salty never married.

Where would Kathleen fit in?

She plopped down on the top step of the porch, wondering what to do next. She figured Gnat would be here. Missus Abu told her the door would be locked, but then she hadn't answered Beth's question about whether Gnat could get in.

Beth jumped up. Gnat didn't follow rules. She scuttled down the porch stairs and walked around to the side of the house. She pushed back vegetation and squeezed between the house and undergrowth. She unhooked a thorn from her shirt and ignored the scratches on her arms and legs. Behind a tangled wall of errant bushes hid an expansive veranda with an empty, moss-covered swimming pool littered with blown-in debris.

Large glass doors with heavy draperies, when opened, would create an outdoor living space inseparable from the house. Next to the glass doors stood huge bay windows.

She tried each of the glass veranda doors—locked.

There were no screens on the windows. The windows held tight when she pushed up on them. The middle bay windows weren't made to open. Beth found one window that had a pencil-wide crack between the sill and the frame, now filled with dark mold and dirt.

Beth held her breath and pushed up against the wooden frame. It inched up, widening the small slit. She worked her fingers under the window and shoved. It slid up with surprising ease.

Heaving herself up to a sitting position on the sill, ready to swing her legs over, she hesitated and pulled her knees up to her chin.

This was trespassing.

However she knew Gnat climbed through this same window last night. She was positive, but not *positive* positive.

Beth studied the room before she entered. On the wood floor under the window before the carpeted area started were several dark smudges. She looked at her own sandals. Damp soil clung to the sides and bottoms in places. She tingled with excitement. Someone else had used this window as their entrance, and she knew who.

Trespassing or not, she swung her legs into the room. She gently slid the window back down into place. Several large china cabinets and some extra dining-table chairs lined the far wall. She could see some too-obvious vacant spots on the shelves of the cabinets where objects once stood. Beth held her breath, listening.

Silence.

The walls were papered above the wainscoting and hung with framed oil paintings of various ships. The mahogany dining-room table held a couple of inches of dust. Gads, this dining room was big enough to be used as a ballroom. She looked back at the windows where the afternoon sun streamed in and saw dust motes stirring in the air she'd disturbed.

There were no sounds, not even a clock ticking or a refrigerator's whirling motor.

Beth held her breath again. She figured the door to her left would go to the kitchen or pantry at the back of the house. She made her way to the other door, careful to preserve the existing quietness. This wasn't the time for anyone to know of her presence.

She pressed down on the door handle, and the door swung open. Beth moved into a room full of couches, leather chairs, and floor-to-ceiling bookcases, and in the center of the room, dominating everything, stood a white grand piano.

Sylvia's—could this be the little-girl-Sylvia's piano?

The heavy drawn draperies shrouded the dusty parlor in afternoon gloom, making the whiteness of the piano feel larger than life. Beth moved into the room, taking in every detail, from the bronze statue of a rearing stallion on the mantle to a thin, gold and blue French cloisonné vase on a side table.

A book lay opened next to the vase. Beth went over, touched the book, then partially closed it, keeping her finger to not lose the place, and she read the title. Poetry by Henry Van Dyke. She returned the book to its original position.

On the wall opposite the bay windows and veranda doors, a double door with detailed wood carvings of ships, docks, and sea scenes attracted her attention. Beth enjoyed studying the scenes, then decided these doors must lead to the entrance hall.

With care, she pulled the doors open, not making any noticeable sounds, and stepped into a marbled foyer.

Golden afternoon sun streamed in from windows high above, falling on the white circular staircase.

Beth took a deep breath. Now it was time to do what she'd come to do.

She started up the stairs, then stopped. Had she heard something? Something from above? Something cut short, a muffled sound? She wasn't sure. She went up a couple more steps.

A larger-than-life-size oil painting hung above the first landing. Beth halted. She stared, taking in the hint of a lopsided smile, the mischievous green eyes, and the long, slender fingers.

She emitted a tiny whimper of pain. Her throat swelled. She found no air to breathe and sank down on the marble step. Her eyes remained fixed on the painting, a painting of a young woman with a face Beth knew.

Tears slipped out, trickling down Beth's cheeks. She couldn't stop—nothing else mattered. The face staring down at her, but seeing nothing, was the face of lovely, young Kathleen—her mother.

Oh, Harold.

Kathleen's stories, all of their intimate talks, Kathleen's suggestions to Beth for saving her marriage. Everything flooded back into her memory, erasing the white, cold marble stone stairs bathed in the soft yellow light.

White noise and confusion filled her mind. Beth worked to sort out her lost relationships. Kathleen would never have accepted any excuse for Beth letting Harold leave. Beth did love him, but how would he know by all her selfish, single-minded actions?

She wanted his arms around her now, but she hadn't earned his love. She threw it away without value because he gave it to her too freely. Beth's ears filled with her own muffled anguish—sounds rising out of grief. She didn't care.

Warmth of a small arm stretched across her back, a delicate arm. She raised her face and looked into the eyes of a fearful, and tearful, Gnat.

"Missus Beth?" Gnat wiped her own puffy eyes, her face sallow and gaunt.

There is no grief like the grief that does not speak.

—HENRY WADSWORTH LONGFELLOW

39

"Gnat," Beth whispered and pulled the child in, wrapping her in her arms. Beth swallowed back her grief, gently rocking the child. When Gnat started to squirm, she released her. Then Beth wiped her own tears and blew her nose. Untangled from the child, Beth stood. She took Gnat's hand and smiled at her.

"Would you care to show me your room?"

After all, the purpose of Beth entering this home was to comfort the child who had been hiding in her bedroom sanctuary, and not for the child to find Beth and comfort her. Beth flushed, even though she knew Gnat paid no attention to such things.

They climbed the stairs to the second floor. Beth pointed down to the painting of Kathleen. She fought to find noncommittal, unemotional words.

Gnat watched her and waited.

"Was that your grandmother?"

"My grandmother is there. She's the painting on the second landing." Gnat pointed to another oil painting of an older, olive-skinned woman with dark hair. Gnat swirled around and pointed again. "And there's the painting of my mother, Lily Jack, and me."

The painting with her mother hung in a large space across the hallway's upstairs landing between two doors, one slightly ajar. Gnat darted over and stood, studying it like she'd never seen it before.

Beth joined her and examined the painting too. This painting surprised her because of the paleness of the young woman. She held a toddler, Natalie Bowman, who clutched a colorful, stuffed-toy fish in her lap, and a slightly older boy in a white sailor suit stood beside them, holding a blue sailboat.

"This is a beautiful painting of all of you." Beth studied it some more and, except for the skin coloring, could see strong resemblances. She took Gnat's hand again. "Would you like to show your room to me now?"

Gnat led Beth to the partially opened door, pushed it wide, and waited.

"May we go in? I have something I need to tell you."

Gnat led Beth in, dropped her hand, climbed up on her bed, and sat cross-legged. Beth remembered her own wreck of a room when she was Gnat's age. Her mother, adopted mother, rather—constantly nagged about the clothes, books, and toys scattered everywhere. Except for the slightly mussed bedding, nothing appeared out of place. Did Gnat keep her room clean, or did she have her own maid?

Gnat patted her oversized bed, indicating Beth should sit with her.

"I like your room. You keep it quite orderly." Beth sat on the edge. "It's not even dusty like the rest of the house."

"I do this for my mother." Gnat's face screwed up, and she pushed her fists into her eyes. Her chest heaved in and out. "Now I don't even," she gasped for air before saying, "have a father—"

The dam broke on Gnat's emotions with her guilt, tears, and wails rushing out, flooding her room.

"Gnat, Gnat, your father is alive." Beth hugged her, whispering in her ear. "Trust me, I know. Let's not cry anymore. We've cried enough for one day."

"He's not alive. I saw the ship go down."

"Missus Abu told me the soup was fine, and your father wasn't on the ship when it sank."

"But she made it to take care of those horrid boys. She gave it to him to give to them. Instead, he ate it. He didn't give it to those boys. Jana only had the cookies, not the soup." Gnat twisted the coverlet between her hands.

"Gnat, listen. Stop crying and let me tell you a funny story about

[202]

Sam. He ate all of Missus Abu's soup." With an animated voice, Beth spun the nightmarish experience into something vibrant and entertaining for the depressed child.

Gnat's eyes widened, and soon smiles crept over her face, and she even clapped when Beth explained the allergy and hive situation.

Beth lowered her voice into soft tones and said, "You know Missus Abu would never hurt anyone. She takes care of people. That's the kind of care she meant when she talked about those bad boys. Think about why she would bother to make food for boys who threw rocks at her and who tease you."

Gnat screwed up her face, then stared back into Beth's eyes. "Missus Abu put her kindness into the soup and cookies to get some of her kindness into those boys."

Beth nodded. "She didn't poison any food."

Gnat frowned. Beth held her breath.

"Then where is he?" Gnat almost shouted. She lowered her voice. "Where is my father? No one's seen him." She whispered, "He's gone, and like my mother he won't be back."

Beth pulled some tissues from a box next to the bed and wiped the girl's cheeks.

"He's been on Virgin Gorda making a deal for someone to buy the *Dusky Angler*. A boat he no longer has, thanks to you." Beth gently poked the girl.

Gnat squirmed but did not smile or giggle.

Beth took a breath and said, "I bet he heard you've been missing, so he's searching for you."

"You truly and positively think he's alive?"

"I know he's alive. I know you didn't kill him." Her back felt cramped. She stood and stretched. On one wall of Gnat's room stood a white-painted built-in bookcase crammed full of books.

Beth gazed at the books. *Wind in the Willows, Uncle Wriggly*, a whole shelf of Dr. Seuss books, *A Child's Garden of Verses* . . .

"My mother used to read those to Lily Jack and me. They were my baby books. I only read the ones downstairs now."

"Are you reading the Van Dyke book of poetry?"

"Some, but not so much."

"Come with me." Beth opened the doors to the veranda.

Far below were the tiled rooftops of Charlotte Amalie and the ocean beyond.

"See that big ship sailing out?" Beth said.

"The whitish one with the two smoke stacks?"

"That's the one."

Beth stood behind and put her arm around Gnat. She braced herself for another of the girl's crying jags.

"You told Missus Abu you knew your mother died in the ocean."

Gnat didn't move.

"Keep watching the ship while I tell you something about your mother."

Gnat's body stiffened, but she made no sounds.

"Can you still see that ship?"

"It's almost to the horizon now," Gnat said.

"Look at how small it is."

Gnat nodded.

"Yet is it really small? Did it shrink?" Beth knelt so she could be even with Gnat's face.

"Just looks that way from here." Gnat said.

"When we see it as small, it's only small in our eyes, but not in our heads."

Gnat shielded her eyes with her hand.

"She's gone now, Missus Beth."

"Like you believe your mother is gone," Beth said. "Let me show you a different way to think about your mother being gone."

Gnat kept rigid, her eyes on the ocean.

"If you finished the Van Dyke book, you might have read his poem about a ship sailing beyond the horizon. Maybe in some way he might have been writing about what happened to your mother. 'There she goes!' is what he wrote about the ship, and when you saw the ship disappear you said pretty much the same thing, 'She's gone now.'"

Gnat looked into Beth's eyes and waited.

"Do you know what he wrote next? He wrote, 'Gone where?'"

"But I want her here." Gnat sucked in a sob and leaned into Beth.

"He says in his poem the ship is only gone from his sight, and when someone says, 'There she goes,' there are others out beyond where you can't see who will say, 'Here she comes.'"

Gnat tilted her head up so she could study Beth's face, then she turned her gaze back to the ocean.

Beth wondered what the child was thinking. She waited for her to speak, but then Gnat turned and bolted back into the house, across the bedroom, and out the door.

Dammit, not again—

"Gnat—"

Beth charged after her. When she'd reached the stairway she looked over the banister and saw Gnat sprinting down the steps.

"Gnat—wait—"

"I'll be right back, Missus Beth."

A wave of exhaustion swept over Beth.

"I'm getting us that book." Gnat darted down the middle section of stairs to the first landing.

Beth leaned against the railing, waiting. She studied the painting of Kathleen from her position high above. The artist captured her beauty, not as classic, but more exotic, making her intelligence and wisdom radiate through the rich oil colors.

Gnat disappeared into the parlor.

Beth noticed a shiny brass plate in the lower-center-front of the painting's frame. She started down the stairs.

Gnat shrieked and yelled something unintelligible. Beth scrambled down the stairs. She heard more hollering, scuffling, and then something break. When she reached the bottom few steps she heard an ear-splitting crash and silence.

Gnat backed out of the parlor holding the rearing stallion statue like a baseball bat.

Vengeance has no foresight.

—NAPOLEON BONAPARTE

40

Gnat's jaw was set firmly, her legs spread solid, and her elbows held out away from her body. This girl meant business.

Beth whispered Gnat's name. She didn't want to startle her. Gnat acknowledged by nodding her head toward whatever was in the parlor.

Beth peaked over Gnat and saw someone across the room, sprawled facedown on the Persian carpet. On the floor nearer the door where Gnat entered lay an upturned end table along with a cut-glass table lamp in shatters. She put her hand on the doorframe and glanced around the room—no other intruders.

She went over and knelt. Joman. His knife lay behind him by the windows. She felt his carotid artery. The boy lived. She checked him visually. He sported a large bleeding goose egg on his forehead. The cloisonné vase next to him, not the lamp, had done the trick for Gnat.

"Gnat, get me a damp cloth, please."

Gnat followed Beth's directions. By the time she put the damp cloth into Beth's hand, Joman was showing signs of reviving. He moved his legs a little, moaned, and his eyelids fluttered.

Beth put the washcloth on the back of Joman's neck. Joman rolled over.

"Shit."

"Shhh," Beth said. "You'll be fine."

"Not if I can help it," Gnat said.

"Gnat, you shush too." Beth pressed Joman's chest back down on the floor. "Don't get up yet."

"Just pull him up so he can get his poophole out of here."

Beth looked at the angry girl and sighed. She focused back on Joman.

"Gnat, do you have any ice cubes?"

"Nope."

"Then please get another wet washcloth."

"We don't have any more for him." Her lips formed a thin, tight line.

"Nonsense. Scoot. Bring me one."

"Look at his machete." She grabbed the knife and made chopping motions. "He planned to hack me into pieces. Why are you being—?"

"It's the right thing to do. He had no intentions of killing you."

"Did too."

"He hid behind those drapes when he heard you heading to this room, right?"

Gnat glared at her, not answering.

"Then you saw him, or some movement, and screamed. He yelled something, and the two of you scuffled. One of you knocked the lamp off the table. You broke away, grabbed the vase, and clobbered him on the head. He fell, knocking the table over too."

"So?" She lowered the knife to her side.

"So if he'd wanted to kill you, why didn't he? He could have plunged that eighteen-inch weapon right into your gut when you first screamed. But he didn't. I bet he didn't even have it in his hands when you two were wrestling before one of you knocked the lamp off the table."

Gnat stared at the lamp. Joman now propped himself up on one elbow, focusing his eyes as best he could.

"Now, would you please get me another damp washcloth?"

Gnat nodded. Keeping the machete with her, she turned and left.

"My head . . ."

"Let me look." Beth turned his head into the light. "It's only a bump, you'll survive. Why are you here?"

"Sam's angry. He wants Gnat dead."

"Sam said you'd take care of her. I'm calling the police."

"I've been searching for her, to warn her. No way am I killing someone for him. Especially not someone I know. Shit, I didn't expect her to let loose like that. Goddammit, my head hurts."

"Stop cussing. It doesn't become you." Beth glanced up and saw Gnat standing in the doorway.

She still held the knife and now a washcloth.

"Did you hear?" Beth said.

"He's still a murderer." Gnat gave a pout when she handed her the washcloth. She scooted back into a chair seat then busied herself making reflections bounce off the knife.

Beth cleaned the wound, stood, and extended her hand to help Joman up.

"Here's what you need to know, Joman," Beth said. "You're close to being locked up with your friend Sam."

"Ha! They'll never pin anything on Sam."

"Already have. He's behind bars as we speak."

Gnat smirked and waggled his knife at him.

Joman's face drained pale.

"I could call the law right now—get you for breaking and entering."

Gads, what a hypocrite I am.

She continued, "They'd think you were here to kill Gnat, too, because of your knife. They know Sam cut the hoses when we were in the bay at St. John. Knowing Sam, I bet Sam told them you were the one who did it."

Beth checked Gnat's behavior out. The young girl sat stone still, not even waving the knife. She must be listening to everything.

Joman's pale face now had a green tinge—nausea.

"Don't you dare throw up in here. Tell me, and we'll get you to a bathroom." Beth handed him the wet cloth and motioned for him to wipe the cold sweat off his forehead and neck.

"Whatcha' going to do now, Joman?" Gnat said. "You don't have a job, and your best friend's in the clinker."

Joman ignored her. He held the cloth over his eyes.

"According to one of your mother's friends, you used to be a pretty good kid until you got mixed up with Sam's gang. Your mother's rather blind to what you've been up to. Don't you love her?"

He sighed and looked away.

"Guess not. If you did you wouldn't be this disrespectful toward her."

"I'm a good son. You don't know crap."

"Most good sons make their moms proud."

"She is, she brags about me. I've heard her."

Gnat bent over laughing. She slapped the machete on the arm of the chair several times.

Beth gave Gnat an evil squinty-eye look. Gnat straightened and settled back in silence.

"Joman, your mother brags based on the lies you tell her, which only demonstrates your lack of respect." Beth held up her hand to stop him from speaking. "Telling her you've signed to work on a fishing boat would be great, except the fishing boat's cargo didn't come from the sea. It came from the air. Transporting and selling illegal substances would never make your mother proud. You're breaking her heart, this woman who loves you unconditionally. She's the only person in the whole world who will stand by you and pick up the pieces when your life crumbles. And the way you're headed, she's going to have lots of pieces to pick up and glue together. Why do you hurt her?"

Joman crawled over and slid onto the couch. A few seconds later he covered his face with his hands.

Beth waited, hoping no smart-alecky remarks would come out of Gnat's mouth.

Joman mumbled something.

"You sound like you're talking with marbles in your mouth. Please repeat more clearly," Beth said.

"I do love her, Missus. But I hate seeing her scrub floors and work in those office buildings late at night after she's worked all day. For what? Money, it's always that. She's making herself sick with all she has to do to pay rent and buy food. This boat stuff . . . we were supposed to make lots of money. Then maybe she could stay home with the little kids. She shouldn't be leaving them on their own night after night."

"Good try, but your behavior doesn't support your words. You're old enough to babysit your brothers and sisters."

And this kid did save that little butterscotch mouser.

He stood up and faced her, starting to say something.

Beth interrupted, "Come on, you can't scam me. You kids did so much crap, throwing rocks at Missus Abu, bursting into that church with machetes, and who knows what else. You're nothing more than a juvenile delinquent."

"Yeah, you got that one right, Missus Beth. But you forgot about my mother's murder."

"You're wrong. I'm good. It's just that—"

"You've got no excuse, sonny boy." Now that Beth had spelled it all out, she wondered why she didn't call the island police. These kids were hoodlums.

"Lady, you don't understand. When Sam said to do something, we did it. He promised us big money, but if we didn't do what he wanted we'd end up being fish food."

"Like you did to my mother." Gnat leaped out of the chair and charged at him, waving the machete. Joman's face grayed.

Beth grabbed her around her waist from behind—suffering visions of the knife slicing through her own neck.

She held Gnat tight. Heat flooded through her.

"Put it down, Gnat," Beth said. "Now!"

Gnat stood sobbing, but she held tight to the machete.

What in the world had Beth gotten herself into? She reached around and pried Gnat's fingers from the handle. Then she made the girl sit back in the chair again. Beth swiped the sweat from her own neck with the back of her hand.

"I didn't kill your mother. I swear." Joman's eyes were still wide and staring at the knife in Beth's hand.

"You," Gnat said, "Lily Jack, and Sam did. You're all murderers. Lily Jack even wears her necklace."

"Are you sure that necklace was your mothers?" Beth said. "Maybe it just looks like hers."

"She let us hold it. She said someday I could have it." Gnat sniffed and wiped her nose on the back of her hand. Beth handed her one of the washcloths to use.

"Don't you think many look the same? Look at the carvings they sell here at the vendors' stalls."

"She told Lily Jack and me stories about it. Like they each are made with a special meaning. Grandfather gave her a fish hook one. Hei-Matau, she called it. If it's given in love, then the spirit of the one who gives it remains with it forever. Now Lily Jack took it." Gnat stared into Beth's eyes and whispered, "He killed his own mother for her necklace."

"Naw, you're stupid," Joman said. "He didn't kill her. He found it."

Beth felt a cold chill, something she remembered Sam saying. Was Joman right? Would Sam feed Jack and him to the fish? She put her free hand in her shorts pockets and touched the nut.

[210]

"Where did he find it?" She wrapped her fingers around the nut and squeezed.

"Before he varnished the deck, he'd need to sand it first. He started in the bow, but he's pretty little. He needed my help to move a pile of moldy ropes. There it was, stuck down between the ropes and the bow."

Gnat sat expressionless. Beth guessed it was her way of processing information.

"Here's what I suggest you do, Joman." She let go of the nut. "Go home, give your mom a hug, and tell her you're setting out on a different path for your future. Cut off all contact with the rest of your little gang. Stay away from them completely. Gnat's grandfather will probably let Jana and Gnat's father turn this home into a school where you can come, learn a skill, get paid to work, and make your mother proud by being an educated person who can get a good-paying job."

"You serious?" He tilted his head and studied Beth's face. "Coach would really come back and teach—here? In this house?" He swept his gaze around the large, plush room.

The tightness in Beth's muscles released. She drew in a deep breath and handed Joman his machete. He looked up at her in disbelief. Gnat let out a howl and jumped up with her fists balled.

"You can't give that back to him." She screwed her face up. "He'll kill someone."

"If he's going to kill someone, he'll do it with or without this. It has to be his decision. At his age it serves no purpose for anyone but himself to be the policeman of his own behaviors."

The machete lay flat in both of his hands just as Beth had handed it to him. He turned his gaze to Beth's face, and his eyebrows crinkled.

Beth motioned him to follow. She strode into the hallway, unlocked the front door, and opened it. "You're almost a man now," Beth said. "Go talk to your mother. It's time for you to be responsible for your own actions."

Things do not change. We do.

—HENRY DAVID THOREAU

41

"Gosh, Miss Beth, you sure told him." Gnat relocked the door after Beth closed it. "Do you think he'll change?"

"Neither of us can guess. You've had to manage a huge change in your life this year, and you've struggled. It's hard."

Gnat lowered her gaze, not responding.

"Let's get Van Dyke and read him up in your room." Beth nodded toward the stairs.

Gnat dashed back into the parlor, stopped, peered out, and said, "Hold on a minute. I'll meet you upstairs."

Beth didn't know if she should trust this child not to disappear again, but then she had trusted Joman with a deadly weapon. She started up the long staircase, stopping on the first landing in front of the painting of Kathleen. The brass plate's inscription read, *Kathleen McPherson—1941*, and below those words, a quote from Shakespeare: *For where thou art, there is the world itself.*

"Are you okay?" Gnat pulled on a couple of Beth's fingers.

She hadn't heard her come up the steps. Beth steadied her breathing, gave the painting another look, then she pasted on a more pleasant face. She followed Gnat, continuing up the staircase.

"You really like the Kathleen painting." Gnat pointed at another painting. "My grandfather likes paintings of ships in storms. My mother paints, mostly flowers and birds. We could go upstairs to the third floor and see her studio, but I want to read Van Dyke first."

When they reached the landing, Gnat skipped to her bedroom. Beth cherished this glimpse of a once-happy child.

They settled on Gnat's bed with the box of crackers between them that Gnat had grabbed from the kitchen. Beth thumbed through the pages of the book, found the poem, and gave it to Gnat to read on her own. She watched the child, head bent over the pages, silently studying the words to make sense out of them. When Gnat finished, she looked toward the sea, out through the veranda doors.

After a few minutes she asked if he wrote any other poems about death.

"Let's look in the table of contents." Beth turned pages back to the beginning and started reading her the titles.

"Shhh . . ." Gnat grabbed her hand.

Beth listened.

She might have she heard something, like a click, or a turn of metal against metal, but very faint. Gnat seemed frozen. Beth patted the girl's knee.

"We're both jumpy after the Joman thing." Beth started in with the titles again.

"I heard someone come in the front door," Gnat whispered. "I know I did."

Then Beth heard the heavy footsteps on the marble staircase.

Gnat looked up into Beth's face, then back at her opened doorway. Beth stood, glancing around for something, anything, to protect them. Gnat slid off her bed and stared at the door. Beth pulled Gnat behind her and pushed back toward the closet near the veranda.

Stupid, she needed to secure the bedroom door—

Beth sprinted forward. She got as far as the bed when a looming, dark figure plunged through the doorway.

William! Oh, God! Not him—

Beth's stomach flipped—no escape. She thrust her hands out behind her to keep Gnat away from this man.

"Stop!" Beth voice boomed with authority as she spread her stance. He'd have to kill her first to get to the child.

"Daddy—" Gnat flew around Beth and into William's embrace.

William dropped to one knee, and he buried his face into the little girl's hair.

Of course, one and the same.

"Natalie, we've searched everywhere for you, child." He held her out at arm's length. "I should have known you'd be here. Let me see, are you okay?"

"I thought—" She sobbed, then said, "I'd killed you."

Of course. William owned the Dusky Angler. *William, the son-in-law of J. M. Davies. If Martin is my father, then, geesh—we're all related.*

"No one's going to kill me, unless it's that crazy tourist lady standing behind you." He winked at Beth.

Beth sank down on the child's bed. She didn't know what to say or what to do.

"Come on. We need to do some soul baring and clarifying." He patted the floor next to him, and Gnat sat.

"You sound like a school counselor." This guy had stolen from her, hurt her. Beth considered him dangerous.

"Always wanted to be one, but I'm just a teacher gone astray. Natalie, girl, I can't be losing you or Jack. You're all I have." He took his thumb and wiped a smudge from her chin, then he hugged her for a long minute. In a barely audible voice, he said, "And you have this woman to thank."

Beth mouthed, *Me?*

He pointed to Beth's cheek. "Aw, Sam—But then I hurt you, too. Damn."

"You did, bully." Gnat gritted her teeth, jumped up, and swatted his arm as hard as she could. "I hate it. Why are you so mean all the time?"

Gnat was shaking, her fists doubled tight. Beth thought the child might bolt out of the room.

William must have thought the same. He pulled her in close and gave her another bear hug. He hung tight to her and murmured words into her face and ears that Beth couldn't hear or understand.

"You're not mad because I burned it up?" Gnat's voice was hesitant and soft.

"You had good reason. My reasons were bad." He released her.

Gnat reached over and whispered something into William's ear. He grimaced, studied his gold watchband, turned it around several times, then cleared his throat.

"Miss Beth, right? I've been ordered to set things straight between the two of us," he said. "I deeply regret my ungentlemanly behaviors when I smashed your camera. I lost my temper because I didn't expect you to fly at me like some Tasmanian devil needing a root canal. You, woman, were supposed to be frightened by me. Now I'm the one who has to say he's sorry for all the distress and pain and loss I caused. Will you accept my apology?"

"And why should I? What's changed?" Beth knew she was pushing it again, but she also knew she was right. "You're saying all of this because Gnat and I are friends. What if we weren't? Where's the regret then?"

Gnat jutted out her chin and glared at her dad.

"Man." He wagged his head side to side and sighed. "I've gone cold turkey, been clean for almost a whole week. Your snooping around, asking all those questions, taking photos—you were getting in the way of my business, woman. Instead of taking the next flight home like I'd hoped, you started chatting it up with Missus Abu—you even went to the police station—and then you actually bought another damn camera. Those boys saw I couldn't get rid of you. Looked like Sam, Bucky, and the gang decided to do what they thought I couldn't. Had no idea those boys would be doing the things they did. Man. Totally my fault. Poor, sweet Missus Abu. She'd never harm anyone."

Gnat punched him in the arm again. "I hate those boys."

"Lily Jack and Joman throwing rocks at Missus Abu was bad enough, but I knew the five of them had done something even worse the next day. I cornered them that evening and made them confess about the snuba-diving incident." William rubbed his temples. "Those boys—they followed me, wanted to be like me, and look at what I did. I betrayed my I and I."

He pulled the child in close and wrapped his long arms around her, cradling her. Beth could see Gnat relax into him. He obviously did love the child.

"I'm supposed to be upstanding, be their role model, keep the world up-looking and positive, yet I mistreated your mother, misguided those boys, and lost my connection with Jah."

"Dirty Poopholes. Murderers, throwing rocks at Missus Abu. They're the worse poopholes ever."

"They aren't murderers. They cut tubes to the oxygen regulators on Miss Beth and her husband's diving gear, causing it to be close to murder. Still can't believe Lily Jack's involvement. I had no choice after that. These two kids—they're my world." He ruffled Gnat's hair and hugged her tight. "Only thing in life I care about now that Frangi is gone are Natalie and Lily Jack."

Silence wrapped around everything.

Beth cleared her throat, then said, "Do you have a plan?"

"Salty and Jana do, so I'm ready to dedicate myself back to helping youth."

"Gnat and I talked about the difficulty of making changes."

"Not a change for me. It's who I am. I should've gotten rid of the *Dusky Angler* and the weed business before I even started." He lifted Gnat's chin. "Won't have you kids running wild anymore."

"You're out of the business?" Beth slid off the bed and sat on the floor next to them.

"Except for one problem. Got to figure out how to cut my connections."

"Your boat for transporting is gone," Beth said. "Could be an in for cutting some of those ties."

William sat silent.

"Let Sam-the-Poophole take over the business." Gnat patted her dad's cheeks. "Tell them all he and Bucky are in charge. Maybe they'll put a hit out on the big bullies."

Beth refused to let the corners of her lips curl up.

"Sam's an easy target," William said. "He's still a minor. Can't do that to him."

"Especially since he's locked up." Beth raised an eyebrow and flashed a thumbs-up to Gnat.

"Heard about it—his attack and his threatening you. Afraid he won't be in for long."

"Maybe, maybe not. Tell me about the last time your wife boarded the *Dusky Angler*."

"Old story told over and over," he bent his shoulders back, stretching them.

"To some, but I've not heard it."

"Frangipani never went on board—at least not after her dad turned the boat over to me."

Gnat grabbed the book of poems off the bed and settled down into her father's lap. She turned the pages slowly, ignoring the worn-out conversation.

"What changed?"

"My views. Women and men have separate duties and places to maintain. Old sailors will agree a woman on board brings bad luck."

"The necklace Jack wears, is it a duplicate of his mother's?"

"Didn't know Jack wore a necklace. Around here, anything less than gold would be—well, not considered manly. Still Lily Jack has a few more years before he enters manhood."

"It's my mother's." Gnat didn't look up from the book. "She always wore it. I keep telling everyone. He killed her for her necklace."

William took an exasperated breath and stared up at the ceiling.

"Gnat, we need proof." Beth touched William. He looked at her. "When did you last see Jack?"

"After the snuba stunt. Assigned him the task of varnishing not just the deck, but the whole interior of the boat, as punishment. Besides, a newly varnished boat sells better than a neglected one." He punched Gnat gently in the shoulder. "Or one at the bottom of the sea."

Jack had worn the necklace every time Beth saw him. He must have taken care to hide it from his father.

Gnat leaned into William with her head against his chest. She continued to read.

"Jana told me you and the two younger boys played softball on the night Frangipani disappeared." Except for his views on womanhood, William seemed to be a decent kind of guy.

"Baseball, a practice, we had a big game coming up."

"Where did Sam spend the evening?"

"Crap! You ask more questions than any cop."

"Probably."

"No one knows where Sam went. He took the boat and didn't come back until morning. He said he likes night fishing."

"Did you know Joman and Jack found Frangipani's necklace, or a look-alike, under some old rope up in the bow a few days ago?"

William's mouth opened, then shut. He waited.

"When Sam threatened me, he said Joman would take care of Gnat, but he wanted to know where to find Jack." Beth waited until she had the attention of both of them. "He said Jack had something he wanted back."

"Mother's necklace?"

"I think so," Beth said. "Jack told his grandfather he didn't steal it. He had asked Sam if he could have it."

"Sam probably didn't think," William said, "about it being important until the boat burned. He'd be afraid lots of questioning would happen. Maybe that's when he figured out who the owner of the necklace was."

"Bet law enforcement would enjoy knowing what you now know." Beth stood. She needed to stretch.

"No more questions, Tourist Lady." William hugged Gnat, then he stood. Gnat stood too.

"One more. Where's my stuff you stole, poophole?" Beth's hand slipped into her pocket and closed tight around the nut.

"Memory card's somewhere out to sea. Sorry, but I really don't know where all your jewelry went. Seems I'm not the only family thief."

Understanding is a two-way street.

—ELEANOR ROOSEVELT

42

Beth said her good-byes, leaving William to tell Gnat how wonderful their future would be. Closing the heavy wooden front door behind her, Beth stepped back into her own uncertain future. Her life held no meaning if she couldn't share it with Harold.

Afternoon shadows lengthened. Exhausted, she sauntered back down the hill of broken sidewalks. Beth had never experienced such emptiness before. Her stomach complained about not eating all day, discounting Gnat's crackers, coffee with Jana, and tea with Missus Abu. She would find a restaurant and eat dinner, then go to the hotel and sleep. She sighed. Food wouldn't fill the hollowness inside her.

Harold.

The events of the afternoon had preoccupied her, but now the emotions of his leaving tumbled back. She had experienced drowning. This was worse. Harold walking out of her life more than suffocated her, it broke all of her happiness into tiny, sharp shards of pain. The lonely idea of eating by herself hadn't encouraged Beth's stomach to stop growling.

She needed more than just food to satiate her appetite. She needed sustenance for her soul.

The rooster crowed, as predicted. The gate opened. Missus Abu invited her in.

Beth went to the chair where she usually sat, picked up a hen, and placed the fat bird in her lap, stroking its rusty feathers.

Missus Abu took her teapot and poured steaming, hot tea into two mugs. "You be looking a little more content after your time in the big home."

Beth's solemn mood broke into laughter. "Missus Abu, you *do* know everything."

The older woman sipped from her teal-colored mug and fixed her twinkling eyes on Beth.

Beth took the iron-colored one and said, "Gnat's going to be fine. I've formally met William, and his apology's accepted. However, I am rather put out about my broken camera, and I really want my watch back. He doesn't know what happened to it. We think we've solved what happened to Gnat's mother." Beth told Missus Abu about all of it, including Joman.

Missus Abu nodded, sipped tea, and waited.

"You're waiting for my questions."

Missus Abu smiled.

"I'm betting my father is Martin Davies, but I can't figure out how Kathleen fits in with Gnat's grandmother and her mother. Why, if Martin and my mother, Kathleen, loved each other—why did Kathleen give away their baby, to be adopted by her sister, my aunt?"

"Mister Davies be a good man. His wife in the USA fell off a horse and never walked again. He would not abandon her. He bought the lovely home you visited and brought us here to help him. He be a sailorman, traveling all over the world. When he brought Miss Kathleen here to live with him, they be happy for many months, but she be lonely. His shipping work took him away for weeks. When Mister Davies said he could not be marrying her because of his other wife, she be sadder and sadder and sick. The sickness she said be allergies. But the housekeepers and I know it be the morning sickness. She left. Miss Kathleen didn't tell him she be with child. His heart hurt from losing her. He could not find her anywhere. Years later a sweet woman came to live with him, and they have Frangipani. She be Gnat's and Jack's mother."

Frangipani would be my half-sister, and Gnat is my niece . . .

A rush of conflicted emotions washed over Beth, keeping her from speaking. She sipped her tea, swallowed hard, then after a few minutes she pulled the buckeye out of her pocket and examined it.

"What is this supposed to do?"

"What has it done for you?"

"Not much."

"You be so certain." The woman tilted her head and smiled.

"It's made me wonder—about what it's supposed to do." She put it back in her pocket and picked up her mug.

"Wondering be good. It keeps the mind fresh. More?"

"It gave me a chance to show off my knowledge to my husband." She sipped. This tea tasted different from the other two teas. She wanted to tell about the conversation on the ferry about the nut, but sadness fell over her. His leaving hurt.

"Did the two of you be talking about this?"

"A little. He teased me. Your nut did bring me comfort at times." Beth found the flavor of this tea not as bold as the earlier one and a bit more tart than the second one. She should ask what's in these teas.

"Then all be good, except for the husband who now be not with you."

Beth's throat tightened with the familiar lump. She stared at Missus Abu.

"This not be magic." Missus Abu put her hand up to her cheek. "You believe so, but there's no magic except what our minds know."

"Then you have too many tricks. You make me wonder how your mind knows so much." Beth put her cup down and crossed her arms.

"No tricks, no mystical knowing, your face tells me your heart be breaking into little pieces. I see your husband get off the ferry early this morning with his luggage. You come on a later ferry with your suitcases. I be guessing what caused the bruise on your cheek worries your husband."

"I need to believe in something magical right now, and you and your tea—" The lump in her throat hurt. She stopped talking.

"What have you lost, child? What you be looking for?"

"Harold's love."

"You do not lose what you have. Let's sip our tea and listen to what we know."

Missus Abu, clever in her calm ways, had told Beth to be quiet once again. What was Beth supposed to do? Sit and be content with

Harold's leaving? She sat back and turned her mug around, feeling its texture and studying the variant tones of grays, silvers, and blacks.

Beth sipped. She examined her mug again.

How had she missed the faint gold streaks behind the gray and silver? The gold paint contained minute dots of blue here and there. As a scientist, Beth noticed the smallest of details, but she'd missed all this.

Maybe her sorrow over Harold had blinded her to her surroundings. She finished her tea, set her mug down, and looked up into Missus Abu's smile.

Except for my work, I have been blind. Kathleen had warned me. Harold told me I never valued what I had, but I didn't want to hear.

"Missus Abu, I *have* lost something today, and it's a good thing to lose. I've seemed to have lost my obsessive need to control. I'm adept at taking control and keeping it, sometimes to the detriment of others. I decided Gnat needed a family, but she'd never adjust to life with us. I've been desperate to learn about Sylvia and my biological mother, and I've wasted much of our vacation looking for my biological father. Now I don't care about any of this. It holds me in the past. It's my future that matters, and I want it to be with Harold." Beth bit her lip, then continued, "Without Harold, I've lost my chance to be happy."

Missus Abu's intense, dark eyes latched onto Beth's.

Beth's throat ached. "I could really use your guidance."

Missus Abu didn't move.

Beth looked away, sighed, and slipped her fingers into her pocket. She pulled out the worrisome nut, scrutinized it, then turned it over several times. Beth closed her fist around it and shut her eyes. "How I wish this magical little nut of yours would help me find Harold's forgiveness."

Science is not a collection of facts; it is a process of discovery.

—ROBERT ZUBRIN

43

If she hurried, Beth would be back down to the center of Charlotte Amalie before the sun completely set. Considering the events of the last two days, she could understand why she had a headache and no energy. If she ate something it might help.

Every time she thought about forcing herself to eat, she visualized sitting alone in some restaurant. An empty ache without Harold shut all her systems down except for her annoying *Center for Uncontrolled Sorrow.*

Beth continued down the hill, listening to dogs bark, mothers call their children, and traffic noise from below. She watched lights twinkle on below her from the shops and ships. The stream of traffic moving on Veterans Drive and its shops along the harbor near the ocean threw dancing lights on the evening's dark water.

When she finally came to Wimmelskafts Gade, she stopped and glanced around into the shadows. Uneasiness swept over her. But then, she *was* close to where the boys threw rocks at Missus Abu, and not too far from the park where William had accosted her.

In the damp, heavy night air, Beth could smell beef and fish frying, along with onions and spices being prepared for evening meals. She followed the street east to the park and headed across the grass to Hotel 1829.

Saxophone music.

The irony of it all. Sylvia?

Beth let out an audible huff. She just wanted to go to her room and get a good night's sleep before her morning flight to Puerto Rico. She hoped she had enough energy to climb all those blasted stairs.

When Beth tugged to open the gate onto the veranda, she could tell the saxophone playing came from the bar. The crowd had overflowed out to the tables and seating on the veranda. A man, sitting near the door, got up and held the gate for her to come in. She did, and he left.

No way could she maneuver through this mob to get her key or to the stairway leading to her room. She collapsed in the man's empty chair at the varnished table and picked up a flyer announcing Sylvia's presence at the bar tonight.

Music flowing from Sylvia's silver saxophone certainly attracted an attentive crowd. Everyone seemed lost in Sylvia's talent. There were no vacant seats on the long veranda. The bar must be packed. This told much about Sylvia. She sounded like a true professional, coaxing her saxophone to bemoan such soulful emotions.

The music stopped, and the air filled with disjointed conversations punctuated with laughter, the clinking of bottles, and chairs scuffing on the wooden floor. A few minutes later, customers shuffled across the veranda and out the gate. The long table where she sat cleared.

At last, Beth could go to her room. Clean sheets, and sleep—tomorrow night at home, she'd straighten things out with Harold. She started to stand, but a firm hand grasped her shoulder.

Beth froze.

"I have something of yours." A soft, deep voice with a hint of accent—Salty leaned close to her face. "May I sit?"

Beth nodded.

He handed Beth her stolen watch—the one her adopted mother, Mary, had given her. The watch Beth's biological mother, Kathleen, had given to her sister Mary at probably the same time when Kathleen gave Mary a baby girl.

Beth turned it over and rubbed her thumb over the inscription.

For where thou art, there is the world itself.

She cleared her throat, then managed to say, "How long have you had this?"

"A few hours. Couldn't find my granddaughter anywhere on Virgin Gorda, so I checked out our home. She kept it hidden there because she said it didn't belong to you. It belonged to the woman in the painting."

"The woman in the painting . . ." Beth glanced at Salty.

Tears pooled in his eyes. "Granddaughter told me you liked the painting, but it made you upset and sad. I suspect your lovely mother has passed on then."

The lump came back. Beth could only nod. She wiped her eyes with the back of her hand, then grabbed a napkin and dabbed her nose.

Salty cleared his throat.

"I gave the watch to Kathleen many, many years ago. It tickles me to see it still runs. Beth, sweet lass, stay here with us. I can see you're fond of the wee children. You're so much like her . . . stay."

Beth slipped her watch on her wrist and looked at the time. It wasn't as late as it felt. She pushed her palms tight against each other to help steady her conflicted thoughts and shut her eyes until her mind and emotions settled.

She opened them, and said, "Kathleen told me Martin was her one true love, and Missus Abu told me why you two didn't stay together. Finally, I understand why she gave me up for adoption. I also know, because she told me many times, she loved you, and after all these years she missed you terribly."

His face turned gray, and he seemed to age before her eyes. A whine of sorts came from somewhere. It must have been from him. He placed a hand over his eyes.

Beth didn't know what to do. She held still and waited, which amplified her awareness of the carefree laughter coming from the bar.

Salty coughed, and he, too, took a napkin to dab his eyes.

"She didn't tell me she was carrying my baby. I couldn't marry Kathleen, because I had a wife in New York, an invalid, she—my fault. No man with a heart could divorce her."

Beth reached over and touched his arm. "Kathleen once called you a most honorable man. I am grateful to have my watch."

"Please," he said, "you and your husband—I'll give you your own room, several rooms. You'll have all the privacy you want. It's a large home—we'll open the swimming pool, hire staff, and it will be full of gaiety again, full of joy. The two of you will live here in paradise with us. We'll go sailing and fishing—"

"Salty, I'm not Kathleen." A wave of comfort spread over her. Nothing mattered to her except going home to be with Harold. "You're charming, intelligent, and funny. I know why Kathleen loved you. You know I love Gnat, and these islands feel like paradise, but I'm leaving in the morning, going home. Martin, may I ask three things of you before I go?"

He shook his head. "All those years of agony, hunting for her— Kathleen simply disappeared. Now you're going away, too. I canna' stand anymore."

"Hey guy, you're strong." She swallowed hard. "I'm not asking for the moon. Jana has my contact information. Would you, Gnat, and Jack, even William if he wants, come to the United States and visit us?"

Beth waited. He didn't respond.

"Okay, Jana's dream of your house becoming a school needs to happen. Gnat, Jack, Joman, and even William need this." Beth stood.

"You said three. What's the last one?" Salty stood too.

"Before I leave, would my father please give me a hug?"

'Tis not the many oath that make the truth;
But the plain single vow, that is vow'd true.

—WILLIAM SHAKESPEARE

44

Beth stood at the veranda gate and watched Martin Davies descend those horribly steep steps. She shuddered, not knowing what she'd do for a man his age if he fell.

He strode down them like a king. She bet Mad Dog would do the same.

Agile old peacocks.

She smiled. This man of Kathleen's showed depth of character. He paused, looked back, and waved to her when he had reached the ground. Then Martin disappeared into the night.

The noise from the bar sounded less boisterous. She walked across the veranda and headed toward the door to the bar to get her luggage and the key to her room. A short but stout woman with unruly golden, sun-bleached, graying hair blocked her path with a black saxophone case.

"You again?" Sylvia elbowed Beth on the arm. You're some fucked-up woman." She held up her mug of beer, took a sip, and continued. "You've wasted your vacation stalking me and interrogating poor old Salty. How can you neglect that handsome guy of yours? What's with you anyhow?"

"Excuse me. I'm on my way to my room." Beth nudged past Sylvia.

"Okay, your guy said you weren't stalking me. But every f-ing time I turn around—well, here you are. So there it is."

Exhausted, emotionally drained, and growling-gut hungry, Beth couldn't take this. She whirled around and said, "Do you drive a green, beat-up old truck? I bet you do. So, lady, who's stalking whom?"

"Whom? My, you're a la-de-da, girly. My mother told me you would be."

This wouldn't end until Sylvia ended it. Beth took a deep breath and slumped down at her previous place at the table.

Sylvia slid in across from her. "Your man said you had questions for me . . . about the cemetery. Right. I don't normally play jazz at funerals, but it seem a fitting thing to do for Kathleen."

"Playing jazz in a cemetery when family members are grieving— you call me messed up? What squirrel controls your brain?"

"Woman, where's the music for her? You didn't bother to at least get a quartet. Her—of all people. What kind of funeral is that?"

"An appropriate funeral for a sophisticated lady. Come on. Jazz?"

"Yeah, girlie, jazz. Kathleen lived, breathed, danced, and drank to jazz. Her life required it, so she needed a jazzy sendoff. Climb out of those ruffled panties and get real."

Beth watched mesmerized as Sylvia set her empty mug aside and pulled out a cigarette. She lit it and puffed, staring the whole time at Beth.

"Ha—look at you. You even disapprove of smoking. Figures. Poor Kathleen. Her last few months with you must have been hell."

Sometimes the best defense is no defense.

"Sylvia, I can't do this one-upmanship anymore."

Sylvia blew a smoke ring and watched it rise to the ceiling. Beth glared at her.

Beth lowered her voice and asked, "Tell me why on earth you showed up at the cemetery, and how you know so much about Kathleen. And you said your mother—your mother—"

Beth gasped. Sylvia took another puff and smiled.

"You're Sophie's daughter."

"Yeah."

"But . . . I don't understand any of this." Beth studied the daughter of Kathleen's best friend. "Why bother to follow me all over Denver?"

"I'll give you the short version of the story. Some thugs kidnapped and beat my mom up pretty badly back in Chicago, years ago. Your mom evidently kicked their asses and rescued her. Kathleen sent my mom here to the islands with Salty to recuperate. Mom returned home months later to Minnesota. She lived with grandma, taught piano and voice until she married dad. She died last year."

Beth soaked in Sylvia's words and their meaning.

Sylvia chewed at a fingernail, glanced at Beth, then said, "My mom brought me here once when I was little. Seems Salty, desperate to find Kathleen, thought my mom owed it to him to tell. My mom would never betray your mother."

Beth couldn't find enough air to speak. Every molecule in her body danced.

Sylvia glanced around, surveyed the veranda, and stared out at Charlotte Amalie. "Before she passed, she made me promise to keep an eye on your mom—'Keep Kathleen safe,' she said. Kathleen would have busted an artery if she knew. So I got some gigs in Colorado and kept watch. She did well until you stepped in and made my job hell."

"You played the white grand piano here in Martin's parlor, back then."

Sylvia laughed. "You have spies too. I didn't want to leave. I'd never been in such a beautiful home. At that time we lived in a two-bedroom, white-framed house in Minneapolis. I don't remember much about my dad—he died in World War II—in England—from the flu."

Beth stood. "I'm sorry about your mom and all that happened to her."

Sylvia also stood and held out her hand to Beth. Beth accepted it.

"It's over. I've completed the vow I made to my mom, and I'm damned glad of it."

Beth nodded.

Sylvia ended it all by saying, "Hey, doll, I'm sorry about your mom, too."

~

Beth stood next to the bar, waiting her turn for the bartender–desk clerk to finish with other customers. This day started out lousy, turned crazy, and ended in a tangle of assorted emotions and sentiments. A pervasive ache deep inside since early morning still lingered. She knew it came from her part in driving Harold away.

One more person in line ahead of her, then she could go to bed.

Beth touched the perplexing nut in her pocket. She still couldn't make sense of its purpose, adding confusion to her list for this day. She pulled it out to examine it one last time.

The magic of it all, what a waste. Science is science. No opera-loving fish, no protection from evil, no saving her marriage. It all stems from our own actions. It's us, not a nut. If this little seed gave me special power I wouldn't have lost Harold.

The desk clerk acknowledged her. She said, "Beth Armstrong, you're holding a room for me." She switched the nut to her other hand so she could sign in. "I left my luggage here earlier today, and you said—"

"Of course, let me get your key. We put your suitcases in your room earlier this afternoon." He reached into one of the wooden cubbyholes behind the cash register, while saying, "Mr. Armstrong already went upstairs."

Beth's ears rang. "My husband—he can't be—he's—" She glanced at the stairway.

"He checked in a little while ago and asked me let you know he's waiting for you in your room."

She started for the stairs.

"Wait, here's your key."

He was holding out the key for her. She ignored it and dashed up the stairs. Not caring who heard, she yelled, "Harold! Oh, Harold! You didn't leave . . . You waited!"

A door above banged opened, and Harold strode out, smiling down at her.

Beth took the last few steps two at a time. Before she reached the top, she shoved the little brown nut down deep into her pocket.

EPILOGUE

St. Thomas, 1997—One Year Later

Ninety-eight tiny flames blazed on top of a butter-cream frosted, chocolate cake. If anyone had asked, Beth would have said the cake couldn't possibly hold so many candles. She didn't mind being wrong.

Sylvia started playing "Happy Birthday" on the grand piano inside the parlor. With the veranda doors open, the party guest on the terrace followed her lead and sang with zeal.

Gnat's voice rang out the loudest of all the "Happy Birthday" singers. When they finished signing, the elfin girl scurried over to supervise Jana's scooping the ice cream on the slices of cake. William stepped in to pass out the dessert to the party attendees, with the first one going to the Birthday Boy, Salty.

Joman and Jack dove back into the pool, splashing each other and anyone unconscious enough to get near. Some other children Beth didn't recognize played in the shallow end. Several older boys leaned against a palm tree or squatted near Beth's table, discussing something controversial about sports. Harold took his cake over near the veranda doors where Salty had held court all day long at his custom-made bar with high-backed stools. He had greeted everyone who came to his party with a freshly mixed cuba libre.

Mad Dog offered several times to take over the bartending duties, but Salty owned it all. William, finished with his cake dispersing, sauntered over to the bar and pulled up a few more stools scattered nearby.

Beth couldn't hear their conversations, but she could see the camaraderie. Sylvia continued playing—evidently for the sheer joy of being back at *her* white grand piano.

Beth excused herself from Missus Abu, Malaka, and Shalee, and she left the umbrella table to make her way around the small clusters of chattering guests. Jana, swiping frosting off the knife, looked up and smiled at Beth.

"I'm so happy, I can't stand it." Jana licked her finger, then wiped it on a wet cloth.

Beth hugged her and said, "Martin seems pleased with the renovations of the study and other downstairs rooms. He kept dragging me around, pointing out which books needed to stay as reference books and which classics you'd want the children to read and where he'd have more bookcases built. Salty even escorted me down the hallway to show me that other new bathroom—off the old pantry. I had to laugh because he and Mad Dog are like two little kids vying for attention. Mad Dog kept interrupting, because he wanted to show Harold and me the playground and baseball diamond he designed."

Jana wiped up some crumbs. "When Harold sent his plans for renovations, I wish you could have heard the excitement in those two geriatric kids' voices. They stayed up late into the night for weeks studying them. Hey, we're up to twenty-five students right now. I think our capacity will eventually be forty."

"William seems to be hanging in, from what I can tell." Beth glanced at the guys sitting around Salty.

"It's like old times, but better."

"Would you cut me another piece of cake with some ice cream? We missed someone." Beth held up one of the plates.

"I wish you and Harold would stay another day. There's so much we have to talk about." Jana put on a pout.

Beth laughed. "Next year we'll plan our lives better. I have to give adequate advance notice. As an administrator, I can't take off for longer than a few days without lining up coverage. The good news is Harold's business is doing well, and he's got some great backup guys who are geniuses when it comes to construction. He can practically leave whenever. We're both dying to repeat that snorkeling trip off of Little Dix Bay."

"Here you go." Jana plopped a scoop of ice cream on top of the cake.

Beth thanked her and carried it over to where the guys sat. "Salty, I need another cuba libre."

"Aah, sweet lass, ask and it be yours." He poured Coke over the ice, glugged some Barbados rum on top, squeezed in lime juice, and decorated the rim with a fresh lime slice. Beth nodded her thanks.

Hands full, she carried them into the parlor and held them out to Sylvia. Someone had placed large bouquets of hibiscus, red ginger lilies, wild orchids, frangipanis, and other colorful cut garden flowers on tables, filling the room with sweet tropical fragrances.

Sylvia glanced up, stopped playing, and shook her head, smiling. She took the drink and dessert from Beth. "Hey, doll, sit here next to me." Sylvia scooted over.

Beth sat. "Boccherini's String Quintet in E Major."

"Piano doesn't do it justice. You know your music."

"Guess you didn't play this at the cemetery because your saxophone can't replace a good violin."

Sylvia smirked, took a bite of cake, then held her cuba libre out to Beth. "Go on, take it. We're sharing today, babe, because you and I have lots of wild stories to compare."

DISCUSSION QUESTIONS

1. The first three chapters center around Kathleen's funeral and death. Could you identify with any of Beth's feelings?

2. Have you ever gone on a trip or vacation with someone who had a different agenda than you did? Did you discover something you never expected?

3. If you could ask any character in this book a question, who would it be and what question would you ask?

4. Some real places in this book were devastated by the hurricane of 2017. If you've been to any of these locations, or lounged on any beach, or snorkeled, or snuba dived, how did the story compare with your memories?

5. Beth, as a scientist, thought and talked about behaviors of animals, poisonous fish, and plants. Did you skip over these parts or did you find them interesting?

6. Beth considered the adoption of Natalie Bowman. What were your thoughts about her doing this?

7. If any of the characters in this book surprised you, why?

8. Who was your favorite character and or place and why?

9. If you've vacationed someplace and wished you could actually live there?

10. Missus Abu denied she or the nut were magical. What did you think?

11. What did you think about the book title before you read the book?

12. As the author of this story, I couldn't bring myself to end the book with Beth at Hotel 1892, so I added the epilogue. As a reader, would you have preferred to imagine your own, "one year later" moment?